MORE FROM MINDLESS MUSE, PUBLISHING

After the Plague Series

BROKEN: 1

LOST: 2

FOUND: 3

SAFE: 4

City of a Thousand Lies Series

OUTLAW

WANTED (coming soon)

CAPTIVE (coming soon)

Dirty Little Secrets by Award-winning Imogen Keeper

TALK DIRTY TO ME

FIGHT DIRTY WITH ME

DRAW DIRTY FOR ME (coming soon)

BREAKING

The

Alien Warrior

GENESIS KEYS

"It tastes so good," she moans around my finger, her free hand nearly dropping the glass. I catch it before she does, and her hand instantly goes between her legs, sliding up between her thighs. Her eyes snap open, find me, and she groans out a long protracted, "More."

"Yeah."

She falls back on the pillows, her legs sliding open. I try not to look as one of her hands slides between her legs, the other stroking her breast through my shirt. "More," she pants. "More."

"Oh, right." This time, it's my finger dipping in, loading it up, sliding up between her parted lips. Her liquid tongue coasts over my fingers, as I roll it back along the flat of her tongue, her fingers moving.

I load up another finger load and bring it to her lips. This time, when my serum hits her tongue, her hips lift up off the bed, she cries out around my finger, and I swear on everything sacred in this universe, I've never seen anything sexier in my entire life.

PROLOGUE

Summoned from my sex dream

AJAX

I close the door carefully, leaving my patient alone. She's finally asleep. Exhausted. Irreparable.

Nissa of Triannon, my best friend's ex-wife, trapped in the throes of a broken Bond. She just sucked his serum off my finger in a bizarre simulation of a sex act I know from holo-vids alone.

I've never cried like that in my life, not even as a kid during the Plague of Days when half my family died. I've never seen anyone cry like that, shuddering and soundless, as if her soul were separating from her body as if her bones were breaking and her skin fragmenting into a thousand tiny pieces.

That's what the breaking of a Bond did.

Bonds were never meant to be broken.

If I'm ever lucky enough to claim a woman and

form a Bond, I'll never let it break.

The thought of Bonding immediately brings an image of vibrant yellow-green eyes to the front of my mind. Feola. And as always, my body responds.

I run my hands through my hair, my cock jutting in front of me like a fucking flagpole. I lower my hand, right there in the hallway of Healing Bay, maybe to tuck it away, maybe just to squeeze the stupid throbbing monster. I don't even know, I just know that I can't think because I keep seeing Nissa orgasm around my finger, and Feola's eyes, and it's confusing as hell.

I've just laid the flat of my palm along the shaft when … there she is. Like I summoned her from my own sex dream, standing in an open doorway directly across the hall, watching me with those eyes, yellow-green and open wide.

Feola.

I've never wanted anything in my life like I want her.

I swallow and jerk my hand away, but there's no disguising the wildly inappropriate bulge in the front of my pants.

"Ay-shocks." Even the way she says my name makes my nuts throb. Like she's singing and whispering and moaning all once.

Her gaze drops to my dick, the look in her eyes saying she knows exactly what it is, and exactly what it's for, and exactly what I want to do with it. Her mouth drops open. Her skin flushes a really fucking pretty shade of pink.

I don't think. I do something I have never done in my entire life—just act. I stalk across the hall, reach out, take the back of her head in my palm, and move in close. As I slide my other arm around her back, her body bows.

She gasps, but her gaze stays locked on me. When I lower my mouth to hers, she whimpers. Her lips are full, and she tastes like summer on my home planet, Argentus. Like sweet fruit and fresh water. Her tongue against mine is as soft as velvet.

"Ay-shocks. I—"

I kiss her again, silencing whatever she was about to say with my tongue, and she leans into me on a moan.

My cock pulses happily against her stomach, feeling the press of a warm body for the first time in fifteen years. I back her up against a wall, tugging at her skirts, and push my hand up her dress, along silken thighs. When I find her pussy, so warm and so wet, I nearly come in my pants.

Her clit is rock hard under my thumb, and she keeps repeating my name, crooning it out, breathless in my arms. It sounds like a prayer. Ay-shocks, Ay-shocks, Ay-shocks.

I've never felt so powerful and so humble in my life. Like I'm as big as the entire universe and as tiny as a quark, all at once. Nothing matters. Everything matters.

I stroke my thumb over the slippery button of her clit, sliding a finger deeper inside her tight, wet passage, hooking it in.

Her hands rove through my hair. I slide my free hand over the rise of a perfect little tit and the turgid rise of her nipple.

The walls of her pussy flutter around my finger, soft as the wings of a butterfly, and my heart swells. Holy gods, I swallow her moans as she bucks out an orgasm right there in the hallway. Her moans echo, ricocheting and rising in a crescendo of their own.

My cock throbs against her, demanding attention, but I ignore it, slide my finger from her body, and stroke her dress back into place, tracing kisses along her cheekbone up to her temple. Her breasts heave against my chest, her wide eyes staying locked on me.

"Feola," I murmur against her lips. "I…." I pause, right on the cusp of declaring… what? My undying devotion? That's not fair. I'd need to clear the proper channels, make sure my superiors won't forbid a union with one of the few precious remaining women.

I need to make sure she's thinking clearly, that the aphrodisiacs in my saliva didn't cloud her thinking, give her time to process before I ask for a Bond. She can't think with my tongue in her throat. She needs space. "I'm sorry."

She freezes. Her brows drawing together.

"I didn't mean to do that. I shouldn't have. I—I just lost control."

Her cheeks flood with heat, and she backs away.

As soon as I get clearance, I'll talk to her. And pray to every whispering power in the universe that she says yes.

CHAPTER ONE

A parasite in the marrow

Four months later…

FEOLA

I have a comm of my own, a thin transparent disk the size of my palm. It even buzzes sometimes, too. Just never for the reasons my friend's does.

Samila's comm buzzes as we walk through the lacy purple reeds in The Fields of Romeo-Two. Like the rest of the women on the base, Samila is Bonded and nauseatingly blissful in her union. Samila's mate calls her to check in, to say he loves her, to hear her voice. The smile on Samila's face is unmistakable. It's the same smile I see on all the faces of the women from my home planet, Triannon, who have been mated. It's the smile I dreamed of wearing myself one day.

The smile says: I love—and in turn—I am loved.

I wore that smile for a sum total of seven days.

Seven days of serum-induced, mind-blowing, unnatural joy. I lived for my mate during those days.

For his smiles and his kisses. For the intoxication of his serum and my own unnatural addiction to it.

Then it all changed.

It's not a smile I will ever wear again. I know that now. I accepted it long ago. I'll never have that smile again.

When my comm buzzes, I feel only fear, and lately, a newfound rage that simmers below the skin and terrifies me with its intensity.

Utto's presence pulses in my chest, where our Bond unites us permanently. His emotions, as always, seethe and ripple, oily and viscous across my sternum, like a parasite that has taken up permanent residence in the marrow of my bones.

He's the only person who ever calls my comm because he's the only person with my number, and my comm can't contact anyone else. He made sure of that.

He checks in too, but it doesn't make me feel safe or comforted. He calls to make sure I haven't contacted anyone else in his absence, haven't seen anyone else, haven't even thought of anyone else.

He wants me alone, weak, and pathetic. Desperate for him.

Sometimes he tells me he loves me, but it is a lie. He doesn't love me. He hates me. The line might be a fine one, but I know the difference now. I learned the difference between love and hate the hard way.

So, Samila and I meet at The Fields occasionally to walk for a stolen hour together while our mates train. It's the only guaranteed time that Utto won't show up at random. During his training exercises, I sneak across the hall to Samila and her mate's chamber. Our friendship is just one of the many secrets I keep from Utto.

If he finds out, he'll forbid it.

He'll do worse than forbid it.

"Let's sit by the water awhile," Samila says with a sly smile. "I'm a little sore from last night."

I nod, tuning out the senseless chatter. Samila is nice, but she's oblivious as she saunters down the grated path through a patch of solar light that filters in through the crystalline domed ceiling of The Fields.

She sets her comm negligently on the steel bench overlooking an irrigation canal dug into the artificial terra of the base's hydroponic farms.

The crops spread before us in tidy rows of yellows, blues, and pinks. I sit beside Samila, so close the comm rests only a few inches away from my pinky finger.

With the wide smile that always calms Utto when the tempers take him, I point at the tiny fluttering birds around a flowering cerulean bush. "What are those? Do you know?"

Samila turns to look, and in that moment, I slide the comm into the pocket of my prim lacy white dress. Samila prattles away about the birds, and I make all the appropriate noises.

Samila doesn't notice her missing comm.

Oblivious. Stupidly happy.

We sit for a while. I nod and smile, and all the while, the comm rests against my thigh, a smooth, light weight that will either save my life or end it.

Samila finally notices it's missing. We spend precious time retracing our steps. I furrow my brow and look under the bench and behind the bushes, careful not to get any dirt on my dress. If Utto sees stains, he'll know I left his chamber.

"I can't think where it could be," I lie with pursed lips. I've become good at lying. A necessary skill. I ignore a vision of my mother's face in my mind's eye, sad and disapproving. Mamma always said lying was bad, but Mamma died a very long time ago.

And, Mamma never met Utto. It's impossible to know Utto and not become a liar.

Samila laughs gaily. "Jamar is going to tease me *ruthlessly* when I tell him. That's the second comm I've lost."

"He won't be angry, though?" I can't help but ask and, when Samila frowns, instantly regret it.

"Angry? Over a missing comm? Of course not." Samila looks for a moment as though she might ask about Utto.

I rarely discuss him, so I laugh to distract Samila. It sounds loud and shrill in my ears, but it does the trick, and Samila joins me. "Can you imagine any of them ever getting angry at us?"

I laugh. Yes. Yes, I can. "Of course not." I lie through a grin. "We're their angels."

I'll need to hurry across the base to Utto's chambers to have any chance of using the comm before he returns.

It's not the first thing I've stolen for my secret stash. Mamma wouldn't have approved of theft either.

I refuse to accept the surge of guilt. Resist the anxiety that comes along with it. If I permit the excitement to affect my heart or my breathing, he'll feel it through the Bond.

I never quite know how much he can actually feel of my emotions or how clear they are to him, but I do know he can feel my terror. My sorrow. And he likes it.

A tiny flare of hope sparks, trilling along my spine. I stamp it down. He'll feel that, too. And then he'll know.

I need the comm far more than Samila does, with her safe and loving Jamar, and her thighs sore from a night of tender lovemaking.

When I enter, the chamber is empty. Clean and cool. Sterile, just the way Utto likes it. I move to the sink, enter the code I stole from the base's Healing Bay to contact a man I knew several months ago, the only person I can trust to help me now, the only person I know isn't connected to Utto or his family in any way.

There's a short series of ticks and a moment of silence. Then a man's deep voice. "Hello."

Ajax. His beautiful, rumbling voice swirls in my ears, bringing back so many memories. My breasts tighten instantly. That voice, his beautiful bright eyes. They'll be crinkled at the edges now with concern.

I swallow thickly, eyes closing, calling up his face, the hard jaw, the gentle smile, his pale, soft hair, the velvety touch of his tongue to my lips. The seductive flavor of his kiss. Utto will feel my arousal—but he'll never know the reason.

Self-loathing tears through me, and my eyes burn.

For a moment, my throat refuses to function, won't shape the sounds. I dig my fingernails into my palms. "Ajax? I didn't know who else to call."

A hot tear escapes to roll down my cheek. Even across the distance of star systems, the frail radio connection of our comms makes me feel safer than I've felt in months. The only connection to the last person in the universe who might still be able to help.

"I need your help."

Over the line, he sucks in a breath.

As my body remembers that day so long ago, my stomach coils, heat pools between my thighs. He backed me up against a wall and plunged his tongue into my mouth like he wanted to swallow my heart and fuse our souls.

If only he had. I'd have let him. I've never wanted anything more than I wanted him at that moment. He was so big. And so hard. So desperate for me. He touched my body in a place no one ever had, and he made me feel the first burst of strident, unadulterated, breathless pleasure in my life.

I was terrified. I hung in his arms like a ragdoll after, as he stroked and petted and kissed my face.

And apologized, which was humiliating beyond belief.

And then nothing. He turned away.

For days, I wondered, waited, hoped for him to ask me to Bond with him. But he did nothing more than nod politely.

Utto did plenty though. Utto told me he loved me, and he'd die for me. He asked me to Bond with him. Brought me tea. That stupid fucking tea. He kissed me. Whispered promises I was stupid enough and blind enough to believe. And maybe a small part of me wanted to prove to Ajax that someone wanted me, even if he didn't. And always, that sweet, steaming, spicy tea.

My body responded to the unknown call of Utto's serum snaking its way through my system.

I part my lips now, to tell Ajax I'm sorry, that I made a mistake, that I should have waited longer. But my throat won't obey.

"What do you need? Are you okay?" That voice again, and all the warm shivers that come with it.

Behind me, the chamber's hatch hisses, no more than a split-second warning.

My heart jumps into my throat.

Utto. He returned early.

Moving in the fluid, practiced motion I've learned in my time here, I open the drawer that holds our plates and mugs.

Smooth, deft motions draw no attention. Jerky behavior garners suspicion.

With my thumb, I end the connection with Ajax on the comm and drop it at the back of the drawer, where Utto will never find it. He hasn't stepped in the kitchen more than once in our entire time here.

"What are you doing?" His voice sounds from the entrance, distrustful as ever. His suspicion slithers in my chest through the Bond.

The door slides closed with a hiss.

"I thought I'd make some *eeffoc*." I pull two mugs from the drawer and slid it closed with a hip, wiping my damp cheek calmly.

"You drink too much of it. It'll stain your teeth."

He unstraps the holsters that hold his *rezals*.

"They can be whitened if they bother you, can't they?"

He makes a face at that, somewhere between a scoff and a snarl, jerking his head in a sharp motion that sets his dark-blue hair shimmering. I loved that thick, shining hair at the beginning. So different from my own. I loathe it now.

I load the fragrant, brown-black powder into the machine and set it percolating. Lifting one of the mugs, I move to put it back in the drawer.

"I didn't say I didn't want any," he bites off.

I picture Ajax's soft eyes.

Utto's tone speaks to impending violence. Experience has taught me that although his anger can only be staved off for so long, I can sometimes soften the intensity of it by forcing myself to remain gentle and sweet.

"Sorry, my love." The false words taste bitter on my tongue, but the smile I offer is sweeter than the *lintorippi* berries they grow in The Fields.

"My cousin, Rennie, is going to come for a while. He'll stay in one of the guest chambers, but he'll eat meals here. I expect you to make him feel welcome."

I don't want to ponder the meaning behind those words too deeply. "Of course. Please let me know what his favorite meals are. I can find recipes."

When the *eeffoc* is ready, I pour it into the mugs, pouring cream in his, just the way he likes it, and bring it over to where he sits in the lounge.

He puts his mug on the table in front of him and meets my eyes with a look I know too well.

I smile for him again—the big, wide-eyed, vapid grin that he loves, the one that probably got me into this mess. With Ajax's turquoise eyes in my mind, I drop to my knees in front of the man I chose.

He speaks, but I ignore his words, conjuring up the sound of Ajax's deep rumble across the distance of space.

I'll find a way to call him again soon.

CHAPTER TWO

Yellow as the Argenti sun

AJAX

"Ajax, I didn't know who else to call."

I haven't seen her face or heard her say my name in months, but a single sentence and my heart goes arrhythmic and skips about five beats.

"I need your help."

"What do you need? How can I help?"

The line goes dead. It's a waste of time, but I try anyway. "Feola?" Nothing. "Feola."

I drop my comm to the glossy black surface of my desk.

Ay-shocks. Nobody else says my name like that. Like a song, a perfect melody that sucks me right back to the day I saw her open her eyes for the first time.

I inhale sharply against the memory of her slim body draped in the white sheets of Healing Bay, the soft rise of her breasts with every breath, the delicate scent that filled the air around her. After we brought her aboard S-6, she slept for five days. She slept through the warming of the cryo pod, slept as I bathed the gel from her body, slept as every machine at my disposal monitored her vitals, tracked her health.

And after five days of waiting, there was finally a change in her sleep cycles. I waited, ready to reassure a lone woman as she awoke after five hundred years in cryo-freeze aboard an alien spaceship.

A soft murmur sounded at the back of her throat, and she tossed her head, sending a lock of pink-orange hair across her forehead. When I brushed it back, she turned her cheek into my palm and smiled in her sleep.

Those lids snapped open, revealing the most incredible set of eyes I'd ever seen. Yellow as the Argenti sun in the center of the irises and emerald at the edges, with thick black lashes. She opened her eyes and looked at me.

That's all it took. I think I smiled. I'm not sure.

She squealed and lurched upright, clutching the sheets.

It took a few minutes for her to calm down. I spoke softly, knowing she couldn't understand. "Ajax," I said, pointing at my chest. "My name is Ajax."

After a long moment, speaking in a voice as soft and fluid as flowing water, she said my name for the first time. "*Ay-shocks.*"

It sounds a hell of a lot better her way.

I drop my head back, jaw clamping tight.

Help. What the hell did she need?

She chose Utto. She Bonded with Utto.

She doesn't belong to me.

The thought burns like acid in my throat.

I trace my hands over the clear surface of my comm's screen, tempted to return-contact the device, but she hung up for a reason.

She spoke fast, a little breathy. Fear?

Am I fabricating? Finding excuses to think about her? *For sure.*

Thick, curling hair and wide eyes. Hot, wet skin, and the sounds she made, breathy moans as she writhed on my fingers the one time I let myself touch her—really touch her.

I can't stop a wry laugh that comes from the back of my throat. It's too perfect. Today, the papers arrived, offering me permanent healing detail on Feola's home planet, Triannon. And today, of all days, she calls.

I pull my comp open and enter the access codes for the Tribe's medical mainframe onto the screen, narrowing in on R-2, and finally locate Feola Upranimus, mate of Utto Upranimus.

I scroll down the screen, past her medical information.

She's made three visits to the healers in R-2's Healing Bay. Once to request information regarding fertility, once to set a fracture of the radius, and once to acquire contraceptives.

Fertility drugs *and* contraceptives.

That made no sense.

Feeling like the saddest, stupidest bastard in the universe, I contact R-2's healers.

"Healing Bay, Romeo-Two. Captain Rashard Wells speaking."

"Wells, this is Commander Ajax Willo from Sierra-Six. Requesting information on one of your female residents, Feola Upranimus, mate of Utto Upranimus."

Wells pauses. There's no set protocol for relaying private information about a woman to a strange male, hasn't been in decades. Almost all the Argenti women are dead. "Shall I connect you with her mate, sir?"

"Negative, Wells. I'd like to know the details of her three visits. This is a confidential request for information. From the Commander of S-6 Healing Bay to you. Just following up on her health after cryo."

Wells pauses again. He could refuse the order, insist on putting the R-2 healing commander on the comm, which would cause delays and could cause trouble for Feola.

I hold my breath.

Wells sighs. "What do you need?"

"She's made three visits to the healing bay. I don't have access to the healer's notes. Was she alone when she came in?"

The line is silent for a moment as Wells accesses

the system's data. "She was alone once. Her mate came in twice."

"Which time was she alone?"

"When she asked for contraceptives."

I don't want Wells to spend too long thinking about what that means. "Are there notes about her injury?"

Another pause. "It just says she had her arm set after a fall. Fractured radius. There's a note about extensive bruising of the other arm. Mate apparently injured her attempting to stop the fall."

A thick weight settles on my shoulders. I can actually feel my blood pressure spike.

"Is there anything else you need, sir?"

The silence stretches. I've stopped breathing. "No, that's all. Thank you."

I disconnect and sit for a long moment, staring at my desk.

"Fuck." I shake my head and tap out a message to the admiral, accepting the new position as Chief of Healing on Triannon. The political movement will make my father happy, at any rate, since it will help him in his machinations back on Argentus.

On the way, I'll stop at R-2, the nearest colony of mated warriors and their women, Feola's new home.

I'm sure she's fine, and I'm insane, chasing ghosts, windmills, and the bright-red skirts she wore during the month she'd spent at S-6.

And no doubt I'll humiliate myself and break my own heart all over again. Maybe she and Utto decided to wait on a baby. Maybe she truly did fall. Maybe she was calling for healing help.

Don't ask me to help you get pregnant with his baby.

There are some things I can't bear to fix.

She'd better have goddamned tripped.

As soon as I confirm she's okay, I'll get as far away from her as I can. Maybe I'll find a mate on Triannon to block out the image of those gorgeous, haunting, lingering eyes and the big, beautiful, happy, flashing smile. *Ay-shocks.*

A thrill ripples through my bloodstream at the thought of seeing her one last time.

If Utto hurt her, he's a fucking dead man.

CHAPTER THREE

A thousand secrets behind my eyes

FEOLA

I've told so many lies I start to lose track of them.

Utto doesn't find the comm, but he does find a tiny spec of dirt on my dress. The dirt came from the market, I say. No, the piazza. No, The Fields. No, the potted plant in the kitchen. I lie until he loses interest and gives up on the truth.

But it means I can't leave the chambers for days. People will ask questions if they see the bruises that stain my skin.

When I don't stop by for more than two days, Samila comes over, inquisitive and sincere, and jeopardizing my very life with her presence. I whisper through a crack in the door that I have a cold.

The future is as clear as the catch in my friend's sweet, innocent voice. Samila will tell Jamar something is off with the Upranimus couple, and Jamar will tell his CO, and it will get back to Utto, who will be humiliated and enraged, and I'll be the one to suffer the consequences of that rage.

Time is running short.

So, I stay in Utto's chambers, isolated by impotence and fury. Pacing the grated floors, exercising on the sofa and bed, toning my arms and legs, preparing for what will come, and planning. Always planning.

I rehearse the plan so many times I fear I'll recite it in my dreams.

The bruises fade to greenish-yellow, just in time for Rennie's arrival. He'll only notice them if he looks closely and the light is just right.

Rennie is built very much like Utto. They could be brothers. Tall and solidly muscular, with the telltale Upranimus blue hair, dark, thick, and shiny. Matching eyes, too. Handsome men. At least on the outside.

Unlike Utto, Rennie oozes outrageous charm, with an easy smile and a mischievous set to his eyebrows, as if he's eternally on the verge of making a joke. He reminds me of who I thought Utto was. Maybe Utto is still like that with other people, but he only reveals the darkness of his soul to me within the privacy of his chambers.

The first time Rennie touches me is after breakfast the first morning after his arrival. He brings his *eeffoc* mug back to me at the sink, thanking me politely, and his hand lingers on the dip of my spine, his fingers splayed over the rise of my ass. It's not the touch of a cousin.

Neither of us comments, and the moment slips

away.

I almost convince myself it never happened until later that night, when he and Utto return, ready for dinner.

Utto opens a bottle of expensive Argenti liquor, dark green, and smelling of trees and dirt. It makes my stomach shudder, but they seem to enjoy it, clinking their glasses, belting out toasts, and swallowing it down until it stains their lips and tongues green.

Dinner passes quickly. They largely ignore me, discussing some man with a strange name and something they called *septusine*.

Being ignored is fine. I let myself drift and pretend I am somewhere nicer.

"She's cute." Rennie tilts his head in my direction. "Like a doll." As if I am not even in the room.

Utto sucks his teeth. "Cute, maybe, but don't trust her. She's sneaky as fuck."

Rennie laughs. "This little thing?" His hand comes down to rest on the bare skin of my shoulder, brushing the hair off my neck. "Nah. She's a sweet little one."

I raise my eyes to my mate's.

His face holds only shadows, but something new lurks in the creases around his mouth. Something I haven't seen before. "Trust me. There are a hundred lies hidden behind those eyes."

Wrong, Utto. There are a thousand lies hidden behind my eyes.

Rennie's fingers drift along my collarbone, hitting a spot that makes the skin of my spine crawl. I shrink away from his questing fingers.

Utto's brow quirks, and again that unnamed gleam lights his eyes. The Bond tightens, quivering and enraged.

"Who cares if she lies? You don't need to talk to her." Rennie's hands follow my withdrawal, seeking, pulling me back with a firm hand curled around my shoulder. His touch remains gentle, but there's an edge to it. Rennie's mask has slipped, the charming façade melting away under the heat of six cups of Argentus's finest. He's a monster. Just like Utto. His gaze drops to my breasts.

Utto smiles, sipping his drink. Not a nice smile. A nasty green-rimmed smile. "That's true. You never need to talk to them, do you? You lucky fuck. You aren't stuck with this one."

Rennie laughs, and the sound turns my stomach. I don't know what they're talking about. Them who? There aren't enough women in the Argenti world for them to talk or not talk to.

He traces his finger along one of the straps of my dress, tugging until it hangs loosely, the top of my breasts exposed. His fingers stroke lower.

Utto's jaw tightens, but he doesn't say anything. Anger ripples across the Bond. He's furious, but he doesn't say a single word to stop his cousin.

"Look at these little tits. Nice and firm."

I close my eyes, focus on sucking air into my lungs. I thought I was long past feeling betrayed by Utto.

Rennie's alcohol breath reeks as he scoots closer, his fingers tugging at the other strap.

Cold air touches my skin.

"Ha. Look at how she tries to pull away. No, no, no, no, no. Open your eyes, little one."

The bastard will deny me the escape of darkness. I open my eyes to see Utto knock back the rest of his drink and pour another.

"Smile for me," Rennie coaxes, sliding his hand down to paw at my breast. "I like it when they smile."

Utto's jaw tightens, but he nods at me, eyes blazing.

I turn to Rennie and smile at him vapidly. Who is he talking about? Who is *they?* When *who* smiled? I focus on the riddle so I don't have to feel what he's doing to my body.

He tweaks my nipples, plumping up my breasts as if I really am nothing more than a doll.

Utto laughs angrily. "See. Such a liar. She lies with her smiles. With her eyes. Go ahead. Look at Rennie, Feola. Look at him while he gropes your tits, and smile for us."

I widen my smile even as Rennie's pinches harden and his gropes grow more aggressive.

Someday, I will not be so weak. We'll see about retribution then.

But for now, I only smile up at Rennie's odious, handsome, leering face.

"Fuck. I love tits," Rennie breathes.

They go back to their joking, with me seated

beside them, ears buzzing like sirens had taken up residence within my skull, my breasts bare for their gaze. They talk of women, *septusine,* and Rennie's father, a senator on Argentus. And all the while, I grin like a vapid, brainless fool and try to escape to some other place in my mind.

I'm ashamed to admit to feeling sickening gratitude that Utto doesn't push it further. But it is only a matter of time before he decides to share more of me with his cousin. The clock is spinning.

He and Rennie prepare to leave to get drunker at one of Romeo-Two's bars.

Soon, I promise myself. Soon, I will be gone from here, and he will never touch me again.

The next time Rennie touches me is after breakfast the following morning while Utto is in the bathroom.

Rennie follows me to the sink again, where I'm washing the dishes from breakfast. His breath is hot behind my ear. "He'll let me do anything I want to you. He's afraid of me." He licks my ear.

When his teeth close over the skin of my neck, my hands shake so badly I have to set down the plate lest it break.

I don't even notice when the water gets so hot it steams and scalds my hands, turning them raw and red.

He backs away slowly.

When Utto returns from the bathroom, Rennie is already seated nonchalantly on the sofa, staring at the news, and I have the tap on cool, soaking my burning hands.

"Ready to head to practice?" Utto asks.

I don't turn around as they rustle and clink behind me, gathering up their knives.

Utto kisses my cheek in passing.

"Goodbye, Utto," I whisper, and it is another lie.

I will see him again. Someday. I swear it.

The doors hiss shut behind them.

With shaking hands, I slide open the drawer that holds the comm. I charged it yesterday when he left.

Just holding the comm—a link to the rest of the universe, a promise of escape—steadies my nerves. I want to contact Ajax with a physical pull that sets my heart pounding.

Clutching a white pillowcase, I drop the comm into it with the canteen and rations I amassed in the last twenty-two days, and the towel-wrapped slicing knife I took. Just in case.

The comm rattles against one of the ten small vials containing the viscous white fluid that makes my stomach twist with revulsion, but will likely provide the only hope this ridiculous plan has of success.

I take a deep breath and head to the back of Utto's chambers, to the bathroom where I step atop the small raised dais that holds the toilet. Reaching over my head, I slide back the grated black hatch that leads to the base's air ducts.

The access panel isn't large, not at all. Utto would barely be able to get his fat head through the rectangular opening, but it is just large enough for me to wiggle my shoulders through.

I practiced, did hundreds of pull-ups over the toilet every day, until my arms grew strong enough to drag the rest of my body into the duct.

It will be so simple to check that nothing was out of place, replace the panel behind me, and drag myself down the ducts and away from the biggest mistake of my life. But first, I have to lift myself inside.

A soft thud sounds in the main room. I freeze. Didn't even breathe.

A footstep. A boot hitting the hard grates of the main living area.

There isn't enough time. I can't be found.

Heart thundering, I drop the panel into place, easing off the toilet to turn on the water in the sink.

Rennie pops his head around the doorway, grinning broadly.

CHAPTER FOUR

Stockpile

AJAX

It takes me five days to get to R-2. Way too long. Five days of silence and nothingness surrounded by great stygian space. I'm bored, frustrated, confused, and most of all worried.

She doesn't call. Not once, though she said she would.

Every second of the journey, I will the comm to buzz. Sometimes it does. But it's never her. My father calls to discuss his election back on Argentus. My brother, Spiro, calls to discuss investments. Healers call to discuss cases. But never Feola.

I sleep with it by my side, lurching awake to check it. A hundred times, I consider return-contacting the device, but on the chance that something is off with that fuck, Utto, I can't risk it.

I work out in the ship's gym, listening to the recording of our conversation over and over and over.

The healing bay at R-2 is larger than the one at S-6, despite a population that is less than a quarter of the size. An entire wing is devoted to pediatrics, and another to the female population aboard. Women are rare. Their lives represent the future of the whole Argenti species. Their lives are to be protected at all costs. Always.

I hesitate at the entrance to the healing bay.

An infant cries from somewhere down one of the long, gray halls. When was the last time I heard a baby's voice? Probably during training. There are far too few babies in the Argenti population.

A healer rounds a corner and greets me with the same suspicion with which I would have greeted a stranger standing in my own healing bay back at S-6. I school my face to neutrality as I nod at her.

I've never seen a female healer. Didn't know there was a single female healer in the entire Argenti world.

There are no laws or customs to prevent women from working in any profession, but after the Plague of Days twenty-three years ago, there were so few women that it's become strange to see them at all, let alone professionally.

I have to resist the inclination to stare. She's pretty in an older kind of way, with deep purple skin, shimmery black hair, and wide topaz eyes.

She raises an impatient brow at me.

I clear my throat, extending my arm, ready to clasp her forearm in greeting. "Ajax Willo, former Head of Healing at Sierra-Six."

"Healer Irees Rillard. Head of Healing right here." She angles hard eyes my way and doesn't clasp my offered forearm. "What are you doing in my bay?"

She must be relatively new, or I'd surely have heard that R-2 had taken on a female healer, especially as the head. It's impressive. "I wanted to check on a patient."

"A female patient?" She snaps the digi she carries into the pocket of her lab coat. "Let me guess. You think *you* can help her?"

I frown, unsure how to answer that. "If she's fine, then she doesn't need my help. I just want to make sure."

She narrows her eyes. "Ever worked on a base with Bonded pairs?"

"Not since I was in training."

"Ever spent much time on Argentus with Bonded pairs?"

The thought slices deeper than it should after two decades. The sympathy in the woman's eyes implies she knows the question is loaded. Everyone lost someone in the Plague of Days. Mothers. Sisters. Daughters. Spiro and I lost our mother and baby sister, Clari. Father has never been the same.

"Not for a while."

"We get a fair number of males looking to 'check' on women. Just to make sure they are *okay*." Suspicion laces her last word.

"It's not like that," I say, but maybe it's a lie. "She called me. She asked for my help. There's something weird about her visits here. I'm not trying to cause trouble for her, or for her mate. I'll leave once I know she's not in any trouble. I just...." I trail off, scrubbing a hand through my hair, sucking in my cheeks.

Healer Rillard sighs. "What's her name?"

"Feola Upranimus."

Her eyes widen, and she stalks past me into the body of the bay.

I follow. It's empty, unlike the halls with the occasional passersby. Private.

"Hand over your credentials."

After a long pause, I pull out my comm and remove the small ID chip that holds all my information.

She shakes her head as she plugs the chip into her digi. "Hand." She gestures at the scanner.

I press my hand over it so it can read my DNA and confirm that the chip is mine.

"Do you have any idea who he is?"

"Yeah. It doesn't matter."

She taps her digi, eyes scanning the screen, and suddenly her brows shoot up. My heart hardens.

Something is off. I may not know anything about Healer Rillard, but that look is universal. She doesn't like whatever she sees.

"What?"

She tilts her head. "It may be nothing. It's just—"

She chews her lips. "I wasn't here back then. It was a couple of months ago. She came in for fertility drugs. Then for a break. They happen. Occasionally. It's not inherent evidence of spousal abuse. I'd disregard it, but she came back for contraceptives at a later date. Solo."

"I saw that in the system. Right after she called me."

"You think he's hurting her?"

"I don't know what to think."

"He's a big deal. Like his father could have us reassigned to the Fringe."

It's true. Utto comes from old money. His uncle is a high-level politician, a senator back on Argentus, far more influential and connected than my father.

"Do you know him?" Healer Rillard asks.

"Not well. I won't lie. I didn't like him before I met Feola." I clear my throat. "But I'm hardly impartial."

"I can tell." She makes a weird face as if she just had an idea and isn't sure if she liked it.

"What?"

"They're a fairly new couple, right? Only a few months?"

Three months and twenty-six days, but who's counting?

"So, she still needs serum frequently. If you were a woman who needed regular doses of serum, what would you do?"

"I'd stockpile serum so I wouldn't have to rely on

him."

"My thoughts exactly. I've seen a woman do it, once."

"Me too. So has Feola. Back at Sierra-Six. We used vials to break a Bond."

"Let's check the inventory for the days after her visits. See if anything went missing. She'd have a hard time coming up with storage vessels any other place."

About an hour later, we discover that, sure enough, a box of vials had gone missing.

She must be terrified.

Feola didn't tell the healing staff anything, nor did she go to the Guarda. Probably because she didn't trust they'd believe her. Or help her. And then where would she be? Alone. On a strange base, full of strangers, with a dangerous man.

She trusted me. I need to find her before they do, and find her in a way that won't anyone know she called me. But how. I look around the healing bay like it might give me answers, trying to think like a small foreign woman in hiding. Where would I go?

My comm buzzes.

I look down at the screen. The same contact display on the screen as before.

It's her.

Thank fuck.

I nod an apology at Healer Rillard and duck into the hallway outside, a long gray corridor.

My heart thwumps in my throat. "Ajax speaking."

"Ajax?"

I lean against the wall. "*Feola?*"

"It's me."

I speak quietly, just in case anyone might overhear. "Are you okay? I'm here—at Romeo-Two."

"You came?" Her voice is breathless. "I knew you'd come."

"What happened? Did he hurt you?"

A pause. "It doesn't matter, *Ay-shocks.* Can you take me away from here?"

"Yes." I have no idea how I'll manage that. The base's sensors will register the presence of not one, but two lives aboard. But I'll figure out a way. I'll find her. We'll get off the base and away from Utto forever. We'll find another universe if they had to.

"Thank you—" She breaks off with a sharp gasp. "I—"

"What are *you* doing here?" a loud voice shouts over my left shoulder.

I turn. Feola's blue-haired, massively muscled mate barrels down the hall toward me. Thick neck. Beady eyes. Utto. Bold and blunt as ever—only he seems weirdly nervous, sweating and jittery. His eyes dart in every direction. Two Guarda march behind him.

I slide the comm down my right side and dropped it along with my hands into my pockets, careful to keep it out of sight. Feola's musical voice trills from the microscopic speaker.

I face the approaching angry Utto. I may be a healer, but I've trained as a warrior, just like Utto. I don't always wear a full arsenal of weapons. In fact, I rarely do, but this morning I'm dressed for a solo flight between S-6 and R-2, in keeping with Tribe protocol for all solo in-space flights, fully armed.

I don't match Utto for sheer muscle mass, but I'm a good three inches taller, and I've trained hard.

But Feola? She can't weigh more than a third of what Utto does. Head and shoulders shorter.

Utto storms up close, stopping a few inches away. "It's no accident that you're here. You took her, didn't you? That lying bitch."

For a second, my vision darkens until I only see a single image at the back of a long, dark tunnel—Utto, mouth flapping.

"If she didn't do it, then he did." Utto's voice rises to a holler. "It's no coincidence that he showed up today."

I have no idea what he's talking about, but I smile thinly. "Watch it, Captain Upranimus. You're speaking to a superior officer. I'd hate to have to write you up."

Utto snarls, shakes, his dark hair gleaming blue under the recessed lights over their heads. "You came for her, didn't you?"

I glance over at the Guarda, who shift uncomfortably.

Utto outranks both of them. I outrank them all. None of which should matter. The Guarda function outside of the normal chain of command. Still, the instinct to respect one's superiors frequently lingers.

Utto's face darkens, ugly and enraged, shaking with withdrawal symptoms of a newly Bonded mate with a severed tie ... He's in for a load of pain. "You started vomiting next?"

Utto steps closer, breath bursting, nostrils flaring, chest heaving. "Where did you hide her?" He plunges a sharp finger into the air toward my chest.

Hotheads lack self-control—and they know it. It makes them angrier. Anger makes them dumber.

Utto inhales sharply, marshaling a semblance of control, but still vibrates with irrepressible rage.

"I assume you mean your mate. I have no idea where she is." I let a deliberate, mocking smile curl my lips, leaning closer. "What happened, Utto? Did you lose her?"

Utto glares at me, sucking in a breath.

I lower my voice to barely a whisper. "She ran, didn't she? It's all over your face."

Utto stiffens. "She killed my cousin. She's a fucking murderer."

What?

Wide eyes, pale skin, but no deceit. Whatever his other crimes, Utto genuinely believes Feola killed his cousin.

What the hell happened here? And what the hell did his cousin do to her that put her in a situation where anyone might even think she'd have killed him?

Staring at his sweaty, seething face, there are so

many things I'd like to do in this moment. I do none of them.

"I'd start hydrating if I were you. A broken Bond is rough on the GI tract." I shake my head and turn on my heel, giving Utto my back, and walk away.

Utto doesn't matter. He's not important.

Feola matters. Feola is important. And she's hiding somewhere on this base. Fuck. She must be terrified.

I have no idea where she is, but I won't risk her freedom by calling her. What if it buzzes and someone hears?

I just have to wait. *Call me back, baby.*

CHAPTER FIVE

A hundred panting women

FEOLA

It's not the inability to stretch that bothers me. I can reach my arms out over my head or my feet below if my knees get stiff. It's not the echoing noise that bothers me. I've gotten used to that, accustomed to the constant whir of air moving over my skin.

What bothers me the most is the need to be silent. It terrifies me. One mistake, and I'm through.

I can never relax. Terror keeps me on rigid alert. Sleep is evasive, and when it does pay a visit, it brings hideous dreams that send me bolting awake, sweating and crying, clapping a hand over my mouth, terrified I'll make a peep or a snuffle.

A wayward sound could lead to discovery. A random warrior won't just ignore a snore coming from the vents. I can't believe they haven't already dismantled them to search for me.

Strange noises on space bases are never ignored. They'll find me eventually. I'll end up back with Utto… waiting for trial. He'll hardly welcome me back with open arms. More likely, an open hand—or a closed fist—basking in the glow of terrified apologies and pleas for mercy.

A sneeze could lead to my capture. A cough. A sniff.

For three days, I hide in the vents, crawling like an animal, moving when no one is around, nausea tingling in my belly.

I drop into the chambers of strangers when they leave for the day to use their toilets, bathe in their pools, wash away the blood and sweat and tears, steal food, refill my water.

I leave no trace.

Sometimes, I hide in the vents over the busy—and noisy—main hallway that leads to the Guarda's main office, unable to resist spying. Utto paces and rants, furious, his face alight with something close to fear.

Good.

I smile grimly.

Other times, I crawl on my belly, through the vents to the large, open piazzas where I feel safest from anyone overhearing a stray heavy breath or sneeze. There's too much ambient sound, and the vents are too high.

Happy people, mostly men, but a few women bustle about their days, laughing, free. One couple laughs together, the man bending low to press a warm, doting kiss to her temple, and nausea slices through my belly.

This piazza is off the main hall that leads to healing bay.

He said he came. Healing bay is the first place he'll have gone.

I bite down on my lips, bracing against the overwhelming surge of hope that rides my blood at the thought of it.

He came to Romeo-Two. For me.

Lightheaded, I peer through a grate, watching, waiting.

And, an answer to my prayers, eventually he comes. One second there's empty space at the entrance to the hall. The next second—Ajax. Larger than life. Pale golden-white hair, tan skin. Calm. Even from this far away, I can feel it.

He wears calm like other men wear clothes.

There's a stillness to him, a steadiness that is softer, warmer, and safer than the best blanket in the universe.

Ajax is hope. My coiled nerves unwind, everything inside me easing at the sight of him. What will he say now that they've told him I'm a murderer? Will he abandon me?

I have to believe he won't. He is my only hope. A part of me longs to call him, arrange to meet now. But I'm in no fit state.

Instead, I reach for a vial, the milky fluid inside filling me with both disgust and longing. My mouth waters. My nipples harden in automatic response, chafing against my dress, on Utto selected, and has only collected dust and grown more hateful in my time in these vents. My body thirsts for Utto's serum, even as my mind and heart recoil from it. The fever is real, though. I have no choice. I'd like to burn it, but I know exactly how sick a woman becomes without access to her mate's serum.

The serum will buy me more time. I need to be healthy to find Ajax. To run. To put as much space between Utto and me—and the Guarda—as possible.

Keeping my eyes on Ajax, far below, I uncork it and tilt the vial to my tongue. The serum tastes of pure Utto. I swallow it down, every last putrid drop.

Gritting my teeth, I squeeze my palms to keep my body still, to silence my cries. An orgasm rolls through me like a riptide, so hard and rough my eyes water, and I bite my tongue. Like an inferno, it blazes through my veins. My panting breaths echo down the endless metallic chute like a hundred women panting in the aftermath of putrid ecstasy instead of just one. All the while, my eyes stay locked on the piazza below, where Ajax pulls his comm from his pocket and frowns.

The orgasm leaves me shaking. Weak.

Replete. For now.

And hating myself. And Utto, the treacherous, conniving bastard. It took a long time to learn exactly how he did it. He didn't play fair. He fought dirty in the days I waited for Ajax, bringing me cups of tea as if he cared. What had they called it? *Septusine.*

Bile surges in my throat.

Life is not fair. Mamma said that, too.

I detest that I still need any part of Utto. I'd give anything to be free from the feel and *taste* of him. I'll end that as soon as I can.

I can fight dirty, too. I am not the smiling girl I used to be.

The metal ducts around me hum.

It's time. I grab for the comm.

Through the vents, I watch as, a few stories below, he lifts his comm to his ear. "Finally. Hey."

His voice reverberates in my ear, raising all the hair follicles, arching my back. That hot place between my thighs pulses in response to the unique pitch of his voice. My body wants more than satisfaction born of serum alone.

It always has. Every time Ajax ever spoke to me in that deep, rumbly voice, I've gone all soft, wet, and silly.

"Ajax. Are you under suspicion from the Guarda?"

"No." His voice is so deep—and for the first time in too long, I don't feel alone. No matter what, Ajax will help me. He turns away from the hall behind him, tilting his head down, a hand tucked in his pocket as was always his custom. Broad shoulders, slim waist. Even at a distance, he is so beautiful.

How did I ever choose Utto over him?

I *know* how. Using serum like that against a woman is illegal and dirty and vile, and I have no proof, but I still know it.

The knives on Ajax's chest gleam, making my ears throb and my palms sweat with bad memories.

I squeeze my eyes shut. Don't think about it. Don't think about it. Think about Ajax.

"Can you leave Romeo-Two?"

"Yes."

"Can you get me out of here?"

He pauses, and I hold my breath.

"Not without alerting about five different failsafe systems that will register a second body aboard. They'll know I've taken you. You know Utto's uncle is a senator, right? His family's got a lot of cred. They'll hunt us. Everywhere. They've got a long reach. We'll have to go far away. Really far."

It isn't anything I haven't heard from Utto. I had hoped he was exaggerating though. "I can't ask you to take that risk. You'll lose your job. I'll find another w—"

"The hell you will. Where are you? I want you off this base ten minutes ago. I ju—"

"I can't let y—"

"You can't stop me. I'm here. I want to help."

I should let him. A stronger, braver woman would say no.

But I'm not stronger. And I'm not braver. I used up all my strong and brave.

Maybe it makes me a bad person, or a selfish person, letting him risk his job. And I swear I'll find a way to clear his name later. But for now—I just need to get as far away from Utto, and Rennie's body, and this whole horrible base as soon as possible.

"Okay."

He sighs, his relief so palpable that little particles seem to swirl out of the air he breathes, to pour through the comm and imbue themselves in the synapses of my brain, scattering hope.

Utto will feel that. So, I think hard about Mamma, the sound of her voice in song, the way she always, *always*, found a way to look at the beauty in life. The grief stabs home. *Let Utto feel that. Let him wonder at the new emotion.*

"We need to get to your ship."

"Can you meet me at the docks?" His voice sends shivers, like a thousand tiny bubbles running up my spine.

I don't want to agree—it feels too much like a promise, a nasty dare to a cruel and hateful cosmos.

"Hey? Answer me."

"Okay. Yes. Sure."

His shoulders stiffen. "You and me, okay? You and me. We're going to get you out of here."

I hold my breath to make sure I don't cry.

"Okay?"

"Okay."

He smiles, a flash of white teeth in the distance.

And so do I, but only because no one is around to see it.

CHAPTER SIX

A smile as wide as a mile

AJAX

I'm more confused than ever.

Feola sounds nervous on the comm and worried and scared. But not panicked, or anywhere near as hysterical as I'd expect.

"Are they watching you?"

"I don't think so," I say. "They've got an AI system combing the base now. Where are you?"

Her breath threads across the comm's speaker. I picture her face, the sharp chin, the enormous eyes widened in fear.

"I'll find you there. At Dock 3."

"H—"

She disconnects.

Moving as nonchalantly as I can, resisting the urge

to sprint, I walk through the base. I stop on my way to the train system, sip a quick shot of *eeffoc* at a shop on the way, careful to give the impression of a guy just going about his business.

At the R-2 docks, the entrance doors hiss open, and I step onto the wide cavernous gray platform.

The station is empty, which immediately makes me uncomfortable. Dock 3 lay just ahead and slightly to my left. I stand there after the train continues on its way, humming down the tracks and into the bowels of base.

No unusual sounds. Just the constant background din of base life. My boots echo on the floors as I walk toward the docks. I press my index finger against a scanner, and another door opens. This one leads to the lot where I parked my ship.

How the hell would Feola get in here?

A faint swish sounds over my head. I frown upward.

I head down the main aisle stop at my dock. Still, no one appears. I'm half shocked that a bevy of Guarda aren't jumping out of the woodwork, but maybe they're waiting.

Moving slowly so as not to alert any Guarda who might be watching through cameras, I shift my stance, so my hand rests near my *marsollian* blade.

The ceiling clinks. A second later, a vent flap slips open.

Feola's face appeared in the square. "Ajax."

The comm didn't do justice to the sound of my name on her lips, in my ear, face to face.

I gird myself to study her face, dreading what I'll find there, evidence of how bad it's been.

Pink-and-orange hair shining, a flash of a quick smile—and even though it's nervous, it's the same big, blindingly beautiful smile as before.

I step toward her. She drops something, and I rush to catch it. A white pillowcase full of lumps, tied up with a knot.

Standing right beneath her, I look up at her face and catch my first glimpse of those eyes in far too long.

A punch to the gut.

She lowers down, arms reaching toward me, until her whole torso hangs down, only her hips and legs still inside. For a single second, she hesitates, withdrawing her arms, flinching inward.

A wealth of information right there. She was never afraid before. Not of me.

I lift my arms up. "It's okay. I'll catch you."

Her arms stretch forward.

I take hold of her at the armpits.

She slips out of the vent, and her legs rush down fast to tangle with mine, and for a split second, every muscle of mine touches every curve of hers.

I suck in a deep breath that smells like flowers and woman and—Utto.

I lower her to the floor. There are so many questions I want to ask her, but this isn't the time. "Let's go."

Some wall behind her eyes falls into place. "First,

let's close the vent. So they don't figure out how I moved around base, in case something goes wrong." She looks up at the ceiling above them. "Do you mind lifting me again?"

"No." I close my hands around her tiny-ass waist and lift. Her hand comes down to rest on my shoulder. I lift her higher and heaven is my nose between her breasts. The small, soft rise of them through her dust-covered dress rubs up my cheeks. She's alive and well and safe. The outlines of her nipples stand out sharply against the fabric, and it takes all the strength I have not to lean into it.

I squeeze her just a little tighter than I should.

She feels so right in my arms. Simple as fact.

Even better when I need to lift her higher. I have to adjust my grip, lower on her hips, and my fingers dug into the soft flesh of her ass. She wriggles, working her arms over her head, and all her wriggles only move her body, so the valley between her thighs is right there, inches in front of my face.

A better man may have done any number of things, maybe turn his head away, maybe lift her higher. I definitely could have. She doesn't weigh much. But I don't.

I closed my eyes against the warm fabric of her pants. She smells nothing like Utto there and everything like perfection. She scissors her thighs, trying to get higher. My hands flex.

She stops moving. "I'm all done," she says quietly. "Will you lower me now?"

I slide her down my body until her breasts are

about even with my face again, pause looking up at her. I flicker of a smile, and her hands flutter over my shoulders.

That's when it happens.

A door hisses open behind us.

Utto steps out, with the Guarda in tow.

CHAPTER SEVEN

Spices and hope and everything nice

FEOLA

I squeal at the sight of Utto's furious face. All the rage and terror from the morning of my escape comes out in a single ridiculous squeal. I can't help it. All the old, pathetic fear floods back.

Shame heats my cheeks, but it's too late to take back the sound. It echoes off the walls of the wide docking bay, as pitiful as a wounded animal. Long and high-pitched.

Ajax lowers me gently to the ground. The second my body leaves his, cold air rushes between us. I have to repress the ridiculous urge to close the distance, tamp down on the instinct to flee. There's nowhere to flee without Ajax. And he isn't moving.

He shifts, pressing a hand low on my belly, so he stands firmly in front of me, blocking me from Utto.

It's sweet. He clearly wants to protect me. But

unfortunately, he also blocks my view of Utto, which is intolerable. I learned long ago never to take my eyes off him. Life is easier if I see him coming.

I sidle a small step to see around Ajax's wide shoulders. Several inches taller than Utto but leaner, the broad muscles of his back ripple and flex through the thin, black flight suit he wears. Leather straps hold sheathed knives to his chest, crisscrossing the deep valley that runs down the center of his spine.

And he smells so good. It shouldn't be legal to smell like that.

I'm about even with the bottom of his shoulder blade. It's frustrating to constantly be the smallest, scrawniest person in any room. If we get away, I'll ask Ajax to teach me how to fight. I can learn to aim a *rezal* or properly hold a knife.

Knives. Just thinking about knives makes me shake. I flex my hands, sweaty and cold at the same time.

Utto stands across the massive docking bay, all polished metal surfaces and dull concrete, with ships parked in a rainbow of colors and shapes. Which one is Ajax's?

"Step away from her, Willo." Utto's voice echoes darkly. "The Guarda are going to arrest her."

That noise pounds in my ears, splitting across my skull.

"For the murder of Rennie Upranimus."

Murder. The word resounds in my head. Rennie dropping to the floor with a thump. Blood spreading beneath his face, dripping through metal grates.

I shake my head. Fast. Trying to shake away the images.

I won't go with the Guarda. I won't. I don't belong here. I should be back home on Triannon, where no one wanted to hurt or own me.

"For what?" Ajax growls. "She didn't hurt anyone."

The wailing in my ears intensifies. Sweat drips down my spine as I stare at the Guarda. Their gazes shift to scrutinize me until my skin itches. One of them speaks, low and muffled, into a comm on his shoulder.

We need to leave, just me and Ajax. *Now.* While we still can.

"Then step away because she's my mate. It's illegal to step between a man and his mated wife."

Ajax makes a weird noise—halfway between a laugh and a snarl. It's a mean sound. Nasty. Chilling. Unlike anything I've ever heard from him before. "Your rights were forfeit the second you raised a hand against her. It's illegal to use violence against your mate. You know it. You relinquished all claims on her."

Claims on me? Like I'm a belt or a boot.

Not anymore. The pounding noise recedes, replaced with the same eerie calm I felt when Rennie's grinning face peeked around the corner. I squeeze my palms together, struggling to focus my scattered thoughts.

Fury pours across the Bond from Utto, bucking in my chest.

I should have known he was planning something. Should have felt it. I was just so distracted by the feel of Ajax's body against mine.

The heat in his eyes surprised me. He always seems so cool.

Well, not always. That one time, he was anything but cool. Back then, I didn't know how to read a man. I saw arousal, maybe, but I didn't understand the rest.

He was as affected by me as I was by him. He was hot and heavy, and if I shut my eyes really tight, I can remember the feel of his hand, cupping the damp skin of my sex until I felt like I might pass out from the desperate need. It was so much better to think about that than the waxy feel of Rennie's hands on me, his rubbery lips on my neck, the sound of his panting breaths in my ear.

My stupid, stubborn mind won't give me a break.

Ajax sends a weird, questioning look over his shoulder that says, *Are you ok?*

"I'm fine."

He lowers his brows but turns away.

Utto scowls, shifting his weight, glancing over at the Guarda. They all ease forward a few steps.

Ajax steps closer, too. "You're not getting anywhere near her. Not ever again."

"She needs to be locked up. Chiefs and the Admiral of R-2 can decide what happens to her."

"No."

The Guarda shift awkwardly, stepping to stand between them.

My knees shake. Nausea slices through my belly again. I won't make it thirty feet if I run at my fastest. Argenti function on a different wavelength than Trianni.

I creep closer to Ajax until I can feel the heat of his body once more. Unlike when Utto and then Rennie touched me, I feel only peace at the connection. "I'm not going anywhere with you, Utto. They can arrest me, but I'll scream so loud everyone on the base will hear me. I'll never go anywhere near you again. I'll die first."

Utto's face darkens, and my mouth goes dry. I've seen that look before. *So many times.*

"You little fucking liar. You belong to me."

There's a difference, I know now, between wanting someone, Bonding with them, letting the chemicals take you away to a special place, and not really wanting someone at all and having the chemicals override your body's natural responses.

"It wasn't real. None of it."

Ajax stiffens. Then he pulls me closer to him, into the cage of arms, wraps me up tight in hard lean warmth. What is he doing?

Deliberately enraging Utto.

He nuzzles his nose against my ear, and my eyes lock on Utto's furious face. Ajax smiles against my temple and presses a kiss to my skin. I shiver, letting my neck arch back, and my eyes find his. The motion parts my lips.

"How long has it been, Utto?" Ajax's voice, silky with dark malice, sends heat pooling in my lower belly, his lips brush over my skin. "How long since you smelled your mate? That's how it works, you know? Pheromones are what Bond you to her." A low-level hum sounds in the back of Ajax's throat. "She smells like flowers." He trails his nose down my temple, and I can't help it—I hum out a noise that sounds exactly like a purr, tilting my neck to the side, exposing my throat to him. "And woman."

Utto growls.

"Too long." Ajax presses a kiss to my temple. "I bet you need her so badly right now that you can't eat. You can't sleep. I bet she's all you think about. Did you kill Rennie yourself? Did you get jealous?"

Jealous? How does Ajax know Rennie touched me? He closes his hands over my waist, and I press up and into him until my sex rides his thigh and my breasts rub against his chest, something hungry, something feral rising up inside me.

The Guarda edge closer, lifting their weapons slightly. Utto's face contorts.

"Do you know why that is, Utto?" Ajax strokes a path down my spine, fingers resting just above the flare of my hip, pulling me closer. A soft moan forms in the back of my throat. Unlike Rennie's gropes, I crave Ajax's hands on my body. They belong on my body. He doesn't make me feel sick; he makes me feel safe. And alive.

This isn't an Ajax I've ever seen before. This is mean Ajax. Cruel Ajax. Terrifying Ajax. But he isn't being mean to me, and I know he never could be. I like this Ajax.

He clearly wants to infuriate Utto. It shouldn't be

so easy to help him. I've spent months learning to avoid upsetting Utto, but now, I gave in to nature and let my body respond to Ajax's touch. I breathe out a slow moan and rock into him.

Rage storming across the Bond. Utto's blue hair gleams against the metal walls of the docking bay.

It's taboo for a man to even touch another man's mate, and here Ajax is doing far more than innocuously touching me. He's caressing me, seducing me right before the eyes of my vile mate. I trace my fingers down the corded muscles of his shoulders, across his back, pulling him closer, drawn by his scent.

Ajax smiles again. "I shouldn't have let you take her last time. I should have fought you tooth, nail, and bloody bone for her." He slides his hand down my back, over my hip to cup the round curve of my ass.

Maybe he only says it to make Utto angry, and it does—his side of the Bond thrashes and vibrates dangerously—but something burgeons within.

I lean in, breathing in his smell. Not Utto's disgusting, oily sweat. Not like Rennie. Not like blood. Ajax smells like spices and hope and everything nice.

Warm, wet heat floods between my legs. Ajax's nostrils flare. The corners of his eyes crinkle as he looks down at me. "Get ready to run," he whispers.

I smile up at him—great big and wide and the first genuine smile I've felt in months, and for just a moment, there's nothing in the world but the two of us. I feel like me again, the girl who got in a pod, terrified and hopeful, and woke up five hundred years later to find a blue-eyed alien god smiling down. I feel … hope.

I wet my lips, the undeniable draw of this man calling to me.

Utto lets loose a bestial roar, his fury ripping across my chest like a blade. In a smooth, even motion, he pulls his *rezal*.

"*Rezal!*" one of the Guarda shouts, moving faster than I can blink.

And I take off running as they tackle Utto to the ground, hands behind his back, *rezal* confiscated. "Are you out of your *fucking* mind? You can't fire that in a base."

"The ship five down on the left!" Ajax calls, running beside me.

We race past sleek white ships and dark black ones to a small silver one. The Guarda shout I don't turn to look.

I just ran as fast as I can. Ajax is faster. His legs are so much longer. He scoops me up and runs so fast everything blurs.

Seconds later, he drops me inside the hatch of his ship. "In the co-pilot's seat. Go."

I scurry to take a seat at the front of the ship, my hands shaking. Behind us, the Guarda shout. I glance back.

One of them stays with Utto. He thrashes, his shoulders rotating, face red with indignation. The Guarda pull their swords.

Ajax punches a final button, and the hatch slides shut.

He runs through the ship, throws himself in the seat, and glances over at my buckled straps. He puts the ship in motion with one hand, working his straps with the other.

The ship moves away from the bay, flying open toward the closed doors at the end of the dock.

I'm about to ask if they'll open, but the words freeze, as a tiny opening in the wall cleaves apart. A second later, we're in a dark metal holding chamber, as doors close behind us, and new ones open in front of us.

And then we're out, loose in black space, and I don't care where he takes me. He can take me straight to hell for all I care, so long as Utto isn't there.

CHAPTER EIGHT

The slap of examination gloves

AJAX

Holy shit. What the fuck did I just do?

I just resisted arrest. That's what I did. While making an illegal departure from R-2, with another man's mate, a woman suspected of murder.

I'm in breach of a few dozen Tribe laws that I could name off the top of my head. There are probably a few hundred more that a solicitor will include when the time comes for me to stand trial.

I've spent my whole life following the rules, checking the right boxes, taking orders, fixing people. And now... I'm a criminal. An outlaw.

To make it worse, the man whose wife I stole is the nephew of a senator, and worse than that, the man she's suspected of murdering is the *son of that senator*. That family is one of the wealthiest in Argentus. There are only about fifteen people in the universe with more power than the murdered man's father, and half of them belong to the enemy planet. The Vestige.

I'll most likely end up in jail. Probably Insuractius Colony, where I'll shrivel up and die young of lung corrosion from working the mines.

And Feola—she'll end up right back with Utto.

I glance at her. Vibrant hair curls around her shoulders, wild and careless. She bites her full lower lip, and I feel that bite like a punch in the muscles right above my groin. Those yellow-green eyes reflect the low lights of the ship's controls.

All worth it. Best thing I've ever done. But what the hell am I supposed to do now?

We've been cruising at maximum speed for a couple of hours. I turned off the ship's trackers, but I'm pretty sure AI back at R-2 can reactivate it.

Hopefully, we're too far away by now to be temporarily untraceable.

I close my eyes for a moment. Where the hell can we go?

I need to talk to someone who knows about breaking laws. I've never broken a law in my life. We need a plan.

I'm good at plans.

"Find the second nearest sat-portal and set coordinates as destination," I tell my ship.

And a minute later, her tinny voice confirms retrieval and entry. From there, we'll be able to jump into another system and contact Tam.

Tam can contact Reyback, officially the shiftiest guy I've ever heard of. If anyone knows how two fugitives can hide from the Tribe's Guarda, it's him.

It will take another two hours to get to the sat-portal. "You doing okay?" I ask her.

She nods blankly.

"Feola?"

She turns to me, eyes fever bright. "Of course, I'm fine. I'm *free*. I've never been so happy." Her voice has the familiar sing-song quality to it, but her face has lost its sweet softness, and been replaced with a harder, more mature edge that, while no less beautiful, sends a pang through me. She's been unhappy.

"Maybe one time before I felt this happy." She smiles at me again, flashing white teeth sinking into that full, pink lip.

I shift uncomfortably, unsure what to make of that statement. It's easy to hope she means when we kissed, but also hard to believe given she chose Utto. "We're going to a sat-portal now. From there, I'll be able to talk to someone who can help us."

The happy smile fades. "Do you think we could be safe on Triannon?"

Her home planet.

"Maybe." It's possible. Tam and his Bonded mate, Nissa, were part of the royal family there. It isn't a bad idea—but we'd need to let the situation cool down and figure out if there are extradition laws in place on Triannon.

"Would you be happy there?"

"As happy as anywhere. The Guarda couldn't get us there, right? But Utto could. He will kill me if he finds me." Wrinkles form between her delicate brows. "You too, if he can."

"He can try."

"He's not dumb."

"Even if he finds us, he won't hurt you again. I won't let him."

She cocks her head, eyes wide, clear, and framed by dark lashes, hiding a wealth of mysteries.

"This time, I'll take care of you. I promise."

A wry smile curls her lips, and for the life of me, I couldn't have hazarded a guess at her thoughts.

"Don't be offended when I say this, Ajax. I'm grateful for everything you've done for me. And I will never be able to repay you." She chews her lips, wringing her dainty hands together. She straightens her shoulders, and her eyes harden. "But—I'm past the time when I'd ever trust anyone to take care of me again."

A hard pit grows in my gut.

What had I expected? That she'd open her arms and beg me to Bond with her and keep her safe forever.

Kind of. Yeah. Hoped anyway.

"Fair enough, Feola. Fair enough."

She rises in her dusty dress and sets her pillowcase on her seat. It clanks as she walks away to the bathroom.

I glance at it just in time to see a vial roll out and

slide to the crease at the back of the seat, filled with thick white liquid.

There's no one to see, so I let myself grimace.

A few hours later, I'm sitting in my seat, staring out at space as we steadily put distance between us and R-2.

It shouldn't bother me. I'm a grown man. A healer. I should be capable of rising above childish, irrational jealousies—but somehow, the knowledge that Feola's pillowcase contains myriad vials of Utto's serum makes me want to throw the sad sack into the waste-ejector.

It's not her fault that she needs his serum. If I'm honest, I'd obviously prefer we opted to break her dependency with a surrogate donor. I, for one, would be quite happy to do the job.

But hell, if I'm making wishes, I'd wish for a lot more than the humble role of serum donor.

I glance over at her. She's still wearing the same dusty dress she wore when I found her. Maybe she didn't take clothes.

The neckline reveals the tops of her small, round breasts. I try not to look.

"Feola, what happened back there? With Rennie?"

"I don't want to talk about it." Her response comes immediately, almost rehearsed-sounding, like she's been expecting it. Her gaze slips away like liquid.

"At some point, you really should." I clench my

fingers against the frustration of wanting to help. I heal people. I fix them. That's what I do. And this … not an easy fix.

Her face closes off entirely. "I said I don't want to talk about it." She turns fully to look at me, her eyes widening. "Please, Ajax."

"Okay."

"I've been thinking." One of her breasts presses against her arm as she shifts, pushing it, so the curve swells. Just an inch or so, and I'd probably be able to see the color of h—

Don't look. Don't. Look.

I look. Smooth, creamy skin. I drag my gaze back up to her face.

"I don't think we should go straight to Triannon."

"Neither do I."

Her brow wrinkles, and she chews that full, pouty, pink lower lip. "Can they track this ship?"

"I don't think so. At least not yet. But I do think they can eventually turn the trackers back on, override the ship's mainframe. I'm hoping that's where a guy I know named Reyback can help. He's weird, but I think he'll know a few things about dodging the Guarda."

"You trust him?"

I nod.

Her tongue traces along the seam of her lips. "Ajax …"

I swear, even my dick reacts to the way she says it. *Ay-shocks.* It makes my balls boil. I don't know what it is about her, but I just lose focus the second she's around. It's not just the way she smells, though I swear she's pumping out pheromones.

"Yeah ..."

"I want to ask you for something. You've done so much. I don't have any right to ask you for more. You can say no..."

"What do you need?"

Maybe she wants a sedative or something so she can get some sleep? Then she'd sleep in my bed, her hair all spread out on my pillows, her body all warm and flushed with sleep. *Don't think about that.*

She shifts again, and I don't look at her other breast and the way it's probably thrust forward, all smooth and round... and warm.

And scared, asshole. Remember that.

"I... I don't want any part of Utto to touch me. Never again."

I blink, wholeheartedly agreeing with the sentiment. I try to appear supportive, but her breasts just keep pushing forward, making my head swim.

"I can still feel him inside me."

I grimace.

She wrings her hands. "Through the Bond," she says softly and taps her chest. "I feel his emotions. He can feel mine. I can't change that right now. It would be a bad time to get sick enough to break the Bond, but do you know what would happen if I...." She glances away, her face blushing as bold as her hair.

I suck in a breath. I wouldn't interrupt her even if a whole fleet of Guarda ships had us cornered against a fleet of Vestige, and every one of them had their blasters aimed squarely on us.

She squeezes her eyes shut, her nose wrinkles up, her lips purse tight, and her face turns toward the floor. *"WhatifIgotserumfromanotherman?"*

Yep.

I shift, clearing my throat.

Her gaze drops to where my cock is caught in the left leg of my flight suit. It's clearly defined, and royally pissed at the confining quarters. There's literally no way she won't notice if I stand up, reach into the front of my flight suit, and readjust the thing, though. Crossing my legs is out. I lean forward and screw up my face like I'm thinking hard about the question, resting my elbows on my knees, and touch my fingertips together, wincing as the flight suit stretches tight over my groin.

"That … uh, yeah. That would probably work as an alternative." I try to sound like it's something that hasn't already occurred to me hundreds of thousands of times, but it comes out sort of strangled. "It wouldn't terminate the Bond with Utto, and I've never seen it done, but I've read of some cases."

She sighs, eyes wide, pale, and hopeful.

"It would be unpredictable, Feola. I don't know how your body would react to another man's serum."

"But it's an option?"

I cross my fingers together and lean back in my seat, thinking through all the potential ramifications.

"Yeah. It's an option.

Her gaze drops back to my lap. *Oh, shit.* I try to think of the grossest procedure from medical training. The first surgery I had to perform on an elderly, overweight man's rectal polyps. It doesn't work. The image instantly transforms to Feola, very much awake, not at all elderly, and certainly not a man. On her hands and knees, legs spread wide on my exam table, pink flesh gloriously exposed. He can almost hear the slap of examination gloves against my wrists.

Not the time, asshole.

She's just survived something traumatic. Either saw Rennie killed… or killed him herself. I rotate in my seat, hoping at least to make the bulge less obvious.

"Ajax?"

I glance back at her, seriously hoping I'm correct about where she's going with this.

"Would you let me have some of your serum? I know that's asking a lot, and it's not appropriate, but…"

A weird smothered sound comes out of my throat. "I could do that. Yeah." I cough into my fist. "I could definitely do that. No problem."

Her lips tremble, and her eyes glitter as she stands. "You really don't know what that means to me."

She really doesn't know what it means to me either. I lurch to my feet because it's the polite thing to do. My mother may have died when I was young, but she taught me manners. My flight suit stretches tighter, and it hurts, but I really don't give two shits.

She hesitates, then steps in close, and her arms slip around my waist. "Thank you, Ajax."

I pat her back awkwardly, hideously aware of the massive erection between us, jutting against her belly.

She leans up on the tips of her toes. *What is she doing?* She has to feel the thing. It's solid as stone and fucking throbbing.

She exhales a soft, sad laugh. "You're too tall. Can you bend down? Just a bit. So I can kiss your cheek?"

"Oh." I stoop at the knees. It's awkward as hell, but at least it pulls my cock away from her. She presses her soft lips against my skin, and my fingers slide to the small of her back.

"You are a good man," she whisper-sings in my ear, her breath dancing over my skin.

I doubt she'd still think that if she knew I'd just given her a very unprofessional, very thorough imaginary medical exam.

Maybe I should push my luck and offer her some serum right now.

But a look into her eyes, shuttered, secretive, tells me it's clearly not the time for serum donations.

But soon. In the next couple of days. I pull away, turn my back to readjust my flight suit.

Her breath catches. "I'm so grateful you came when you did... I don't know what I..."

I glance back, but her face is shrouded in secrets as she drops back into her seat, skirts spinning in a rush of crimson.

CHAPTER NINE

Happy to supply it

FEOLA

I'd have thought that as a healer, Ajax would be more comfortable discussing serum. But I guess, to him, it's not a dangerous addiction-stealing substance. To him, there's probably a sense of romance, seduction, allure to the stuff his body spews when he orgasms.

Not so much for me, though I won't lie, the thought of tasting his does pique a certain sense of curiosity. Will his be thick and bitter? Gloppy and sour like Utto's?

I keep my eyes on never-ending blackness. Not only to give him some privacy. But for my own. There's too much understanding written in his turquoise gaze. He sees too much.

I can practically feel questions perching on the tip of his tongue. But he holds back, and for that, I'm grateful. I need time to process. Everything happened so fast.

Too fast.

Rennie came into the bathroom. His hands closed on my waist. He bent me over the sink, pulled up my dress. Shoved a hand in the small of my back to hold me still while he worked my dress up over my hips.

And all the while, I was staring down at my pillowcase. Right there on the vanity. With a knife in it.

Because my body is shaking, the air rushing in my lungs so fast, I'm worried I'll grow dizzy, I force my brain to focus on insignificant details, painless minutiae. Tiny specks glint all around Ajax's ship—distant suns through the viewscreen. I count them until my heartbeat slows and my hands unclasp from the armrests. Some of them probably have planets and moons and life. Numbingly big. Terrifyingly beautiful.

Like Ajax.

I glance over at him.

His forearms flex as he taps on the clear screen in front of him. Pale, violet-hued light washes over the floor and ceiling. Green, red, and blue lights glint from the controls. To me, he looked like the statues of Teemo, The ancient moon god of my people. He always did. Pale, fair, and good; sinew, muscle, and bone. Hard edges and cool eyes.

He moves like water. Fluid. Never jerky. Rarely fast. Just careful and calculated. The veins on his hands gleam as they moved over the controls.

When he gives me his serum, maybe he'll want to use his own hand, wrap his fist around the thick hardness that pressed against my belly earlier. Every part of him is hard. His stomach, probably rippled with sleek muscles. I can see it perfectly—arms flexing, his hand pumping up and down the long, hot length. I press a hand to my warm cheek.

How would he want to deliver his serum? I could lick it from his fingers. Or maybe he'd want me to use my mouth on him. I'd hated it with Utto, but somehow, the thought of it, of opening wide for Ajax and taking him deep into m—

"Yes!" he says, voice elated.

Was talking out loud? My mouth drops open, and I turn toward him, aghast.

"I just got through. Look." He points at a lighted hologram projected by a small metal sphere on the dash screen.

I stifle a cry of irrational panic.

A bluish hologram of a man's head flickers in space. "Captain Tycho Van. Triannon."

"Captain Van. This is Chief Ajax Willo. I need to speak with Tam Essinger."

The hologram nods. "He's w—"

"As soon as possible. He'll take my call. Get Reyback, too, please."

The holograph shimmers for a moment. "Ten. Twenty minutes, max."

A muscle ticks in Ajax's jaw. "Thank you."

Tam was the future king of Triannon. I feel a stab

of nerves at the thought of seeing one of the leaders of our people.

A few moments later, Tam appears, and though I only saw him briefly, I recognize him. Hard jawed, dark-haired, roughly featured. Beside him hovers the holographic head of the other man, who I assume is Reyback. Gruff and gray with the mischievous expression I associate with naughty children, not older men.

"Ajax—what the fuck, man? I just heard you took off with Upranimus's mate. What the fuck were you thinking?"

I inhale slowly.

"Tam," Ajax said, a laugh in his voice. "Nice to see you, too. How've you been?"

"You dumb shit. Upranimus is the second richest guy in the galaxy. He'll send bounty hunters and assassins. Every asshole in Argentus will come looking for you."

The corner of Ajax's mouth tightens. "Thanks for the summation of my current situation. I appreciate it."

Tam laughs.

Deep weathered lines stretch around Reyback's mouth, and when he talks, he reveals a slightly crooked front tooth. "From what I hear, Ajax's father is no slouch himself."

Tam grunts, "Not like Upranimus. Ajax's father is a senator but from a smaller region. He's got a fraction of the connections of Upranimus. Small bones in comparison."

"Small bones add up. And your brother. Spiro's already made War Chief. A well-connected family. Won't hurt."

"Let's leave my family out of it for now. I'd rather not get them involved." Ajax runs a hand along the back of his neck, and the fabric of his shirt clings to the thick muscles of his upper arms.

My mouth goes dry.

Tam's hologram cocks his head. "What do you need?"

"What's the extradition policy on Triannon?"

Tam grins. "Don't have one yet. Interplanetary laws are still nascent here. I'll get the squad of elders on it, though. It'll give them something new to squawk about."

At the warning gleam in his eyes, my stomach tightens.

"But it will take months to draft something iron-tight enough to man off against the legal shit-storm you're talking about. Senator Upranimus is fierce. I'll need to call in outside help. But Triannon protects its own. If that fuck touched her ..." The hologram pauses, taking a deep breath. "Nissa will kill me if I don't say this: tell Feola she still has a home here, family here. She's not alone, and the Tribe needs Triannon. It needs women. She's got clout of her own. She's got people in the ring with her."

My throat constricts. He never even asked if I was guilty. Tears burn the back of my eyes. Ajax reaches out and gently strokes my knee. I find my hand reaching out, gripping his long, elegant fingers.

"Start now. I bet you hear from him in the next couple days. Triannon's the obvious place for us to go. He'll start laying on pressure fast."

Tam's brows lower. "That's my problem. Don't worry about it."

"So I need to know how to get under the radar," Ajax says. "Where do I go? What do I do so they can't trace the ship?"

Reyback's mouth turns down at the corners. "You don't. You can't."

"So, what do I do?" Ajax's touch on my knee might be soft, but his voice is hard.

"You need a new ship."

"Okay."

"Get to Pilan. Ask for Quasilliaro. He's a mean, dirty, rotten fucker. But he'll trade you a three-hundred-year-old hulk of a junker for that pretty little Argenti ship of yours. From there, hole up for a couple months on some abandoned planet on the Edge and wait."

"Can you send me Pilan's coords?"

Reyback looks down at something offscreen in his hands. "Just did. Along with coords to Araa-Ara, my rec for a hider-planet. It's an old vacation colony that was abandoned when better digs popped up, closer in. Expect it to be rough there. Hotter than balls in an engine. But a nice cozy ruin of a hotel on a hilltop."

No one asks why this Reyback person has the coordinates readily available for 'hider-planets.' They just take it in stride.

Reyback's jaw tightens visibly. "You take that woman with you everywhere you go on Pilan. Every single person there will be willing to kill you to get their hands on her. You keep her close. Dress her like a man, hide her smell. The place is rough. Really rough. Don't let her out of your sight."

Ajax's warm hand tightens around mine. "I won't. Thanks. Both of you."

The holographs say their byes, and the image of their heads implodes in a pinprick of bright white light.

Ajax turns in his seat. "Are you tired?"

"Yes."

"Go on to bed, then. You take the bunk."

"Where will you sleep?"

"I'm okay here."

"In the seat?"

I saw the bed earlier when I used the bathroom. It's big enough for both of us. "Ajax, it's okay. We're both adults. We'll share the bed."

He makes a face like he's about to push the issue.

"Please, Ajax. I don't want to be alone."

He looks like he's about to ask questions again, so I interrupt before he can get the chance. "How long until we get to Pilan?"

"According to the computer, we'll arrive tomorrow afternoon."

I drop my eyes to the floor. I'll need him before then. It can't be avoided, and it will be less awkward if he expects it. He has to be wondering when I'll need him. "I'll need your serum tomorrow. In the morning."

He's silent for so long that I finally look up at him. One of his big hands comes up, his fingertips stroke my scalp, and his thumb traces along my cheekbone.

"You don't need to be embarrassed," he says in a gruff, raspy voice. The deep, rumbly kind that gives me the shivers. A wry half-smile curves one side of his mouth. "I'm happy to supply it." He raises a shoulder, and the smile spreads over his lips into a full grin. "All you need."

I've never seen him so unguarded. For a single moment, I forget we're on the run. I forget about Utto and his uncle and Rennie. And I laugh. I can't help it. All the horrible time on Romeo-Two fades away. Ajax makes it all seem like it happened years ago to some other woman; and if I feel Utto's vicious wrath at the tiny, glistening bud of joy within me, I refuse to let it dampen the moment.

CHAPTER TEN

This is gonna be a long-ass night

AJAX

"Can I borrow your shirt? To sleep in?"

I stare at her dumbly, taking in the smudges under her eyes, the sad turn of her mouth.

"I didn't pack clothes, and this is so dusty." She bares her teeth in a grimace and indicates her dress. "From the ducts."

"Oh. Yeah. Sorry, I should have offered." I glance down, pluck at the white fabric of my shirt. In preparation for bed, I stripped off and hung up my weapons, harnesses, and the flight suit.

So I stand now in only briefs and the shirt, both of which I intended to wear to sleep.

"I don't mind wearing one you already wore." She pulls a soft smile. "It's okay."

"Sure." Dimwitted beyond belief by the sheer idea of her sleeping like that wrapped up in my smell, I grab the shirt by the back of the neck and yank it over my head. "Yeah."

I didn't put a lot of thought into what she'd wear to sleep, but my shirt sounds good. Great.

She disappears into the bathroom, and when she comes out a few minutes later, I have to fist my hands to keep from reaching for her. The shirt falls to the tops of her knees, the arms all the way past her elbows, the shoulders sagging on her smaller frame. The shirt falls to the tops of her knees, the arms all the way past her elbows, the shoulders sagging on her smaller frame. Her nipples press against the fabric of the shirt.

"Your turn," she says sweetly, walking past me toward the bed with a waft of our commingled scents.

I watch over my shoulder, frozen in place, as she lifts a knee onto the bed, the shirt clinging to the round curve of her ass.

As she crawls across it, the shirt shifts, riding high up the smooth skin. My eyes linger on the gap between her thighs. Just another inch or two, and I'd see ...

I groan, biting down on my lower lip, dropping my head back to stare at the ceiling. It's not a good idea to be this hard for this long. I've treated patients for this exact problem.

Blowing out a long breath, I head into the bathroom. Where I get out the glass I put there earlier. She asked for my serum once. I'm not going to make her ask again. Not unless she wants to. So I hold the glass, close my eyes, imagine that perfect gap between her thighs, and jerk my fucking dick into a cup in the bathroom like a pervert while she sits outside.

When I come out a few minutes later, she's lying against the wall, facing me. Curled up, head resting on my pillow.

"Feola." I roll my eyes at myself. "I wanted you to have a choice. So ..." I hold up the cup, my serum inside. "If you want it."

She rises up on the bed, resting on her knees, her hair behind her shoulders, my shirt dwarfing her. Her lips sink into her lower lip. It's like a switch flips. Her cheeks go pink, her chest rises, her gaze locks on the cup, and she nods, holds out her hand. "I want it."

I cross to her, sit on the bed next to her, my hip pressing against the warm skin of her thighs. Her small soft fingers bump against mine as she takes the cup and looks down at it, and licks her lips.

"I guess I should have brought a spoon."

Lips parted, breathing as fast as me. "I can use my finger," she whispers.

"Yeah." I watch, mesmerized, as she reaches inside with her pointer finger and trails it through the serum.

"It's still warm."

I think I manage to blink back at her, but nothing else, as she coats it on her fingers, and brings it to her lips. The pink velvet of her tongue rolls, curls along her long, slim length of her digit, and laps at my serum.

It's fucking surreal. Her eyes roll back, and she hums, her neck arching, her chest rising, her hips rocking.

"Holy fuck," I breathe.

"It tastes so good," she moans around my finger, her free hand nearly dropping the glass. I catch it before she does, and her hand instantly goes between her legs, sliding up between her thighs. Her eyes snap open, find me, and she groans out a long protracted, "More."

"Yeah."

She falls back on the pillows, her legs sliding open. I try not to look as one of her hands slides between her legs, the other stroking her breast through my shirt. "More," she pants. "More."

"Oh, right." This time, it's my finger dipping in, loading it up, sliding up between her parted lips. Her liquid tongue coasts over my fingers, as I roll it back along the flat of her tongue, her fingers moving.

I load up another finger load and bring it to her lips. This time, when my serum hits her tongue, her hips lift up off the bed, she cries out around my finger, and I swear on everything sacred in this universe, I've never seen anything sexier in my entire life.

She collapses back on the bed like a ragdoll and whispers, "More."

Fuck if I don't feed her the rest of the serum in the cup. I'm smiling. I couldn't stop smiling if I tried. She is too, her lips still wet with me.

Her eyes list open as she tugs the covers up over her body. "Thank you. Sorry if that was weird."

"It wasn't." I kill the lights and lie down beside

her, my heart pounding hard enough to shake the bed. "Anytime."

I roll onto my side, so my back is to her, willing my cock to stop throbbing.

After a moment, she moves in against me and presses her forehead against the back of my neck. "Good night, Ajax."

Her breath ripples against the bare skin of my back. My cock throbs so hard I'm surprised it doesn't snap off, sprout legs, and climb across the bed to cozy up closer to her.

It takes every ounce of self-control I possess to keep my hips from thrusting as instinct and intellect fight a silent war in my skull.

What I want to do is roll over, kiss her lips, slide a hand between her legs and give her an orgasm, maybe jerk off all over her, or spread her wide and shove my way inside to the hilt, balls deep.

Fuck. This is going to be a long-ass night.

I bite back a groan when she sighs against me.

She's torturing me. It has to be intentional.

A few minutes later, the even rhythm of her breathing tells me she is asleep ... I am not.

CHAPTER ELEVEN

Sleep-pink and blinky

FEOLA

The dim of Sierra-Six's healing bay echoes in the night. Chilly and sterile. I hesitate outside the doorway to my own room, waiting. Ajax was in the room across the hall for a long time.

It's been a couple weeks since he woke me. I've been among these massive aliens long enough to understand certain things about them. Long enough to see how Bonds worked. Long enough to understand the gleam in Ajax's eyes when he looks at me and the desire in Utto's. Long enough to know their version of marriage is far more profound than anything on my home planet.

Ajax is so gentle. I want to stay with him. To belong with him. I've never belonged anywhere, not since Mamma's death.

When the door swishes open, I jump. He steps into the hallway, scrubbing his hands through his. He looks stressed. And confused. And *hot*.

With a curse that my translation device doesn't bother to interpret, he moves his hand down to his groin, cupping himself.

I gasp.

He freezes.

"Ajax—" My gaze drops to the muscles of his forearm, flexing and cording. What was he thinking about? Me? My cheeks heat.

Something moves behind his eyes, lust, resolve, determination? He crosses the hall in a single stride, reaches out a hand, takes my head in his palm, and yanks me against him. My body bows. When he lowers his mouth, I whimper and part my lips. He tastes like spices. His tongue against mine is softer than velvet.

"Ajax—" I try to whisper, but he kisses me again, silencing me with hard hands on my body, grinding that thick hard ridge against my belly. I can't breathe, but who needs to breathe when they can have Ajax?

He backs me up against a wall, all panting breath, and wild savage need. My head spins as he pushes his hand up my dress.

"Feola," he whispers reverently.

Only it isn't Ajax's hand anymore. Nor is it his voice. It shifts like a writhing beast in my ears and becomes another.

I'm back in Utto's bathroom on Romeo-Two, bent over the sink.

Rennie's hand slides up my thigh over my bare skin, pressing inside my folds, his breath hot on my back. "That's right, spread your thighs for me so I can see your pretty cunt. Utto will be gone for hours. Just you and me."

My hand wraps around the handle of the knife in the pillowcase…

I wake on a piercing inhale, drenched in sweat and breathing like I've been running from an army of Rennies.

Veiled in the safety of darkness, I stare up at the shadowed ceiling above. Rennie is gone. Rennie is gone. Utto can't hurt me. Ajax is here. The taste of him, delicious, sweet almost, coats my lips. I lick away the lingering flavor of him, a dull throb between my thighs setting up a driving tempo that tells me sleep may be hard to find again.

There's no obvious sense of time on Ajax's ship. Without a sun, there's no morning. No night. Only dark time in endless space.

There is surely a clock somewhere, but I don't know where.

It doesn't matter. Every second puts us farther away from Utto.

I'd gladly lie beside Ajax forever, letting the calm flow from his sleeping body into mine, letting him eat away all my sins. He makes everything seem so safe and so normal that I almost forgot about Utto and Rennie and all of it. And let's not forget about the serum. I crave it. I want it. And not just any. *His.*

With a sleepy murmur, he rolls onto his back, and

I curl into his side. His big arm tucks around me, drawing me close until my leg lifts and the cleft between my thighs presses against his hot bare skin.

His big hand palms my ass, the heat burning through my body as if invisible cords stretch between every place his body touches and my burning core.

I pulse so hotly in my *cunt* that my head swims. Rennie's word. Utto always said *pussy*. It always seemed dirty. I don't have another word for it. On Triannon, well-bred ladies always just called it *down there*.

Though, maybe if Ajax called it a *cunt* or a *pussy*, in his deep, mellifluous voice, it wouldn't sound so bad. Or maybe he has some other word for it.

Heat flutters through my belly.

I want him. I want my hands on him. And his on me—all over me. I never felt like this with Utto. With him, it was all serum, but with Ajax, it's constant. He deserves to feel this with someone else. Someone who doesn't look at people and see their potential to cause pain. Someone fresher to love him.

It would be right for him to be with someone kinder, but the thought makes me want to claim him now, take him inside me and tie him to me forever.

The shirt has ridden up to my waist, leaving me bare down below. My hot skin presses against his hard thigh. My hips push against him.

I take a deep breath as my fingers, summoned by a force all their own, slide across his stomach under the covers. Even as he sleeps, his belly is layered with rigid muscles. I rub my nose against his side, breathing in the smell of spices, trees, and his own special man-musk. Addictive.

More pulsing and heat and panting. For once, Utto is silent across the Bond. He must be sleeping.

Ajax shifts a bit, and my knee rises up to bump into something even harder. Something big that calls like a magnet. I want to press against it.

He grunts, and the sound goes straight to that throbbing place.

He stiffens. "Feola?"

The darkness hides the furious blush riding my cheeks. I woke him by practically humping him. What is wrong with me?

"Is it morning?" His voice is sleepy, soft, and gruff. Rumbly. Just like the first time, when I woke to see his face after a five-hundred-year-long nap.

His grip on my ass tightens, and I press my hips against him, can't stop it.

He hisses.

"I don't know. How would I tell?" I keep my voice low, little more than a whisper.

"Has the alarm sounded?" he grunts out, low and raw and rough.

"I don't think so. I haven't heard anything."

"Then it's still night."

"Oh. Okay."

"Are you all right?"

I swallow. *No. Not all right at all.* I need something … him … to fill the emptiness.

He takes a deep breath, that hand on my ass tightening, pulling me closer. "Do you need … I could—"

I shake my head, fast, before I can change my mind. "No, Ajax. I'm fine. Sorry for waking you. Let's go back to sleep."

He exhales something that sounds like a laugh, and that hot, hard length jerks against my knee. I press my bare, damp skin against his thigh. Can he tell?

His hand tightens, pulling my hips closer.

Would it be wrong to pretend to need his serum?

I may not need it, but I really want it. A wave of heat crashes down below.

My chest burns as Utto's emotions buck. There he is, angry, no doubt having endured my arousal beating in his chest. I smile grimly. *Good. Feel it. Wonder.*

Ajax releases a strangled moan and wraps his other arm around me. He presses a kiss to my temple, extricating my arm, and turns me so that I face away from him. He loops a lazy arm around my waist but doesn't press any closer.

I frown at the wall in front of me as my body throbs angrily.

When I open my eyes next, Ajax is exiting the bathing chamber, a towel draped low and loose around his hips. He moves silently, pushing the hatch closed behind him. Light pools along the bottom and sides of the door, washing over the cold, hard surfaces of the room and the warm, smooth surfaces of Ajax.

When he shifts, every muscle—from his corded calves to his ridged abdomen to his sculpted arms—ripples and flexes.

Maybe I should be embarrassed at the way I licked up his serum, the way I orgasmed in front of him, the way I humped him while he slept, but I can't find the emotion, not while I stare at him.

He doesn't have an ounce of fat on him. Not one. Smooth skin clings to taut muscle and bone. Deep twin ridges curve inward from his hip bones in an arrow, headed straight for his groin.

His arms flex as he pulls a pair of briefs from a shelf. He turns, dropping the towel, and steps into the shorts, the full weight of his sack hanging heavily, glimpsed briefly in shadows.

A puff escapes me, and his head pivots toward me. The shorts ride low. A soft, knowing smile lurks at the corner of his lips.

He slow-motion stalks toward me, smooth and easy, graceful as a wild animal, running a hand over still-damp hair, every shoulder muscle and vein sticking out in sharp contrast. "Morning."

I drag my eyes from the dips of tendons and muscle in his shoulders. "Did you sleep well?"

His throat shifts, and his blue eyes warm. "It was a good night. You okay … about what happened?"

I get a vivid flash of my on my back, legs sprawled

wide, begging for his serum. "Yes."

"Good. You're going to need it again soon?"

I swallow thickly, search along my body. I'm throbby in all the places, my blood sings, I think about my Bond to Utto and nausea splices, I think about Ajax, and something else happens. I get more throbby, more blood-singing.

"Soon, but not now."

"Are you hungry?"

"Yes.

His smile stretches. He tilts his head in the direction of the hatch and the galley that lies across the passageway. "Let's go eat."

I pull at the neck of his shirt, hanging loose over my shoulder. "Like this?" The shirt covers me nearly to the knees, but I'm completely bare beneath it. Hardly adequate attire for a meal, but I don't want to put that awful dirty thing back on. Utto picked that dress.

"Why not?" Something moves in his face, almost like he's goading me. "I like you in my clothes." He gestures that I should go first.

I rise carefully from the bed, enjoying the burning weight of his eyes on my back as he follows me from the room.

In the galley, he pours a mug of *eeffoc* and pulls out some *serrichol* berries, while I spread nut-butter on toast.

He leans a hip against the counter, overtly comfortable in his near-nudity.

Something is different about him. Something changed overnight.

He hands the mug to me. Veins run down the front of his biceps as they flex with his motions. A line of hair runs down the center of his belly, darkening and widening to disappear into the waistband of his shorts amid a network of thick veins.

I swallow a big gulp of *eeffoc* and nearly choke at the heat.

Ajax's turquoise eyes narrow at the corners, and a dimple appears for a split second in his unshaven cheek.

He pours a second mug of *eeffoc*. His gaze dipping to my breasts, where my nipples press, hard and tender, against the shirt.

My whole body sizzles. Wet heat rushes between my thighs.

"You're pretty in the morning," he says, deep and velvety. "I mean, you're always beautiful. But ..." Holding his mug, he steps closer to me, invading my space, stopping when his hips are a hand's width away, and his shoulders block out my view of anything but him. He trails a finger over my cheek to smooth back a strand of hair. "All sleep-pink and blinky."

"'Sleep pink and blinky'? That makes me sound like a *splirantu*."

"A what-who?" He sips his *eeffoc* but doesn't back away at all.

"A *splirantu*—fuzzy little animals that live in the trees of the forests back home. They're pink. They sing and blink a lot."

He licks his lips. I catch my foot in midair, trying to step back. That's the old Feola. The new Feola doesn't retreat. Not even from Ajax.

"Sounds like you. Cute." His hand still hasn't left my face. He's just holding my jaw. "I want to kiss you, Feola."

I blink.

"But you know what will happen if I do?" His other hand closes over my hip, his thumb stroking my belly through the shirt. "Your body will respond to the natural aphrodisiacs on my tongue. You'll get hot, and you'll want more." He speaks slowly, druggingly, and he smells so good. My eyes drift half-shut. "And so will I. We won't be able to stop."

He's woven a spell around me. Made me forget all the fear and guilt, and shame.

"I want to give you my serum again, Feola. So badly my balls ache, and I barely slept last night thinking about it."

I go still, trapped in the hypnosis of his vibrant eyes, my heart pounding a primitive beat.

"I realized something last night, lying beside you. Smelling you, as my serum worked through your system, when you rubbed against me. You want me. Even after having my serum. You want *me* and not just for my serum. I want to touch you, Feola. I want to touch you everywhere. Tell me you want me, so I can touch you. Now, while you have a choice. Not later, when your body's sick and you need me for serum."

I blink again, heat rushing straight between my thighs.

He drops his mouth to my forehead, touches his nose to my hair, breathing hard. His morning-stubbled jaw grazes down my cheek. His lips rove my neck, behind my ear.

I gasp, arching up, pressing against his thick bulge. When he closes his teeth around my earlobe, his breath tickles my skin, and I moan out loud. He is the only man who's ever touched me like this, as if I am something special, not an object to be fondled. There is nothing to fear from Ajax. I know that. I've always known that.

"Tell me," he purrs in my ear. "Tell me you want me. I need to hear you say it."

I don't even hesitate. I've wanted him forever. "I want you. Now. Not just for your serum. Not like … to Bond. I'm not ready for that. But I don't want to drink your serum from a cup again."

For a split second he pulls back with wide, hungry eyes, and then he growls, low and savage, his hands curling around my arms.

He keeps his eyes on mine as he lowers his lips. My knees tremble.

His big hands smooth over my back and down, over the rise of my ass, lifting and pulling so my hips rock against him. It isn't nearly enough to cool the burn.

His lips meet mine, and though his hands aren't gentle, his mouth is.

Too gentle. I drag him closer.

His tongue strokes mine, and he lifts me up higher as he straightens, so our mouths are at the same height. I wrap myself around him, giving back every single thing he gives, gasping when he sets me on the counter. With his mouth on mine, I can't think, can't feel anything but him and the hardness that presses into that hot throbbing place that calls to him. It feels like freedom and safety and heaven in a single overpowering dose.

Tearing his mouth from mine, he whips the shirt over my head and growls, his gaze roving my breasts, down, down between my parted thighs.

"You're so beautiful." He steps closer, so my tender, now-bared flesh presses against his thick brief-covered ridge. I pant. He grinds against me, and I drag his mouth back to mine.

He tastes delicious, like *eeffoc* and mint. And him. I remember that from the last time he kissed me. His smooth tongue strokes mine and his hand comes up to cup my breast, his thumb teasing my nipple.

It's so wrong. I shouldn't let this happen. He deserves more, but I can't resist him.

My brain shuts down in that moment.

Maybe the aphrodisiacs kick in—I really can't tell, but I want him every bit as much as I did the first time. Maybe it's not the aphrodisiacs. Maybe I just plain straight-up want him.

I drag his briefs down at the back, pulling restlessly at him, wanting *more*.

"Wait," he grits out, freezing.

"What?" I can't think. The air between us is cold.

I try to pull him closer, but he's too strong.

"It's just—" He points down, at the long length of him, tenting the front of his briefs.

"What?"

"Fuck it." His mouth closes over mine again, and nothing separates us. The molten heat of his silky, harder-than-steel skin presses against my own wet skin.

"Fuck," he breathes, his breath fanning over my cheek and lifts me from the counter, walking with his briefs around his ankles, his hands still roving my body, toward the front of the ship

He lowers me into his pilot's seat. Dropping to a knee before me, he bats away my hands when I try to reach for him. His mouth finds my nipple, scraping teeth and dragging tongue. Rough fingers slide up my thigh, and I arch my spine, closing my fingers around the arms of the seat. His hand is hot enough to brand.

A long finger presses inside, and it feels so much better with him there. Instant relief, but still not nearly enough.

"So wet." He trails his tongue down my belly, over the rise of my pubic bone. His hair tickles over the sensitive rise of my ribcage.

"You're so beautiful." He lifts one of my legs over his shoulder to rest on the heavy muscles of his back, and my eyes drifted shut.

The man—my head drops back—*knows exactly what*—I suck in a deep breath—*he's doing*—my spine vaults higher—*with his tongue.* I moan.

Magic, that tongue, and I have no idea how he

knows what he's doing, but it doesn't matter. I've never felt anything even half as miraculous as his hot, velvety tongue as it dances, even better when he presses in a second finger. "So beautiful, baby. Come with my finger inside you."

His pale hair glitters in the lights of the cockpit, and his shoulders shift as his palm slides up my belly to knead my breast. His thumb strums my nipple, making every nerve tingle and sing and beg for release. My fingers slide through his hair.

He smiles darkly up at me. The moment our eyes collide I scream out an orgasm that tears from some untapped well inside me.

I'm not quiet, and I don't care. We are all alone, surrounded by light-years of nothing, and if Utto feels the joyous, decadent, frenetic release across the Bond, good. *Enjoy it, bastard. You wanted to share me— here you go. Share me with Ajax. He's the one I choose.*

I scream out Ajax's name, and his smiling eyes blaze hot enough to burn, telling me he likes it when I say his name. So I do. I scream it again as my body shakes and contorts around his tongue and fingers.

He brings me down slowly, stroking, humming encouraging words like *beautiful* and *good girl.*

With a dry grin, he leans back, so he kneels between my spread thighs and takes the full length of him in his hands, stroking up and down. The muscles of his arm bulge.

"Ajax, I wa—"

"Shh. I know." His lips curve as he strokes. I want him in my mouth, to taste him on my tongue, want to feel him thick and hot and hard inside me. But I can't move, mesmerized by the sight of his beautiful, gleaming body.

I've never seen anything more wickedly, seductively, intensely sexy than his pumping fist. After a moment, he hisses a curse, his eyes tighten, gaze on mine, the muscles in his neck cord, and hot serum splashes over my stomach and breasts in thick, arcing spurts. Moving as if compelled, I trace a trail of it with my finger, raise it to my lips, but he stills me

He runs his fingers through a stream of serum covering one of my nipples. Moving slowly, he strokes through the remaining splashes that decorate my abdomen, rubs it into my skin.

I sag on the seat, my legs still splayed.

"You smell like me now," he rasps out, low and awed. "I like it."

CHAPTER TWELVE

life is weird

AJAX

I strut back to the galley, grinning like an asshole, which is fine. No one can see me.

The smile on Feola's face after I made her come made me feel deity strong and prouder than I've ever been in my whole life. Forget graduating school. Forget being made chief. Making Feola scream my name with my tongue in her pussy has them all beat. Every single one.

I squeeze my still-hard cock.

She'll need a bath soon, not that I'm in a mad rush. She smells like my own little slice of paradise, all covered in *me*. Bliss would be seeing her just like that—always.

And fuck, if I wouldn't do anything to keep her with me, safe from that bastard Utto and whatever the hell his cousin did to her. I haven't missed the way she keeps catching herself relaxing with me and then curling back into herself. She doesn't quite fear me, but she's not comfortable with me either.

Not for the first time, I wish I had medicine that could erase or heal the past. But it doesn't exist. There's no medicine for what she survived.

They hurt her. If she killed Rennie, it was self-defense. No doubt about it.

I make a new pot of *eeffoc*, and chug down a mug, rolling my shoulders, scarf down toast and fruit, a powdered protein shake, then head back to my pilot's seat, a fresh mug in hand.

I sit in the seat naked. Naked. I've never done that before. It feels ... decadent, obscene, rude, like something I'd never do in a million years. I prop a foot on the dash—something else I've never done.

I feel amazing. Relaxed, but energized. We'll be at Pilan in a couple of hours. And I swear, I'm ready for anything. Nothing in the universe will stop me.

Well ... except Feola. My stomach tightens, remembering the feel of her, the taste of her perfect pussy, dripping and clenching as she screamed out one hell of an orgasm. On this very seat. With her hands in my hair and her legs spread wide, fucking up against my tongue. *Ay-shocks. Ay-shocks.*

Beautiful beyond reason. And mine to protect.

Life is weird.

Fugitive, jobless, headed toward a hotbed of criminal activity—I've never been happier. Not once in my whole damned life.

A few hours later, I know one thing: Pilan is a shithole.

I hesitate in the hallway outside the dilapidated dock where we parked my ship. "Sure you're okay?"

She nods, eyes earnest and clear. I took her temperature, checked her oxygen levels, her heart rate. She's healthy—physically, at least.

Her emotional landscape is uneven at best. Her expressions vacillate between fear, hope, and doubt. It will be interesting to see how she reacts to the presence of strangers. According to her, she won't need serum for another six hours. Which gives us plenty of time. Still though, we don't really know how *mine* will affect hers compared to Utto's. Every male's serum generates a unique response.

I hesitate. "There will be a lot of men." A lot of men who all want the same thing—a woman, in a world with almost none. This is probably the most risky thing I've ever done.

"Ajax, I'm fine. Okay? Stop worrying."

Psychiatry isn't my specialty, but even I know she exhibits the signs. Uneven moods. Shifty gaze. Suspicion. Withdrawal. But then it's all confused by serum and her dependence on it.

Nothing is more frustrating than being unable to help someone you care about.

I can't leave her here and go trade the ship myself. I have to take her with me. What if she has a delayed reaction to my serum? What if someone smells her and decides to take her? What if twenty of them do?

"No tingling? No nausea? No... heat?"

"None. I'm fine. Really."

I doubt it, but whatever terrors lurk in her brain will have to be sorted out later, when we have the luxury of time and safety.

Which we don't have now.

I extricate my palm from hers. Holding hands isn't appropriate. Not at the moment. At least not for the roles we've chosen.

She looks like a short boy. A short, fat, mistrustful boy with a pigeon-footed gait. Though it had hurt ... deeply, right before we docked here, I led her to my ship's bathing pool, gave her her *epicanthu* oil to slather under her arms and between her breasts and thighs to mask her scent.

She even dusted the shadow of a mustache across her upper lip using *momadrac* powder in the galley. Her hair is tied back in a low tail and obscured by a cone-shaped black sunhat. A pillow stuffed up her shirt, and she's pretty effectively disguised.

Hopefully, we'll give the impression of an Argenti aristocrat on a tour with a slovenly servant in tow. Anyone looking for longer than a split second will note those puffy lips, the delicate bone structure, the long lashes.

No one will have call to look, though. Not here.

Pilan is an out-of-Argenti-jurisdiction offshoot. A few hundred years ago, a mess of antique and retired ships were fused together to form one great cancerous mass that functions as a few neutral zones.

Since it doesn't fall under either Argenti or Vestigi

law, it has become a melting pot of drugs, illegal weapons, sex trafficking, smuggling and probably about a hundred other crimes I can't even imagine.

The hall we walk down seethes with unwashed people, unhealthy-looking animals, far too few lights, peeling paint, and market stalls with noisome wares.

Algae, or mold, climbs the walls, green and furry. It reeks of urine. A cockroach as big as my foot crosses our path and Feola sidesteps it, reaching out for my hand.

Instinctively I grip it and pull her closer to me, before we both remember and she yanks her hand away.

"Sorry," I mutter and point down the dank hall toward the main body of the space station.

"Of course," she says. "I shouldn't have done that."

I shift the bag on my shoulders that carries all the items we couldn't leave on the ship.

She falls into step behind me, refusing to meet my eye.

"You should, Feola. You should feel free to touch me whenever you want. Just not here. Later."

She doesn't answer.

The market is endless. And twisted, a warren of branching alley ways.

I have to stop three times to get my bearings.

From a squalid stall, a dirty man wearing stained rags spits at us, a globule of spit landing an inch shy of my left boot, and I have to remind myself that the only way off this ugly heap is to get a new ship. One that wasn't traceable.

Each hall worsens. Deep fissures run along the foundation. Old, rusty stains spread like decaying vines, rotting and climbing up the walls. Blood.

"What's wrong with this place?" she whispers.

"What do you mean?" I pause to look down yet another fetid market alleyway, and she bumps into me, the squashy pillows shoved in her suit pressing against my elbow.

She smells like a woman. Like my woman. Even under the layers of *epicanthu*, I can smell myself. Primitive pride has my hand going to her waist in a way I'd never have touched anyone else.

"Why does it look like it's about to crumble?"

"It probably is."

She touches my back for the briefest of seconds, and her eyes flare with what I swear, looks like comfort. Like she felt fear, touched me, and felt better.

I've spent my life administering medicines, staying up late to analyze the risks to other men's lives— being responsible for others, but never for anyone who was mine.

This is new. I run a hand over my *rezal* at my hip. I've never used it outside practice. The knives either. I'm good with them, I can throw or parry, but the only time I've ever sunk one into skin has been for surgery. All of this feels … new. Overwhelming.

Something's changed. Maybe just serum and pheromones at work, but it feels bigger as I stare into her wide yellow-green eyes. I wanted her from the first second I saw her, but this …

It got real when she trusted me to help her, when she took my serum, when she let me give her pleasure. At least for me. She might need a little convincing.

"Stay close, okay? And be ready to run if we need to."

CHAPTER FOURTEEN

Not anymore

FEOLA

Ajax isn't Utto. He isn't Rennie.

I know it.

Deep down in my bones, I know it.

But still, every once in a while, I look at him, so tall and broad and strong, and strapped with weapons, and I have to remind myself that no matter what Utto did, Ajax is not him.

They couldn't be more different, except for one thing. Utto hated asking for directions too. It infuriated him.

Evidently, Ajax has the same aversion.

This endless circling is frustrating.

Enough.

"Ajax," I say as we pass the same filthy market stall for the third time. "I think we missed a turn. We should ask someone."

"It's just up here on the right. The map Reyba—"

"It's not," I say baldly. I'm done being scared.

An old man sits behind a drooping stall, selling a strange, oozing gray fruit.

"Excuse me?" I mince awkwardly to him, the round swell of the pillow projecting in front of me.

The man has sallow skin, hair the color of iron, and a mole on the tip of his nose. His face wrinkles in suspicion.

I'm supposed to be a man, so I deepen my voice. "Could you direct us toward Quasilliaro?"

He flinches. I shift my gaze to Ajax with all his weapons, his massive boots, and his hard body in the black flight suit. He is truly fearsome. *To anyone who isn't me.* The thought gives me a thrill.

My own personal guardian. Too bad he wasn't there when Rennie… No. I saved myself.

"I'm Argenti, sir," Ajax says in his smooth, mellifluous voice. "But we're just here visiting. We mean no harm."

As my gaze settles on the bulge between his thighs, heat creeps up my neck, and I remember exactly how it feels pressed against me. I turn back to the man. "We just need to find Quasilliaro."

He rubs his fingers together, eyeing Ajax. He points at his knives.

He pulls a small one from a sheath across his ribcage. "My dad gave these to me when I came of age." He strokes along its surface, balancing it on the tip of his finger.

I shake off the memory of another knife. "Maybe we co—"

"It's okay." He hands it over, and it promptly disappears into the folds of the old man's sleeves.

"This wrong floor," the old man says, blunt and cold, in a thickly accented voice.

I bite my lip to keep from saying *I told you*, but can't resist glancing over at Ajax.

His lips twitch.

"Four floor up. Stair there." The man points with a gnarled finger. "Turn left at staircase. Long hall, all the way at end, on right."

"Thank you," I say with a triumphant smile.

From the way Ajax freezes with his hand in midair, I can tell he was about to gesture for me to precede him. He catches himself and stalks toward the door. As his "servant," I follow meekly.

It takes fewer than five minutes for us to find the offices of Quasilliaro. The hallway on the fourth floor is far cleaner than the dank market pit of the lower level. One whole side has a massive view of the center of the galaxy, and it spreads like a cloud of glittering so big that it boggles, shames, and inspires all at once.

The rest of the hall is shiny, lacquered so vibrantly yellow it hurts my eyes. Strange oblong benches rim one side in metallic golds and bronzes. Amorphous lights slither across the ceiling, casting a warm glow.

I try to keep my eyes on Ajax's broad back, but it's impossible not to sneak glances around. So many men. *None of them is Utto. None of them is Rennie. Utto is gone, and Rennie... is... dead.*

"The Seignaraglio is in a meeting," says a secretary behind a gold desk when Ajax asks about Quasilliaro. He's like nothing I've ever seen, with a tuft of feathery hair on top of his head and three eyes.

He's like a bird and a man combined, at the same time, only bottom-heavy.

Behind the secretary's desk, next to twin black doors, three enormous males stand with their backs against the wall. They look like the offworlders who came to my planet so long ago. The Vestige. With smooth pale skin, long black hair, and soulless eyes.

One of them scents the air.

Ajax shifts to stand in front of me. "Tell him I'm Argenti. And I've come to trade for a ship."

The secretary's three black eyes narrow, roaming up and down his body.

The bird-man rises and taps away on feet that look like claws. The sound echoes down the long, yellow hallway. Ajax glances down at me. I try to look fat and mannish. One of the Vestige guards shifts his weight, and I swear his nose twitches.

Oh, goddess. They're all so huge. I clench my jaw, shaking off an image of Rennie's leering face.

"Stay close," Ajax breathes, lower even than a whisper. Sweat slicks my palms.

Tense moments later, the bird-man returns. "He will see *you*, sir. Alone."

My stomach convulses at the thought of being

alone here, away from Ajax, with those three heartless men sniffing at me.

"No."

The bird-man blinks three eyes, his gaze lingering on my face. After a long moment, he parodies a smile with his wide beak-mouth and shrugs.

Ajax's shoulders square.

I move closer to him than is appropriate for a servant, and together we follow the secretary through one of the doors.

As we pass the guards, I'd have sworn one of them sniffs the air, his gaze slithering up my body.

The doors slide shut on a hiss, and I breathe a sigh of relief.

At least, until I see the man behind the desk. He's huge, and his face is deformed. He has no nose and sunken eyes. His face looks like it imploded and then was rebuilt of metal. Wide silver metal plates form cheekbones.

"That will be all, Ssssimmonsss. Pleassse don't clossse the door. The guardss will be alert."

Ajax shifts his weight, blocking me so I can't see. He's always doing that.

I move just a little bit to see the strange man behind the desk.

He sees me and smiles, pinched and weird, and the metal plate over his nose glints.

Swallowing thickly, I look away, toward a blank yellow wall with a long, low fireplace. A faint light gleams along a fine crack just to its left. A hidden doorway?

"Quit hiding back there." Quasilliaro's voice is as cold and sharp as knives. "Ssstep forward. I haven't ssseen a young woman roaming free in a long time."

Bile rises in my throat. My head spins … it's just like with Rennie. I squeeze my hands into fists until my nails dig into the soft flesh of my palms. *I am not that scared girl.*

"I've already ssseeen enough of your pathetic disssguisssse in the feedsss."

I step around Ajax.

Quasilliaro's smile stretches, and the blood stills in my veins.

"Do you know what a woman like that iss worth?"

I glance down at my rotund pillow belly.

"She iss yoursss?"

Ajax's shoulders tighten. "Yes."

When Quasilliaro laughs, it sounds like a hiss. He steeples his hands on the desk before him. "Not anymore."

CHAPTER FIFTEEN

Scum king

AJAX

I study the man across the desk. Quasilliaro's face is *fucked* up. There's no other way to describe it. A mess of crappy surgeries on top of bad healers, and even worse, limited or inappropriate supplies. It's a miracle he's even alive.

"I'll make you a fair deal." Quasilliaro's hands stretch across the table, fingers spreading out like webs. "But she's not leaving thissss station. What do you want for her?"

"She's not for sale."

Quasilliaro slow-smiles and leans back in his ornately carved chair. The gleaming yellow walls behind him are so damn bright it burns the eyes.

"Yesss. She iss," Quasilliaro hisses. "You have

two choicesss. You can make a fair trade and leave here with your ship. Or I can have my guardss kill you. And I can take her. Either way… she iss mine. The question iss really only if *you* leave here or not."

His accent is clearly Argenti but the hiss is not. It's not an affectation either. He clearly makes an effort to hide it by clenching his lips together.

That's why the smile is so creepy, tight, no more than a grim stretch of his lips. More grimace than smile. No teeth.

Suddenly, the hiss makes sense. He must constantly clench his jaw to keep from showing a mouthful of busted or missing teeth. He's speaking through a clamped jaw. Again, shitty healers.

"I'm not leaving her. Not on this shitty dump."

Quasilliaro claps, but his face holds no amusement. "Ah, Pilan. This place may be a hive of sssscum and villainss. But thessse are my villainssss. I am king of thisss sscum hive."

I raise my brows. "Sorry, what? You were talking, I mean I even saw your mouth moving, but I couldn't focus on your words. I kept getting distracted by your mangled robot-turd of a face."

His cheeks turn red around the metallic plate.

"Oh, that's right. You were claiming to be the scum-king. But you aren't, really. You're co-scum-king. You need to check with the other scum-kings before we make a deal."

"I have no *co-sc*… kingsss."

I step closer, trying to get a better look at the bubbling red skin around the edges of the metal plates over Quasilliaro's nose. "Do they have healers on Pilan?"

Quasilliaro props his hands behind his head. "I know what you are trying to do. There is only one exit from thisss room. You're wassting your time."

"He's lying," Feola breathes behind me.

No one like Quasilliaro would have their office at a dead end.

Quasilliaro claps again, a slow, steady rhythm that echoes in the room.

"Ahh, a pusssy with brainsss. Not a good combination." A fat tongue licks along his lower lips. "I would fix that. There are certain drugsss that can remove that negative energy. Make for a 'yesss' woman, if you will."

I don't look back at Feola. I don't need to. I can hear how fast she's breathing how fast her heart is pounding. Too fast. She'll faint if she doesn't relax. "Shh."

Quasilliaro clearly thinks I'm talking to him, because his face twists, but Feola knows. And she listens. Her heart slows.

"I do need a ship," I say. "But she's not for sale. I've got an Argenti ship, two years old. Fully loaded. A *Stella-Scrematrice 55.0*. In prime condition. She's yours in exchange for any space-worthy vessel, stocked and ready."

Quasilliaro smirks. "Why not kill you now? You've annoyed me enough. Take the woman *and* the ship?"

I step closer, until I'm maybe twelve, eleven, ten

feet away. The desk is between us. It's bolted to the floor with great big silver clamps.

"Because, as I said, you aren't the only scum-king on this dump. I'm Tribe, fresh from Sierra-Six. I may not be here on official business, which you know since I want an unmarked ship." I lift my right hand to stroke my lip, trying to look natural even though the move is awkward as hell. "But I'm not without friends. A lot of warriors know exactly where I am. They'd cause a lot of trouble for you and your friends."

"Yet here you are. Alone but for a pillow-ssstuffed, *epicanthu*-sssmeared pusssy with a brain. No, no. I will have the woman. Not negotiable."

Red corrosion blisters along the edges of the metal plates. "Your face really shouldn't look like that," I say with a dramatic wince. "It's got to hurt."

He flaps his hand in the air. "Enough with the dissstraction techniquesss. You can leave alive with your new ship. Or you can die here. Either way—I get her."

I step even closer. The corrosion is a deep red, oozing yellow. "What kind of painkillers do you take?"

Quasilliaro ignores me. "Nothing short of an army of Argenti will sssave you and her—and we both know you can't pull an army, or you wouldn't be here."

He's got a point.

I'd put him at around thirty-five years old, maybe forty. His hands are under the desk and out of sight.

There's likely a weapon within hand's reach, probably multiple weapons. The thing is—with nothing more than windows separating them from space, he won't want to use a *rezal*. That has to be why his office is where it is. So no one else is inclined to use one either.

Breaking that glass means painful death. Fourteen seconds of exposure means loss of consciousness to apoxia as the blood deoxygenated. Then ebullism, as bubbles form in bodily fluids, and hypocapnia as the pH of their blood changes. Ninety seconds max, and we'd all be dead. But the symptoms would be irreversible long before that.

"I could fix your face."

Something moves in Quasilliaro's sunken eyes. Hope?

"How many surgeries have you had? Four. More? Six?" I whistle at the look on Quasilliaro's face. "More? None by me. I'm a very good healer."

"Right. I'll jusst kill you now."

I shift closer. The *rezal* also has the added negative of calling the guards.

Eight feet between me and the desk. Feola can't run very fast. I need her closer to me—and that desk. "What kind of ship can you offer me in exchange for her?"

"What kind of woman are you offering me?"

The most beautiful one in the universe.

If Quasilliaro has a *rezal*, he won't use it. So he has something else. Whatever he has, it isn't out… But my knives are. I'll be able to draw faster. And trust that Quasilliaro won't hurt a woman. Not if to him, she means money. Lots of it.

"Come here, Feola."

She steps beside me, smelling like herbs and flowers and sunshine, and under that, like woman, aroused woman. She needs serum. And soon.

"Take off your hat."

Her chin lifts and her eyes tighten, but obeys. Her slender fingers pull at the black, triangular hat, and all that glorious pinkish-orange hair bounces free.

I try to put reassurance in my eyes, so she'll understand. "Take out the pillows." They'll only slow her down anyway.

The look in her big yellow-green eyes just about breaks my heart. All the while, I keep inching us closer to the clamped-to-the-floor desk.

Her lip trembles and my gut clenches.

She pulls a pillow out through the top of the jumpsuit, and then another.

The soft, black fabric bags around her, clinging to her skin, highlighting her perfect, round breasts.

The pillows flop as they hit the floor.

"Nice titsss," Quasilliaro, the nasty mangled fuck, grunts. "Show me."

The look Feola sends me burns like acid in my gut.

I want to pull her close, tell her I'm sorry. Instead, I make my voice sound lazy and say, "Wait 'til you taste her. Like flowers."

She keeps her eyes on the wall in front of them, shoulders tightening, shaking with all the pent-up rage I can't even imagine, as I tilt her forward, so her luscious ass juts out.

"Hold onto the desk," I breathe into her ear.

"I do love the tassste of cunt." Quasilliaro leans forward, those sunken eyes narrowing as he studies her, lingering on her vivid hair and eyes.

She shudders in my hands.

"I know you." Quasilliaro claps his hands together like a happy child. "The blond healer who ran away with the pink-haired Trianni woman. Her mate hassss money, but more than that… his uncle hass… Power. Asss long asss the sspace between here and Argentussss. Even on Pilan. His reach iss sstrong."

I drop my hand away from Feola's warm hip. "Where's my ship?"

Quasilliaro's eyes narrow. "Ssstep around the dessk, behind me."

Fear simmers in the air around her, but arousal too. She's getting more desperate for serum.

I glance at the windows. The only type of windows thick enough to be blast-proof bow out in the center. These are smooth and flat.

Feola doesn't meet my eyes as she rounds the desk with small, deliberate steps to stand just beyond Quasilliaro's reach, three feet from the escape door.

"Where's my ship?"

Quasilliaro turns in his chair, angling toward Feola. "Not far. Lower level. This quadrant."

"What type?"

Quasilliaro moves closer to Feola. She cringes but

doesn't back away.

"It's a Parsssa. About fifty yearsss old. Red asss blood and uglier than sssin. Sssolar ssstorage for crap, but it'sss fassst. It'll get you where you need to go. Totally untraceable."

"Access codes?"

Quasilliaro holds a key up. "Nah, ah, ah." He waves his hand. "Backup all the way to the doorsss, until you're even with the guardsss, and I'll tosss it to you."

That's the opposite of where I want to be. When shit blows up, I need to be close to Feola, the bolted-down desk, and the closest escape.

But I nod genially.

Quasilliaro smiles.

"That's fair." I turn toward the ornate black carvings that flank the exit, ornamentation disguised as blast doors, stark against the ridiculous yellow walls, and hope there are blast doors at the back entrance too. My boots squeak on the gleaming floors.

Then I pause. "Just out of curiosity, what the hell did happen to your face?"

Quasilliaro's smile melts away. He pauses, hand mid-reach toward Feola.

"It was a *rezal* blast to the face, right?" I ask.

Quasilliaro nods awkwardly.

I move closer, leaning in for a better look. "Who did the reconstruction? A Vestige doctor?"

Quasilliaro shakes his head, mouth tight.

I frown, licking the corner of my mouth in thought. "Because, I have to tell you, I didn't go toward bionics or grafting, but even I could have laid smooth skin over that. What is that? It should be solid titanium. But it's not, is it?"

Quasilliaro doesn't move. I smile and pivot from the core, and on a breath, pull one of my knives.

"Not titanium. Aluminum, right? That explains the corrosion."

Spinning and throwing at the same time, I can tell before the knife even leaves my hand that my aim is off. Something about the feel of it, or maybe something about the way the neurons in my brain fire relative to the motion, but I can just tell.

It doesn't matter.

Quasilliaro does what anyone would do when a knife is thrown at their face. He flinches. And brings his arms up to block.

He's not fast enough, though. The knife hits him hilt first, right in his nonexistent nose, and his head flies backward.

That's all I need.

I take off, fast, vault over the desk, and land on top of him, knocking over his chair.

We fly back. Quasilliaro's head hits the ground, and I sit on his chest, my fist burying itself in his face before he can even make a sound.

Feola makes a sharp strangled sound, covering her mouth and scrambling toward the knife that's clattered across the floor.

I should probably reach for her, help her, but my hands are a mess, still buried in an imploded face.

On a space station with fabricated gravity, Quasilliaro didn't need the same kind of metallic implants they use on Argentus to mimic bone structure. His shitty doctor used sheet aluminum, which was enough for a man who intended to live his life on a space station, surrounded by armed guards. But not thick enough to stand up to the fist of an enraged warrior.

My stomach heaves as I lurch to my feet.

My whole life, I've saved people. Stayed up late, sat by their sides, held their hands, fought *for* their lives.

"We need to go," I whisper.

Gray matter mixes with red blood on a floor the color of the Argenti sun.

"Did you j—"

Banging sounds come from the doorway.

"Don't look."

The guards are running toward us, moving fast, weapons raised.

"Hold on to me."

I grab the codes from the man's desk with slippery fingers, and a single glance tells me they're fakes. Fucker was lying all along.

I wrap an arm around Feola, pulling her against me and wrapping me legs around one leg of Quasilliaro's desk. I raise my *rezal* and fire it at the wall of glass separating us from certain death.

It happens in slow motion. The *rezal* blasts out, deafeningly loud. The glass melts around the hole, shattering into a hundred broken shards, sucking out as if pulled by a thousand invisible strings. The guards, running past the broken glass, lift up and into the air. Loose chairs, papers from Quasilliaro's desk—all of it lifts up as the pressurized air sucks out into the great vacuum of space.

"Take a breath," I shout.

It isn't far. Two or three long steps toward the door, but the air is moving wind-tunnel fast. The traction of my boots and a hard kick off the desk let me get a hand around the slim depression of a handle, to wrench the door open.

I shove her through, yanking the door shut behind us.

Thank every god in the universe, there's a locking hatch on the other side. I seal it manually, locking the breach on the other side of the door, and pray the three-eyed secretary on the other side thought quickly enough to contain the explosion.

CHAPTER SIXTEEN

The illustrious pair

FEOLA

My time with Utto was bad, but I learned one valuable thing from him. I learned how to shut off my mind and go somewhere else, somewhere he couldn't touch. I found this little faraway corner of my mind that functioned like an off switch, a place where I could shut away all the fear and focus on one thing.

Which I do now.

I focus on getting out of here alive. With Ajax.

"Go," he shouts over the roar.

And I do.

My body runs, Ajax right behind me, and Utto buzzing frantically across the Bond, like he can feel the terror lurking just beyond the edges.

Shouts echo down the long hallway we've

stumbled into. A service hallway, maybe. Endless blackness, punctuated by small bursts of light. Black shapes scurry in the darkness. More cockroaches.

Ajax pulls me to the right, down another hallway.

We run. Sirens wail, drowning out the ability to think. No time to analyze the similarities between the scene with Ajax's possessive, appraising hand on my hip and Rennie's on my breast.

Down another hallway.

Down a stairwell. And the sirens wail on.

And another.

And another.

How many? Three, four? I can't be sure.

The wailing ricochets off the walls, multiplying and resounding in my eardrums until my head throbs and my stomach shudders, and my skin breaks out in chills. Ajax grabs my arm, pausing me mid-run. I jerk to a stop, whirling to face him. I can't hear him in the cacophony. He points at a circular disk in the floor, a hatch with a big cross-shaped handle.

"Down," he mouths.

I nod.

He squats down, gripping it's handles, and after a long muscle-bulging moment, the metal unsticks, and the hatch door rotates with a grind. He lifts, and I duck to peer through.

We're maybe ten feet above another dingy market hall, maybe even the same one we were in before, and the wailing is even louder.

I resist the urge to cover my ears.

Ajax hauls my body against his, presses a fast kiss to my lips. I get a fleeting impression of his perfect Ajax smell, and then, as if I weigh nothing at all, he lifts me over the hatch.

I dangle in midair as he lowers me as far as his arms reach, until my feet are only a couple feet off the ground. Not far.

People scurrying past barely even notice as they run past, intent on their own evacuation.

He drops me.

This time, I stifle the squeal in my throat.

I land in a squat under the power of the drop, but I keep my footing, for which I feel proud.

Holding the handle of the hatch, Ajax drops into space, pulling the hatch closed with his body weight. He hangs for a moment, feet dangling in the air, body torquing as he twists it closed, then drops agilely to the floor.

Without pause, he tilts my chin back with a firm hand on my neck. He studies my eyes, takes my pulse, then takes my hand, and we walk together down the market's central aisle, the bag with their belongings bouncing on his back.

"You okay?" he turns to look at me over his shoulder.

And immediately crashes into a wall of men.

Two men, even taller than Ajax and more muscled than Utto, block our path.

"Come with us," says one of them. "Hurry."

Ajax's hands lift, and so do mine.

Guilt rollicks through me.

This mess is all my fault. All of it. The fact we're on the run. The fact Ajax had to punch a man in the face. The fact he's now being held at gunpoint.

Maybe I can reach his rezal. But then what?

I study the men. They don't appear to be Vestige, as Quasilliaro's guards were. They look like Argenti.

I don't know enough about the convoluted politics on this bizarre space station to understand what's going on, but Ajax seems less worried as they hustle us through a scarred door. In my chest, Utto seems almost relieved, the Bond unwinding and relaxing.

We walk for a long time, so long my stomach cramps, my hands sweat, and my mind clouds. I needed Ajax. I need serum. The vials of Utto's rest in the bag on Ajax's back.

Bile surges in my throat. It's almost like Utto is goading me, pulsing in my chest, encouraging, almost loving. *Take my serum, Feola.*

Fuck that.

Hard pass.

Finally, we follow the guards into a wide space with amorphous walls, shiny and black. The guards lead us toward a table and chairs that sparkle and gleam.

"Where are we?" I ask.

"Sit," one of them says in a voice so gravelly I can barely hear him.

"Who do you work for?" Ajax asks.

The one on the left, whose face is more square shaped and whose eyes are less dark, grunts. "Sit. Shepherd will be in shortly."

Ajax sighs and pulls out a chair for me. The walls remind me of flower petals, sinuously curved, molded and shining wetly under low lights. Occasionally the tone of the black lessens and drifts toward colors, dark blue, deep purple. Wherever we entered, I can't see any seams; the doors must be hidden within those folds.

The massive men back out of the room, exiting through a rounded fold that disappears as soon as they're on the other side.

"You okay?" Ajax's voice is soft.

I take a deep breath. "I'm so sorry, Ajax. This is all my fault. You should just leave me. Go back to Sierra-Six. Get your life back."

"My life wasn't all that great."

"You weren't running for your life on this … place. Wanted by the Argenti government. If they catch you …"

"Then I'll have been caught doing what was right. What I wanted to do. Whatever happened back there, Feola, it was wrong. You needed help. I'm here. I want to be here."

He always says the perfect thing. He deserves so much better than me. When this is over, I'll figure out how to repay him. Somehow. But for now … I can't even try to turn him away. If I were a stronger, better woman, maybe.

I trace my hands over the smooth surface of the

table. Up close, it looks like thousands of tiny stars imprisoned within the material. They blink and pulse, pale and golden, under my shaking fingers.

Time to face facts. "I need serum."

"Okay." His hand slides across the table to capture mine. My belly flutters at the contact. He looks at the door.

I don't know what his plan is, maybe to just whip it out right here, or go ask someone for privacy. Either way, it doesn't matter.

A sleek black petal of a door opens at that moment, and a man enters. Muscled, oiled, wearing nothing more than a brief strip of fabric belted around his waist, his body gleams in the low lights. He carries a massive platter laden with food.

Ajax tracks him, body tense.

"Food." The man lowers the platter to the table.

My nipples tighten into hard aching peaks.

Ajax casts dubious eyes over the food. "How long will we have to wait?"

The man doesn't respond and bows low before exiting.

"How badly do you need it?" His words ripple in my ears, and I arch my neck, squirming into my seat.

"Utto withheld from me a few times as a punishment. I think I could make it another couple of hours if I had to." But I really don't want to. I'd rather that than drink Utto's filthy serum though.

Ajax tilts his head back, looking up at the ceiling. "That fucking asshole." His fingers slide up my arm, to my neck, behind my ear.

I lean into his touch.

In the soft, warm light, his eyes are nearly purple. "You don't feel fevered," he murmurs, moving closer so his other arm circles my back. His finger slides down over my jaw, down my throat. "Your pulse is fast."

I'm breathing fast, too, but it has nothing to do with the need for serum. I lean closer so my forehead rests against his jaw and my nose presses against his neck. He smells so good I sigh, rubbing my nose against his skin.

"Feola."

"Yes?" I pull back to look at him.

His gaze drops to my mouth. The corner of his lips angles up, his eyes crinkling. "You still have a mustache."

"What?" I bring my hand up to my lips and remember the *momadrac* powder I rubbed on my upper lip.

I wipe at it, and his eyes crinkle even more. "It's all over your cheeks now."

The door opens again.

An Argenti man enters, with dark golden skin and long ebony hair. He wears a shimmery black suit and has a close-cut beard. His shoes echo off the polished floor.

I move instinctively closer to Ajax, shifting so my chair sits between his spread thighs and my shoulder presses against his chest. His hand closes around my hip, drawing me closer.

"The illustrious pair." A smile stretches across the strange man's face as he approaches, moving with serpentine grace. "I go by the name of Shepherd. *I* owe the *two* of *you* quite a big thank-you."

"Enough of a 'thank-you' to get us off this place," Ajax rumbles in my ear, voice low and velvety.

The smile stretches. "It *could* be negotiated." Shepherd has a way of emphasizing words and drawing them out so they seemed to carry hidden meanings. He lowers his long body into a chair opposite us. He isn't an idle pusher of papers. The man moves like the warriors of the Tribe. His suit hints at hard muscles beneath the fabric. He leans forward and makes a show of scenting the air.

Ajax growls barely audible. Little more than a disturbance of the airwaves.

"The last time I smelled a female, she *wasn't* free. She *wasn't* in heat. She *wasn't* alone in the company of *only* one man." He pours himself a glass of water from the goblet, takes a long sip, and sighs theatrically. "What are you? A warrior who misses knife throws?"

Ajax shrugs lazily.

How does he know about the knife throw?

"A real warrior wouldn't have missed that throw. No. You're something else." His gaze burns with intensity as he scrutinizes us, lingering on my hair and Ajax's face. "More than just a healer."

Ajax stays quiet.

"So those knives are just decoration?"

Ajax shrugs again. "Everyone in the Tribe carries the knives."

"And yet, you took out Quasilliaro and his entire seat of operations. That is no mean feat."

Ajax thumb strokes my ribcage, making it hard to focus.

"You want a way off this space station?

Ajax's nod brings his roughly stubbled jaw in contact with my temple.

Shepherd leans back in his chair, studying me. "And yet—you are Ajax Willo. And this is the famous Feola. So valuable, this woman. I could turn her over to Upranimus. He is so very rich, you see. I could take the money, set up a business somewhere other than this miserable hellhole."

I lean toward him. I learned one other thing from Utto. Men do what they want. This man didn't turn us over immediately. Which means he wants something else.

"Then you would have," I say, earning a curious glance from Ajax. "If you were going to turn me over to Utto and his uncle, you'd have done it by now."

"Ahhhh." It sounded like agreement, but it might just be curiosity.

"So what do you want with us?"

He leans back in his chair. As his head angles back, the light hits his eyes. They're almost amber. So unusual, flicking back and forth between me and Ajax.

I stifle the urge to whimper, or pant, or maybe just

rest my head on the table. My stomach twists. Five minutes alone with Ajax. That's all I need. I dig my fingers deeper into his thickly muscled thigh, and the connection steadies me.

"How familiar are you with the politics on Pilan?"

Not familiar at all.

Shepherd wiggles three fingers. "There are three main political figures."

"The three scum-kings," I whisper.

A whisper of a smile appears at the corner of Shepherd's mouth.

"Correction. There *were* three. Your murder of Quasilliaro has left quite a power vacuum."

"Where is the other?"

Shepherd leans back in his chair, eyes sparkling, and crosses his arms behind his head. "He, too, met a rather *untimely* demise, off Pilan. I have slipped into his role for now. A position that is *highly* useful to me. One I would like to *keep.*"

Silence fills the chamber. *Untimely demise. Off Pilan.* Old memories stir in my brain. The obscure drug references. *Septusine,* the drug Utto used to make me compliant. Something Rennie said about loving tits, and Utto saying he never had to speak with the women whose tits he touched. It wasn't possible. What women? There were too few women.

"Was Rennie a scum king?"

Shepherd's eyes gleam, and suddenly it all makes sense.

"Do you have proof?" I ask, earning a curious

glance from Ajax.

"My fellow *scum-kings* worked in human trafficking. One of them was meant to deliver a *shipment* to Quasilliaro. Who would then deliver the *shipment* to me. Neither of them is alive. Yet my clients are still here. I am in what you call a *quandary*."

A muscle under Ajax's eye tightens. His jaw clicks. Fury veils his face. Or maybe it was disgust. "Not our problem."

"Oh, it *is* your problem. If you ever want to leave Pilan, I *need* your help."

"What do you want?" Ajax's voice seethes with disdain.

"I would like to provide my clients with a *product.*"

"What does that have to do with me?" I ask, tired, sick, and desperate for this conversation to end.

"You would make a perfect slave."

I shiver, the pulsing between my thighs growing too urgent for me to bother feeling fear or anger at his statement. I can too well imagine the life of a slave. No control over one's present or future, moving from one slap to the next. Fear.

"Again," I say, "if you wanted to make me a slave, your bald men would have killed Ajax, and you'd have made me a slave. What do you really want?"

Shepherd sinks his teeth into his lower lip. "Quasilliaro supplied the merchandise. And I took care of sales. The people in the club were promised a slave."

Ajax shakes his head, firm and resolute as ever.

"No."

"You see my dilemma. I have a thousand men waiting in a room. They flew in from all over the galaxy. I cannot simply tell them that the goods are not here."

One more person who wants to use me.

Ajax's fingers tighten on my waist. "No."

Shepherd lowers his palms to rest on the glittering surface of the table. "Then you are not leaving this room."

"You're not selling her."

"I agree." Shepherd's smile is beatific. "I don't *actually* need to sell her. I just need to pretend to sell her. To a specific buyer." Shepherd's eyes grow more intense. "A specific *blond* buyer."

Ajax's face darkens. "How can I trust your word that you won't let someone else buy her instead?"

Shepherd spreads his hands wide. "Would I do that to my new *friends?* After you've so kindly taken out my competition." His gaze flits to me again. "*All* my competition. Of course, it is customary for the new owner to provide a small level of *entertainment* after the auction has ended …"

The words hang in the air, lingering like a bad smell.

Like have sex in front of them? "We can't," I say. "We aren't Bonded."

Shepherd's smile doesn't waver. "You *need* serum. No?"

He has us there, and by the serpentine glint in his

eye, he knows it. "I can keep you safe. And immediately after, you'd be on a ship, flying into the distance."

It would get Ajax out of here safely. No bloodshed. And whatever his qualms, they're born of his desire to be a gentleman, not because he doesn't actually want it. He *would* enjoy it. "The ship will be fully stocked and untraceable?"

Shepherd nods.

"We'll do it," I say at the exact same moment that Ajax says, "No."

"I *do* need serum." My face burns as I glance over at the grinning Shepherd. "We need to get off this space station, and he can help us. Done."

"I'm not parading you in front of a group of men like some sort of trophy."

"Why not? Women and men have been paraded for far less worthy a reason. This will get us out of this mess. It makes sense." I study his tight jaw, hard mouth. "You just don't want anyone else to see me naked."

He closes his eyes at that, inhaling sharply. He turns back toward Shepherd. "You could just be a decent person and let us go."

Shepherd rises. "I'll give you a few minutes to discuss."

"No need. I can't wait much longer. Bring in your hair dye and prepare your club. Tell them to get ready for a performance."

CHAPTER SEVENTEEN

let's get this show started

AJAX

I swivel in my chair to rest my elbows on my knees.

The vein along the side of Feola's throat quivers with every beat of her heart.

I tear my gaze away. The air around her carries the scent of *epicanthu* and her.

Looking at her hurts.

She squirms in her chair. "Please, *Ay-shocks*. I know this isn't exactly what you want, b—"

"This is all I want. It's all I've ever wanted. Just not like this."

She leans in, cups my cheeks in cool hands, forces me to meet her wide yellow-green eyes. "How did you want it?"

I don't even have to stop and think to answer.

"Like the first time I kissed you in that hallway. Simple. Honest. Straightforward. Just you and me. Because we want each other."

A breath gusts out of her like she's been punched in the stomach.

"Then forget it's like this. We're doing this to escape, but we'd have done it anyway. Pretend it's just us. No past. No future. Just now." She sinks her teeth into her lower lip, and all the blood in my body rushes straight to my cock.

A smile ghosts across my lips. "You were right."

"About what?"

"I don't want to share you."

"You won't. Let them look. You're the only one who will touch me."

For now. My throat tightens at the reminder that whatever this will be, it won't be a Bonding. "Fine. But... Feola?"

She nods at me.

"Don't dye your hair. I love your hair."

Those big white teeth flash in the dark room. "Maybe Shepherd can come up with a hat."

Within moments of us telling him we're ready, supplies are brought in. We prep fast, Feola's shivers getting worse with every minute that passes.

"You ready?" Shepherd asks from the door, with at least the grace not to smile.

I offer Feola my hand and tug her to her feet. "You feel all right?"

She shrugs with a quick flash of a grin. "I will in a few moments."

I trace a finger down her cheek. She's pulled her hair back into a tight bun and brushed it with coal powder. Shepherd produced a black mask for me—apparently everyone in the audience wears them to conceal their identity during the illegal proceedings. But none for her. She'll go in completely exposed.

Which makes me feel about as small and pathetic as the cockroaches roaming Pilan's underbelly. What kind of man lets a woman under his protection perform like this in public?

Not my choice. She isn't mine.

She touches my hand. *"Ay-shocks.* Thank you for doing this. For us. For me." The hairstyle makes her skin glow brighter and her eyes burn brighter. They blaze yellow-green and effervescent. Animated. Like she glows. Always. I just wish I understood the secrets hiding behind those eyes.

Her choice.

"Believe me, this isn't entirely altruistic." I trail my thumb over her cheek, run it over that full pink lower lip. Her lips parted, the bottom one mushing up and moving with my thumb. She trails her tongue along the fat of my thumb. I barely suppress the growl building in the back of my throat.

Her cheeks flush, skin heating under my hand, and the air carries another burst of arousal.

"You're killing me." I press a quick kiss to her

forehead. "Let's go auction you off in a bizarre sex club to a bunch of strangers."

She sends me a look.

Shepherd steps away from a leaf-shaped door and gestures Feola through. The black silky fabric of the robe Shepherd gave her shimmers under the light with her every step. I try not to think about what's under that robe. Nothing. Or rather everything. Feola's naked body. Slicked with oil.

Shepherd drops a hand to my arm, his eyes taking in the man's creepy orange gaze. "No one will recognize her. Or hurt her. Trust me." I must make a face at that because Shepherd offered up a low laugh. "She'll be on a stage. Separate from my patrons. They won't get to her."

"And the exits?"

Shepherd sizes me up for a long moment. "There will be one just off the stage. To the left. One of my men will show you when this is over. There's a tunnel. He will take you to your ship. Fully stocked. With all the provisions you could need."

"And untraceable."

Shepherd nods. "Completely."

I grit my teeth, staring at Feola's back while she stands, impatiently shifting, uncomfortable. Needy. Waiting for me.

"Let's get this show started."

CHAPTER EIGHTEEN

I guess you're mine now

FEOLA

I remove my slippers just outside of the door to the stage.

The club is dark as night, punctuated by warm, low lights. Loud, driving music shakes the floors and sends a pulse throbbing between my thighs.

I curl my toes against a sudden burst of ridiculous nerves. Not about Ajax touching me, for some reason that doesn't scare me a bit, but to be surrounded by all those men…. Utto complained constantly about how small my breasts were, how big my butt is. And now thousands of men will see me. Bare. Exposed.

I shouldn't care what they thought, but somehow….

What if they think I'm ugly? What if they boo me off the stage?

I shake that stupid vain thought away with a grimace, and try not to think about the fate of the girl who was meant to be in my place.

As I walk onto the stage, cold air swirls under my robe. Frosty on the damp skin between my thighs. A fresh stab of need coils low and goosebumps spread across my skin. The need is so much stronger now, as is the weight of Utto's apprehension, thick and frenetic in my chest.

Hundreds—thousands—of men sit in chairs like a massive open arena, all of them facing me, faces concealed behind black half masks.

Guards pace nearby.

Black silhouettes eye me as I stop in the center of the stage, alone, washed in blinding lights.

My body rebels when Ajax moves past me, down the steps to take a seat in an empty chair in the front row. I bite down on the inside of my cheeks, forcing myself to relax, to slow my breathing.

An announcer moves around the stage. Talking fast. Saying words that made no sense. *Prime flesh. Choice slave. Unique eyes. Virgin ass.*

I let it all wash over me like the tide in the Green Sea back home on Triannon. Adapting is not the same as surrendering.

I have no choice about this ridiculous public performance, but I can control how it happens. This will not be one more moment in a lifetime of things being done *to* me. From now on, I will be the doer.

With shaking fingers, I untie the knot around my neck that holds my robe closed.

Forget them all. Forget every last person in the room but him. Ajax matters. They don't. Not right now.

I can't see his face. He's just one more shape in the crowd. But I focus on him anyway.

The robe falls to the floor in a dark puddle, and I am naked before a thousand men, but my skin prickles for just one of them. I can't see his eyes, but I can feel them. Hot. Hard. Determined.

Forget about Utto and Rennie and everything that happened at Romeo-Two. Just look at Ajax.

The slithering Bond in my chest twists so tightly I have to rub my hand over the ache. Someday I'll cast Utto out for good.

The crowd claps. And the announcer has to shout to be heard, loud enough in my ears to block out the sound of Utto's taunts and Rennie's smug laughter. The lights are bright enough to blind me to anything but the feel of Ajax's invisible gaze.

Across the theater, blue holograms of me appear. Close up, blue-tinged, and enormous, my body gleams around the room.

The thousand masked faces in the crowd are all leveled right on me. They hold up their hands with numbered flags, and the announcer's voice comes even faster. The bidding has begun.

Ajax's face, eyes shadowed behind the dark mask, looms like a promise.

He waits. So long. Unbearably long. As the price soars. Until finally the number of hands raising lessens. There are three or four. And still, Ajax does nothing. Then just two, number flags slicing up into the air in a staccato beat in time with the announcer's voice.

So long, I start to doubt, to wonder. Is he the man I think he is? Would he abandon me to this?

Then finally, that elegant, long-fingered hand slices up into the air, and the panic recedes, my throat loosening.

The announcer's voice grows excited. "And we have a new bidder joining the fray."

It doesn't take long after that. Ajax rises to a smattering of applause and ribald cheers. Time slows, every single second. All the details fade away. The noise of the crowd. The lights.

He stands in front of me. So big and tall, a breath of a smile at the corner of his lips. "I guess you're mine now."

"Was I ever not?"

His lips part.

A second pulse pounds between my thighs, fervid and incessant. Chewing my lip, I reach up for the zipper of his flight suit over the hard ridges of his collar bone.

The straps of knives will need to go. My fingers slide over the buckles, tugging them free. He holds them, dangling from one hand, body rigid as I tug down on the zipper, leaving his flight suit gaping from neck to groin.

I stroke a finger down his cheek, along his jaw, his throat, over the rise of his Adam's apple. It bobs when he swallows. He casts a wary glance around the room, shifting our bodies so he faces the audience, and they have my back.

His nostrils flare in time with his breathing, his breaths fanning over the skin of my shoulders, my breasts.

It's like my body knows the serum is coming soon. My mouth salivates, my eyes grow heavy. I can almost taste it.

I push the arms of his flight suit over his shoulders. Hard biceps come into view, corded forearms.

The sharp lights of Shepherd's club accentuate the fierce, jagged edges of his body. I suck in a breath. I've never seen anyone so sharply muscled in my life.

He stands head and shoulders above me, and except for the rise and fall of his chest, he doesn't move a muscle. Just waits.

I lick my lips, block out the sounds of cheering from the patrons of the club behind me, pretend I can't feel infinite gazes glued to my bare ass, and trace my hands down from his collarbone, over the thick rise his chest, over the hard bulges of his abdomen, over his navel, and lower.

A roar from the crowd buzzes in my ears, and desire makes me dizzy as I close my hands over the hottest, hardest part of all. The thin layer of fabric is a barrier that needs to go.

A shudder racks through him, his hands fisting, his abdomen flexing.

I've never touched him there.

I undo the snaps and wrap my fist around him.

Scalding skin. Smooth and velvety soft. Silk stretched over iron.

"Feola," he breathes like the breaking of a dam. His hands close around my waist, pulling me closer, higher, so I stand on the tips of my toes. My neck and spine arch back as he bends over me and claims my mouth with his.

Shouts and claps ring out.

His thick length presses against my belly, and I am hungry for it, desperate for it, ready for everything he has to give.

His tongue strokes mine.

"Ajax," I pant against his mouth, desperate for the taste of him, more potent than *eeffoc*. Everything fades away. Utto's Bond heaving in my chest, and all the spectators. Gone.

"I want you," I whisper against his lips. I don't know how, but I somehow know he needs those words. They rush out. "I want you. Even without all these people, I want you."

He growls, and the vibrations ripple along my every nerve. His grip tightens, clutching me against his body. I should be scared at the ferocity of his coiled muscles. From anyone else, I would be. His grip is like steel.

But I know him. It was never like this with Utto. It never felt this right. His body moves over mine, sinuous and sleek. Maybe I even stop breathing.

He moves me effortlessly, dragging me closer. My brain stops.

His mouth moves to my neck, roves down to my

collarbone, his hands rising up and down, higher and lower, gripping my ass, his fingers sliding deep in the valley between my cheeks. I want him everywhere.

I try to help him get the positioning right, or maybe we're dancing, an ancient, hip swirling, steady rhythm. One minute I want my breasts against his chest, and the next it's my throbbing heated flesh I want against the tickling hair of his hard thigh.

Restless hands and even more desperate hips.

I turn my face to the side and vaguely register the thousand faceless men. I forgot about them. I think Ajax did too. One man stands closer, less than twenty feet away. His eyes are shadowed in the darkness, but his gaze is steady, locked on me, stillness surrounding him, like staring at death.

Shivering, my fingers close at the nape of Ajax's neck. He growls against me, grazing my skin with his teeth, his fingers clamping around a nipple, strumming until my eyes close.

When I lift my eyelids again, I see us, Ajax and me, both of us, in holographic reproduction, repeated across the entire club, glowing bluish, moving, and beautiful. Like a single exotic beast caught in a dance.

"Ajax, I need to taste you." I'm on fire.

His growly purr does nothing to cool the burn.

His cock presses hotly against my belly. I've never wanted anything in my entire life like I want him inside me, right now.

His chest vibrates a low rumble that sends a flood of heat swirling. His finger slides down my belly, down between my thighs.

It's not enough. I don't want his finger inside me. I want his body inside me. He presses a second finger in beside it. I want more. I want all of him. Every last bit... which means Bonding.

I tear my mouth from his, turn my face away from him.

My eyes settle on that man in the crowd again.

I need serum.

"Now." I push his hands away, dropping to my knees.

He shakes his head like I've surprised him, or maybe like he's just struggling to focus.

Magnetic heat pulses between our bodies. For a brief moment, embarrassment courses through me at all the strangers staring at my ass of all things, big and fat as it is. The familiar shadow of the man stands nearby, watching, the twenty holograms of myself behind him, on my knees, pilgrim to the muscled man-god that is Ajax.

The thrashing of Utto's Bond grows wilder, a demanding, threatening pressure. My chest aches, but somehow, I know it is an ache that Ajax can heal.

He looks down, his eyes unreadable behind the mask, his lower lip pushed out slightly, every muscle tensed, breathing fast.

The tip of his cock glistens under the blue light. I lave my tongue over the hot, velvet crown, and the flavor blasts through me like an explosion. Sweet and intense and ridiculously good.

Moaning, I suck him down deep, pulling him into the back of my throat.

I scrape my nails over his abdomen, trace them gently over the skin of the heavy sack between his thighs, reveling in the gasps and groans tearing from his throat, the rising appreciative roar of the crowd.

I look up at him, and when I increased my pressure, bobbing my head up and down, his head tilts back, neck arching, muscles bouncing.

His hips buck infinitesimally, and I can well imagine the strength it takes for him to hold his body still.

This man is so sweet. Too sweet. He doesn't need to be so gentle. A part of me wants from Ajax what I never wanted from Utto. I want his power, his need, his frenzy.

I hum around him and suck harder.

He explodes in my mouth with a curse, and a grunt, and a buck of his hips, and then all reason leaves my mind. I swallow down everything he had to give, even as the cells in my body detonate in a violent, screaming orgasm. My eyes roll in a vision-darkening, ear-splitting, deafening roar.

CHAPTER NINETEEN

I can make lots

AJAX

Holy shit. With ears still exploding like a goddamned supernova, I force my eyes open. So many people are staring at us. Oh, gods. She keeps on sucking even after there's nothing left, and the heightened sensation makes me shudder, muscles twitching, toes curling in my boots.

Gasping, I drag my gaze away from the sight of her pretty lips wrapped around my dick and up to the crowd.

The commentator's voice pulses, words drifting across my consciousness. *"...hell of a blowjob. The lady seemed to enjoy it as much as he did."*

Wincing, I stroke a hand through Feola's hair, tugging slightly so she'll release me. Her glittering eyes find mine, and slowly I pull out of her mouth. Cold air hits my skin, and I hiss, yanking my pants closed.

"Let's go." I wrap a hand around her wrist, snagging her robe off the floor to drape around her shoulders as I pull her to her feet.

The lights brighten across the theater's seats, and Shepherd appears, a brow raised in all its sardonic glory. "That was quite a performance."

I open my mouth to tell him to go fuck himself, but Feola speaks first.

"Are you going to take us to the ship?" she murmurs, voice coasting across the airwaves, husky and raw.

My fingers flex to fists.

"No," Shepherd says. "I have… larger problems to contend with." He pauses for a moment, then steps closer to me, voice lowering. The façade slips, and along with it the affected gestures, the coy tilt of his head, and I see only a pragmatic man. "Upranimus hired bounty hunters. One of them is especially good. A Vestige named Torum. He's known to be fairly ruthless and efficient. Watch your back, healer."

It's nothing I didn't already know, but it settles something like determination at the base of my spine. "Yeah."

About an hour later, I'm in the pilot seat, staring out the viewscreen of our new ship.

It's the color of dried bile, rusty, and about eight

decades old, but not in bad shape, all things considered. It's been dismantled and reassembled a few times—probably before I was born. Enormous seams scar the hull where it was grafted together, different colored metal and faded paint jobs combining in a patchwork quilt of ship-skin.

I don't even want to imagine what its engine looks like.

It's noisy, clanking, and groaning.

Feola sits beside me, clutching the arms of the copilot's seat. She's barely spoken since we left Pilan.

"You've been quiet. No nausea? No renewal of the …?"

"Not yet. But it's only been a couple of hours, right?"

The digital reader on the dash says it's approaching midnight.

"I want to throw away his vials." Her voice is musing, unemotional.

That makes two of us. I shake my head instead. "I'm not sure that makes sense. It might be nice to have a steady supply on hand."

"Never. Not after..." Her dainty hands tighten into claws. "I can't ever tolerate the taste of him again."

"What do you mean?"

"It tastes wrong. His serum. It's not right, what it does to me. It's an addiction from him. It always was. Something was always off about the way I responded to it." She flushes and chews her lip. "Now I know

… after … It's different with yours."

I'm not proud, but in that moment, I really do want to puff out my chest and thumb a fist against it. It's not like I play an active conscious role in producing the stuff, but it makes me obscenely proud that she likes the way my serum tastes. "They say that each male produces the ideal flavor of serum for his mate. I wonder if ..."

"He wasn't really my mate?" Her tone is unemotional. She isn't speaking in metaphors.

I frown.

"Is that possible?" Her eyes burn. "It was never right. From the beginning, it was all sour, tainted by …"

"You were definitely Bonded, but maybe …"

"I don't care what the reasons were. I just know that tasting him again would make me sick. I don't want to. Not after you."

There's what I want to say and there's what I have to say. What's *right* to say. "What if we get separated, or captured? We've got no idea what we'll find on this planet."

"You could make some, right? I stole Utto's."

I shake off the burst of lurid curiosity. I really don't want to know how.

I reach out a hand, pull her to her feet to stand between my spread thighs. She's dressed in a pair of tight black pants and a black shirt that Shepherd found for her. I tug her against me, pressing my face between her warm breasts. She smells like flowers and like me.

She melts into me.

"I can make more. I could make lots. I mean … Not right now. I mean I *could*. But you need it now too. And anyway, I'm not sure that's smart. It's more important that you're safe. I just … We aren't Bonded yet. His serum might be more potent if we get separated, since he's still your Bonded mate…" *Which sucks.*

I can barely even let myself imagine that she might be mine someday.

"*Ay-shocks*, I can't Bond with you."

I knew that, but it hits like a blast of icy water anyway. "I know. It's okay."

"It's not that I don't want that. I do. I want you, but after Utto, I won't give anyone that kind of power over me again."

"You don't need to explain. When we get back to Triannon after all this is over, after you are safe and free of Utto for good, I'll see what I can do about ending your addiction. We can do it. It would just take weaning, and it doesn't make sense while we are running from the Guarda for you to be sick for that long."

She nods.

"But Feola"—I tighten my grip on her waist, pulling her closer, so she can feel the thick ridge of my dick against her—"I'm going to do everything in my power to change your mind between now and then. I lost you once. I don't want to lose you again."

She stills in my arms, her eyes going wide.

"I'd never hurt you. I'd never do what Utto did.

There's something wrong with him. The purpose of the serum isn't to keep the woman captive to the man. It's the opposite. It's to bind us to the woman for life so that we'd die to keep her safe, and her children. It offers protection."

"Ay-Shocks." She strokes her hand down my face.

I don't really want to hear whatever she's about to say, so I shift her, lifting her up to sit in my lap so her legs straddle me. She sighs when I kiss her neck, sliding my hand under her shirt to stroke one of her tightly-peaked breasts. "I want to be inside you. So badly."

She freezes in my arms. Afraid? No. She grinds down, pressing that molten heat against me, and all the air rushes out of my lungs.

"I know. I want it, too."

"There are other ways." I tilt her back, bowing her over my arm, so I could rub my face in the soft heat of her breasts. When I suck a rosy nipple into my mouth, she groans and writhes on top of me. I *will* change her mind. I just need time to earn her trust. I rise and carry her toward the bed at the back of the ship, where I lay her down. "This time, there's no rush and no audience. We can take our time."

I do. I trace my tongue along every beautiful part of her body. It's so fascinatingly different than mine. The line from her armpit to the bottom of her breasts, over the ripples of her ribs, along the hollowing dip of her abdomen to the rise of her hip bones. The sinuous curve of her spine leading down to a pair of perfect twin dimples at the base, and her beautiful, perfect round ass.

I hiss, my hands on her hips, imagining how it would feel to rise up behind her, shove inside of her, take her roughly, unabashedly.

I close my teeth over the spot where her neck and shoulder meet. She arches against up, pushing back, moaning. She's hungry... for me, and that makes my dick swell even longer. Groaning, I slide my hands under her, between her hot body and the soft sheets, to slide my fingers through slippery skin.

Some day.

CHAPTER TWENTY

A major fuck-up with a population of 6...

AJAX

A sat-portal, a relic from a few centuries past, is our final pass-through before we hit the periphery of the galaxy and our destination, the planet Araa-Ara.

When we're within an hour of it, I access radio connectivity to contact Tam. The ship's technology is cumbersome, but we get through to Triannon's comm net. Tam isn't available, so I send him a quick message, telling him we left Pilan.

I'd feel better if someone in the universe, beyond a shadow of a doubt, knew exactly where we were, though.

That, and if we didn't have a slew of bounty hunters on our tails.

We slow and do a cursory flyover of Araa-Ara, letting the ship's scanners analyze it for humanoid life forms. The readings are clean. I hate having to trust the word of a man I've never met, but Tam trusts

Reyback. It has to be enough.

The ship spins a lazy arc over the planet, and we watch through the viewscreen. Pale gray, silver, white, and purple. An unknown. I've never spent time on any planet but Argentus.

The vegetation here is largely pale purple, with a wide, silvery sea. A single colossal landmass dominates the rest. Mountains cover a majority of the continent, but a wide open plain offers an ideal landing location near a long, sparkling river, and more importantly for our uses, the ruins of the old abandoned hotel Reyback mentioned, nestled on a hillside. A good, defensible spot should we need it.

Feola points out landmarks. Mountains and lakes. "It's so pretty. I've never been on an alien planet."

"Well, get ready." I shift the thrusters, walking her through it as I go. I've been teaching her the basics of flight as we go, and set the trajectory toward a landing spot that's nice and flat, near a shaded area about two miles south of the old hotel.

"Wait." She puts a hand on my arm. "I want you to leave me here. Give me a *rezal* and some rations, help me find some place safe where I can wait for Tam and Nissa. I'll be okay. But you need to go back. Reclaim your position. Your job. Help your family. I can't let you give up your whole life for me."

I push off from my seat and cross to hers.

She looks up through dark lashes, eyes clear and determined.

"You aren't *letting* me do anything." I tug at a lock of her hair. "Don't worry about my life. I didn't like it all that much anyway. Do you have any idea how bad a ship full of warriors smells?"

A small smile breaks through. "You'll be arrested."

"By your side. I'm not leaving you alone, Feola. I'm in this with you. 'Til the end."

She looks like she might argue, so I squat down to check the straps on her seat.

"They're done correctly. I know how to strap in."

"I know you do. But I'll still always check."

The dirt on the surface of Araa-Ara is white, soft, and shiny. Mineral powder. It billows out from beneath the hulking behemoth of our shitty ship like iridescent steam.

The fucking thrusters died half way through landing.

I glare at the piece of shit, resting my weight on one foot, hand on my hips. I want to punch it, but I'm wary of venting my temper in front of Feola. She's seen enough violence in her life that I don't need to compound it with useless fits.

Her brows are high. She cups her palm over her forehead, blocking the harsh, silver sunlight from her eyes, and sucks in her lower lip.

"Just give me a minute," I say and walk around the ship, out of her sight, where I kick the dirt and punch the air a few times to release some of the pent-up energy.

Life on Pilan suddenly looks pretty fucking cozy.

Squatting down into the dirt, over a clump of plants with tiny white leaves and blue flowers, I let my face screw up and my hands clench. My gaze falls on the rise of lavender mountains in the distance, the gleaming white cupolas of the hotel ruins, the thin shimmering line of a river trailing down through violet woods. *Fuck*.

I scrub my hands through my hair. *Fuck*.

No thrusters means no lift-off. Which means no escape. Which means we are stuck here on the fringes of the galaxy with no ability to contact anyone, and who-the-hell-knows is coming after us.

I pull out my comm and stare at the last message Tam sent, only partially downloaded. *Don't go to AA. Planet abandoned after major fuck up with the population of b ...*

That's it. What the hell was the rest of the sentence? Buffalo? Boys? Bacteria? Barbarians?

Either way, we aren't supposed to even fucking be here and now we're stuck.

I don't even want to think about if the b is for bacteria. The pathogens that could exist on an alien planet is enough for nightmares.

Shepherd's ship is well stocked, but has no medical instruments or machines ... nor does it have functioning fucking *thrusters*.

Whatever the *fuck up* was, it must have been brutal to make them abandon a resort planet. Normally, they'd have just eradicated the problem.

Beyond that, we fried the circuits landing, and the

ship's power cut off. It's hot as shit here, and the beating sun will turn the ship into an oven in a few hours.

So, we can't stay in it, not until the sun sets and the temperature cools.

But at least the air is breathable. Small victory.

A plan. We need a proper course of action. So I stand, and plaster a smile on my face, and round the ship, back to Feola.

She's facing away from me, looking into the distance, the dark black of her clothes a stark contrast to this hot, pale, sunny planet. Her hair is the brightest thing on the horizon, flashing almost neon orange pink in the sun. "Can we fix it?"

I shake my head. "We may be here awhile."

"I gathered as much. Did he do it on purpose? Shepherd?"

"Give us a ship with bad thrusters? I doubt it."

"I was going to try again. To make you leave me. But now you're stuck with me."

"I'd never have left you. Not in a zillion years. Not for anything."

Her jaw tightens. "This is my fault. You shouldn't be involved in this. Any of it."

"I wouldn't change a thing."

We stand in silence for a long time. Finally, she reaches out and takes my hand in hers, cool despite the heat, and smooth.

"We'll be okay, *Ay-shocks*. Don't worry."

A smile tugs at my lips. "That's supposed to be my

line."

She taps her forehead, right between her eyes. "You've got a big frowny wrinkle right here. Tam and Nissa know we're here. They'll send someone for us eventually."

It might be months. I don't say that, though. No need. She knows that, too.

"Let's go check our supplies." She holds out a hand.

It's as good an idea as any.

We can hunt. Assuming there is anything to hunt on this planet. And we can forage, assuming there's anything to forage—and that it isn't poisonous.

And it's time for some god damned luck. An angry buffalo or a wild boy population I could handle. A dangerous bacteria population ... Anything but that.

I watch her because it's something to do other than think about the mess we're in.

She's in the pantry, counting out our provisions. The dip of her spine and the small of her back curve as she shifts. She leans forward slightly, and the round heart of her ass pushes toward me. I give in to the temptation and stroke a hand over it. "I love your ass."

As she glances over her shoulder, a wry smile twists her lips. "You don't think it's too big?"

"Too big?" I frown studying her body. "Trust me, your ass is perfect."

We count through the food together. It will last a few weeks, assuming it doesn't melt in the heat.

"We're going to need more food. There must be something we can eat. There should be game here, since it used to be a sporting planet. I'll teach you how to hunt." And then she can protect herself from buffalos or boys or whatever else starts with a b, if necessary.

She looks surprised. "With a knife? Or a *rezal?*"

"What else?"

Something moves behind her eyes. For a minute, I'm afraid she might cry.

Instead, she smiles. "Let's go."

CHAPTER TWENTY-ONE

I love your screams

FEOLA

"There's less gravity here," I say, lifting my feet experimentally.

"Yeah." A bead of sweat runs from Ajax's temple, down his neck, and over the sharply angled rise of his Adam's apple to pool in the hollow of his collarbone.

It's hot. But more than that, the sun is scorching. We changed before we left, donned lightweight white clothes from the closet. Shepherd provided just about everything.

We have clothes in every color, weapons, and hats, quite a bit of food, blankets. Everything... Except shoes. The only shoes I have are the stupid slippers Utto gave me to wear on Romeo-Two. Ajax scored the bottoms with one of his knives to give me extra traction and lined the soles with leather inserts he tore from own boots, but they're still woefully thin.

The ground is as hot as coals beneath the thin

soles, so I keep my steps light and quick, trying to land on clusters of the tiny blue flowers, grateful for the long white dress he found. Its wide, open sleeves provide protection from the sun and a break from the heat of its rays.

Ajax has on white pants and a shirt, but he long since sweated through them. The fabric clings to his body, and as always, he's strapped up with his knives, and those big boots. Poor thing. He looks miserable.

Triannon, my home planet, was a sultry, humid place. I grew accustomed to the cool temperatures aboard the ship, but the heat here doesn't faze me. Not like it does him.

"At least he gave us lots of clothes."

He scowls back beneath the wide straw brim of his sunhat. He initially refused to wear it. We found two in the closet. I took the one decorated with enormous pink flowers, leaving him with one with a huge yellow bow around the rim.

We stepped about eight feet from the ship into the glaring sun before he backtracked and retrieved the yellow-bowed hat, ripping away the ribbon with a grumpy wrench.

He held the offensive ribbon between his fingers as if it were poisoned, letting it flutter to the floor of the ship.

"I bet you regret tearing off your pretty bow now." I tighten my own pink bow beneath my chin as the wind kicks up.

He slaps his hand on the back of his hat to keep it from blowing off and fires me a dismal glance.

The pale, pearly soil intensifies the sun's brilliance. The dust kicks around our feet as we walk, sending up clouds of blue petals.

"I feel lighter... almost bouncy."

"It's not quite that bouncy," he grumps.

The heat and sun will kill us as fast as hunger and thirst. How long until Tam decides to come looking for us? Weeks, if we're lucky. Months, more likely. We need to find a steady source of food and water, and a place in the shade to spend their days. He knows all that and it makes him cranky.

So I wrinkle my nose. "It's pretty bouncy."

He chugs water from one of the bottles we brought in the pack he carries and offers it to me.

I take it, staring out at the distant trees. They are far slenderer than any I've seen before, swaying in rhythm with the breeze, as gently as if they were underwater.

"There's a larger grove of trees up ahead," he grunts. "We can get out of the sun for a while."

He's right. Shining silvery trunks reflect back at us, like a handful of precious metal.

A silvery tendril of the river curls down the slope of a gentle lavender hill, blinking in the light. Delicate beauty, pristine and unsullied. Untouched by Utto or Rennie or any of the ugliness. Even the dirt is clean and pure. "I like it here," I say.

We continue in silence toward the copse of trees.

The air is cooler in the shade and filled with a sweet smell. The trees rise above them, causing the light to dapple and spread. Long lavender leaves sprout from the tops of trees like feathers, reaching high into the sky, and then trailing down to touch the ground, willowy and soft, in a wide circle like a tent. The feathery tendrils trail into the water on one side. "It's beautiful."

Ajax rips the hat off his head and tosses it to the ground. "It's hot."

There are far worse things than being hot. As if he can read my mind, Utto flickers in my chest. He's been quiet lately. Biding his time. Or planning.

Ajax unhooks the straps across his chest, moving fast, stomping over to dip some sort of measuring device into the river.

He looks miserable, weary and wilted down to his soul. And suddenly my heart feels as light as my body.

A small giggle escapes, and he sends me a baleful glare.

He freezes, eyes gleaming.

"What?" I ask.

"I haven't seen you laugh like that. Not since... before."

At the look in his eyes, my belly flutters, and the heat of a blush rises up my neck.

"The water's safe." He hooks a hand at the neck of his shirt and peels it over sweaty skin, revealing the lean, hard expanse of his thickly muscled back. "Take off that dress," he growls, pulling at his boot.

"Why?"

"If you don't want it to get wet, I suggest you take

it off now." He tosses his boot and sets to work on the other one, muscles flexing and bulging as he shifts.

"Why?" I'm not laughing anymore.

He doesn't look silly. Not at all. All lean and rippling, with a dangerous gleam in his eyes. And naked. And... hard. And big. Heat floods between my thighs.

"Because you're about to get really, really wet."

Too late. The dangerous purr in his voice sends ripples of arousal straight to my lower belly, like a punch in the stomach. I suck in a breath, "Wh-wha—wha..." And off when he straightens and stalks toward me.

He's not laughing. He just looks determined, and it's a testament to him that no part of me feels afraid.

He stops a few feet away. The slight smile hiding at the curve of his mouth keeps me relaxed, easy as I study him, biting my lip.

His eyes soften. "I said I'd teach you how to use a knife, and I will. But I'm too hot to do anything right now. So we're going to get wet." He flashes me a grin. "If you aren't out of your clothes in three seconds, you're going in the water with them on."

I laugh into my hand and shake my head.

"Three...."

"You wouldn't."

"Two...."

I know he wouldn't. He knows arid places like this may be hot in the day but they're cold at night. He wouldn't want me wet and shivering. But I don't wait to find out. I slip out of the slippers and, pulling the dress over my head, run toward the silvery glint of the river.

The brittle soil gives way to slippery white mud and water, blessedly cool on my skin as I run down the bank. Ajax follows close behind.

He could catch me easily, but he lets me run, and for that I adore him.

I part a curtain of trailing, purple feathery leaves, sending a shower of pale petals swirling through the air, and stumble out into the brilliant, blinding world beyond.

Water rises up my hips. The river's a paradise of life. Silky-smooth plants swirl cobalt rich and purple bright around my feet. Vivid fish flash around my legs in a kaleidoscope of color.

I glance over my shoulder to see Ajax barreling toward me, water splashing on the hard planes of his body.

He looks at home here, with his pale silvery blond hair and his golden skin, against the backdrop of a glittering sun and sky.

I dive under the water again, kicking my feet to get away, propelling forward faster than I intended into a school of glassy silver-and-yellow fish that dart and flicker away.

Ajax catches me by the toe and pulls me back against him. I hit the air laughing and sputtering, sending water splashing in a thousand droplets all around. My feet slide on slick rocks below, but Ajax would never let me slip. It's a relief, after all these months of ships and recycled air, to feel the weight of a sun's rays and the slide of moving water over my skin, fresh air.

I've never felt so free in my life.

All the bad memories recede. We may be hiding. Utto is out there. We may be stuck on this planet for an unknown amount of time, but in this moment, right now, I am free and Ajax is glorious, with his mesmeric turquoise eyes.

His mouth meets mine, grinning. Lips and teeth, less kiss than shared air.

He tugs at my waist, and my feet leave the ground, legs circling tightly around him. With a hand on my belly and one below my ass, he presses me back so my body rests on the river's surface.

"Your skin is pale. The sun here is too bright." He walks us back to the shade of one of the willowy trees. "I can't let you burn.'

I let him tow me back into the shade and stretch my arms over my head, a hum rising in my throat.

Lazy and happy.

The thought makes me wary.

Happy. I chew over the feeling, humming louder. Happy always meant laughing with Mamma in the Red Gardens of Triannon, dancing, singing. When did I last sing? On Triannon, surrounded by red ferns and old friends. Long ago. Before the Vestige came and took over the planet.

I let the hum rise into a song. A nonsense one, a children's song from home. I keep my eyes on the cathedral of purple in the tree that arches high above.

My eyes drift shut. Ajax has gone still within the circle of my thighs, his big hands firm around my rib cage. He doesn't move a muscle. The river's current sets us gently asway. If moments could be perfect, this one is.

When I open my eyes to peek, Ajax's face is inscrutable.

A long moment passes. "You sing," he says, voice gruff.

I swallow against the emotion in his voice. "Not in a long time."

"I haven't heard a woman sing in person since … not since before my mom died."

I want to ask what kind of music his mother sang. Lullabies, perhaps? Or happy songs? Learning songs?

Mamma knew a song to suit each mood. She had a song for every type of day, each time, each purpose. I don't want to make him sad, though.

"Your voice is beautiful."

"You'd say that even if I squeaked."

"I'd say that especially if you squeaked." He bends his body over mine. "I like your squeaks. And your squeals." Presses a kiss against my lips. "And your moans." Another soft kiss, as he tows me toward the sandy bank. "And your screams."

He kisses me until I'm weak and pliant in his arms, then whispers against my lips, "Keep singing."

I do, because really, by this point, just to feel his hands dip lower and his mouth close around my nipple again, I'd do almost anything he asks.

Almost.

CHAPTER TWENTY-TWO

A very thorough medical exam

AJAX

Twenty-four years ago, my brother and I had a sister, and our mother was alive. We lived in a big stone house back on Argentus, shaded by great blue *bayeran* trees, with leaves twice as tall as I am now. I ran in the yard with my siblings, Clari's curly golden hair spinning behind her, dancing in the breeze. I can barely even picture her face now. Our garden was filled with songs. We chanted and we played and we danced, spinning and happy and laughing.

Then it all stopped. The songs died, Spiro and our father and I watched as our family had burned in the great stone bier where the dead of our family have been burned for centuries. Silence reigned on Argentus.

I've listened obsessively to recordings and holo-performances by female singers. All of us do. They sang haunting music that gives me chills. Bittersweet echoes from the past, of voices long dead.

Never anything like the simple, joyous trill of Feola's happy song. Her voice is high and pure, and it makes my chest ache as I press her back against the muddy soil beside the river.

Wet, her hair is darker, and her vibrant eyes, under thick spiky lashes make my guts clutch.

The B better not stand for bacteria.

I can't lose another person to an illness.

"You're happy?" I ask, something tightening in my chest, condensing.

She nods, and her lower lip wobbles.

"Me too."

She traces her fingers along my cheek, leans up to press her lips to mine, drawing me down closer, wrapped her legs around my waist, rocking wet hot against my dick.

I torture myself, sliding against her slick folds. It's too much. All that heat, right there, a hypnotic pull tugging at a place deep inside. My dick just takes over, butting up against the entrance it craves, slides inside, just the head, but nothing has ever felt better.

Her eyes widen, and I with a muffled grunt, pull away so my dick slides free. It ... physically hurts, every muscle in my lower body clenches.

She rolls her hips so her clit presses against me, and I wince into her neck, trying really fucking hard to find self-control. It's just her pussy, her fucking wet hot soft *tight* pussy Right there. Like an inch from my dick.

I recited heinous medical procedures in my mind. Wart removal. Foot fungus. Goiters on wrinkled, old Argenti necks. They all contort in my mind, shift into her, beautiful and naked and spread out on my exam table.

I graze her nipple with my teeth, I can literally see myself taking a seat on my stool before her spread thighs, pressing a finger deep inside her pussy, her moans—*Oh, Healer Willo*—echoing off the walls of an exam room.

"Someday," he whispers, "I'm going to give you" —I swirl my tongue around her nipple— "a very" — thrust my fingers deeper— "thorough medical exam."

She tilts her neck back, her hips rocking against me, thrusting her breast into my mouth, rubbing that sweet pussy all over me.

I grit my teeth. It's painful, but I hold my body still and let her take her pleasure from me, rocking her clit against my length. I don't trust myself to move, not even a fucking inch or I swear to god, I'll lose it and ram myself inside. It's the only thing my monkey brain wants. It wants to shift, just a little, get the aim right, push inside that heat. She's so close, gasping against my neck.

Her fingers dig into my back.

She tightens her grip around my body until no part of her touches the ground; she just hangs under me, suspended over the damp soil, sounding out her pleasure against my wildly thumping heart. The low gravity makes it so easy to hold her. She's practically weightless. I slide one hand down, between the cheeks of her ass, to the tight puckered round skin there. Press.

She lets out a high-pitched almost shocked squeal, but my finger slips in and it topples her over the edge.

I wait until her motions grow softer, more languid, and pull my hand free, lower her down, dodge her hands, fist my dick. It takes scant seconds and I'm pumping wild ropes all over her.

Her eyes are sad. Mine probably are too, as I trail a finger through the thick pools on her chest and bring it to her lips.

CHAPTER TWENTY-THREE

Not a chance, woman

AJAX

In our shady spot on the shore, in the dim, silvery light, it's almost cool. The river ripples to our left. There are birds on this planet, we discovered, to go with the fish. Big birds, white with long, blue necks that sing with voices even higher than Feola's. And small twittering blackbirds too, that live in the trees and set the feathered fronds stirring, releasing more of that flowery smell.

"Ready?" I ask a few minutes later, my hand cupping the back of her head, where she rests on top of me.

"For what?" she asks drowsily.

"To learn to hold a knife."

She peeks up at me, all blinking yellow-green and curling pink hair. "Right now?"

"It's as good a time as any."

She bolts upright, breasts bouncing, the soft hair between her thighs tickling my belly. I bite back a groan.

She hops to her feet, face glowing and animated and practically races to pull on her clothes. I strap up again and pull on pants, but ignore the hot shirt and the miserable hat.

I take the smallest knife out. I'll adjust the straps for her later. Maybe one thigh sheath? And one to wrap around her forearm, where she can access it easily? I liked the idea of her carrying protection. Just in case. We still don't know what the b stands for. Bandicoots. Bobcats.

"Do you know why we fight with knives? The Tribe?"

She shakes her head.

"*Rezals* can damage a ship, and then everyone dies. Even the Vestige will rarely draw a *rezal* in space. Mostly, we use knives because it hurts. And death shouldn't come cheaply. Knife wounds are disgusting. People bleed like animals. It's visceral. It's personal. It's not like stabbing a pillow." I take her hand and press it against my abdomen. "Feel that. There's a layer of skin to get through. And under that, a layer of fat. That's all easy to pierce. But beneath the fat is muscle. Thick and hard. You've cut through game before? Right? It's not as easy as you might think." I tap her hand against my skin. "You need enough power to push through the muscle. Depending on where you aim, you can hit organs and take an opponent down." I move her hand up to my ribs, her fingertips cool against my skin. "If your aim is off, you can hit bone, and the knife will glide away. All you'll have done is pissed someone off and let them know where your weapon is."

She nods, her face so earnest and determined I want to smile, but there was something darker too. Memories and secrets swirl like mist behind her eyes.

I move her hand so her fingers trace along my neck. "This is a good spot. Everything in the throat is soft and vital." Lower. Over my collarbone and sternum. "All of this, shoulder, to chest, to ribs. All of this is bone and muscle. You won't achieve much of anything with a stab here." Lower to the base of my ribs, and then down to my groin. "From here to here is good. All soft, squishy organs. Even better if you can angle the knife upward." I shift the angle. "Under the ribs. Pierce something vital."

I drag her hand across the swell of my bicep, to the tendons and muscles on the inside of my elbows. "Strike here, sever these tendons, you can render your opponent's arms useless."

She swallows, gaze locked on mine. She doesn't look afraid so much as thoughtful. Like she's internalizing and memorizing my words.

"You hold it like this." I show her the proper hold. "With your hand, not your fingers. Use the fleshy part of your hand. Just there. Not too tight, but firm."

Her hand shakes as I close her dainty fingers around the blade, and something flares in her face, hope or satisfaction, determination maybe. Like someone who experienced violence and won't be on its receiving end again.

Her eyes widen, meeting my gaze.

Her secrets aren't so secretive after all.

I drop my hand away leaving the blade in hers.

"Knees bent, slightly, arm strong. Like this," I say showing her the proper stance.

She mimics my posture, and I spend a few moments correcting it. "Most important thing, always pull the knife back out. And twist before you do. Your goal is to stop someone, not annoy them. You leave your knife inside of someone, then you've either stopped the blood flow so they can keep fighting you, or you've given them a weapon and left yourself defenseless. In, twist, out." I mime a jab, twist, pull. "You never lose your weapon."

She nods again. I have to give her credit. Happy, singing, river-angel Feola has morphed into no-nonsense ready-to-fight Feola.

"Most important thing about fighting someone, Feola, anyone. Expectations. People respond to what they see."

Her gaze slips away from mine, scanning the distance. "They're going to look at you and see big eyes and a sweet face. Pull a knife on them, they might laugh at you, especially if you look like you've got no idea what to do with it. If they don't take you seriously, that's an opening. The second you start attacking and they realize you mean business, you've played your last card, and they will incapacitate you. Anyone you come up against is probably going to be bigger, stronger, and faster than you."

She chews her lip. "I know that."

"So you wait. Look stupid if you have to. Pretend

to be scared. Hide and surprise them. Whatever it is, don't play your hand too soon."

"Okay."

"We'll practice how to draw it later." I step back and spread my arms. "But for now, come stab me."

Her mouth drops. "I don't want to hurt you."

"You won't."

"I might."

"Not a chance, woman."

She scowls. Glancing down at the knife in her hand, she adjusts her grip, bending her knees, eyeing him with such resolve I nearly laugh.

She studies me for a minute, chewing her lip for a bare second. And charges.

She doesn't hurt me.

But she keeps at it for hours, until she's pink in the face and sweating, and I let her work out strategies for getting around blocks. I'm proud of her and more determined than ever to make sure she never needs to use that damned knife.

Maybe the B stands badger or bankers.

CHAPTER TWENTY-FOUR

B is for ...

FEOLA

The first time Utto hurt me, I swore I'd get away from him and never look back, and never, ever let anyone have the power over my life that he had. But then I looked around with fresh eyes and saw a base filled with men who looked like Utto. Big, handsome, powerful, and joined together like brothers. A mess of alien laws, and my own planet thousands of light-years away.

I was all alone.

And then Rennie came, and suddenly Utto wasn't the biggest threat in my universe. There was something even worse. It all made sense now. The scraps of conversation, the words I hadn't understood. Utto took me using his Argenti serum against me. He may have ruled my world, but *Rennie* had ruled his.

Utto may have stolen one woman, but his cousin had stolen many, many more.

We just need proof that Rennie was the third scum

king.

Ajax is in the water, as still as if he was born there and took root. He bends at the waist and lets his hands dangle. The sunlight strokes over the broad, rippling planes of his beautiful back. Along with the knife and the serum and the company on the run and the ride off R-2, he gave me a tremendous gift today by teaching me. He'd given me trust and safety like no one ever had.

And in return, I just keep on rejecting him.

He's done nothing but take care of me, protect me, support me, share with me, risk his life for me, sacrifice everything for me … and I've offered him nothing in return.

I rest my elbows on my knees and chew my lips. So tempting. I could Bond with him. We have time now. Freedom and safety on this planet. We might even have months before Tam comes to find us.

He doesn't move his body, but he catches my eyes from the river, and a slow cocky smile spreads across his cheeks.

A second later, a fat, white fish sails through the air and lands at my feet on the bank with a wet splat.

It flaps and gawps and bounces wetly.

I scrambled backward up the beach with a stupid squeal.

Ajax lunges through the water toward me and the flailing fish.

When he picks it up in his hands and smacks it against the silver bark of the nearest tree, I hide a wince behind my hand. He's coming alive. Every second he gets deeper under my skin, pulled at my broken heart more. Utto's Bond slithers darkly in my chest, a warning.

"I haven't fished like that since I was eight or nine," Ajax says, grinning. "Hungry?"

I swallow the lump in my throat. I need to know something. Did I go to Utto of my own free will? I know in my heart I didn't, but I need to hear it from Ajax. "Have you heard of *septusine*?"

All trace of a smile vanishes. He stiffens, eyes growing intent. "Not in a long time. Where did you hear that word?"

The look in his eyes is enough. Suddenly, I don't want to know anymore. Not now.

"Let's head back to the ship now that the sun's going down. We'll build a fire."

He pulls on his shirt and dons his boots, moving with the caution of a man lost in his thoughts. "Feola? That's a drug that hasn't been in use for twenty years. Not since the last woman died from the Plague of Days. It's dangerous. Where did you hear about it?"

"Utto and Rennie mentioned it in passing. I think he used it on me back when... back before we Bonded."

Ajax's jaw drops.

"What does it do?" But I know. I've always known.

"Its original purpose was to use artificial serum to heal women without needing the Bonding ritual."

I hold my breath.

"But it didn't work. The women didn't recover from the illness. It did, however, make them dependent on serum. It made them ... malleable."

It's like a thousand weights lifted off my chest. "Could it be simulated? Using real serum. From just one man?"

His gaze intensifies. "Is that what..."

The rest of the sentence hangs in the air between us, louder than if he's shouting the unsaid words. *Is that what Utto did to you? Is that why you Bonded with him? Is that why you didn't wait for me?*

Emotions well in the back of my throat. "Part of it. I think."

He crosses the distance between us in fast, even strides, the fish forgotten. His hand closes around my nape, fingers digging through my hair. His mouth falls on mine, open, and his kiss is almost desperate.

"I should have killed him," he whispers against my mouth. He wraps me up in a hug that is brutal enough to banish Utto from my mind. "I shouldn't have let you leave."

"It wasn't the only reason, Ajax. I was ... I was angry at you, for the way you just walked away after kissing me in the hallway. You said you were sorry and left and then, nothing. I didn't understand."

The corner of his lip tightens. "I didn't either. I thought I was doing the right thing, giving you time."

"I know. I get it now. But back then, I was so embarrassed. And so confused. I thought you didn't want me."

"I did. So badly. You have no idea how badly. I

got permission from the Admiral of S-6 to ask you formally to Bond with me, but I didn't want you to be skewed by that kiss. I wanted your head clear."

My heart thuds. He wanted me all along. I close my eyes tightly, remembering those early days when I lived for him. When every minute of the day after I woke on Sierra-Six, I thought of only one thing, one person. Ajax, and his kind eyes. Ajax and his gentle touch. Ajax and his slow smile. Ajax and his perfect, wonderful body. And while Ajax refused to kiss me in those days, giving me time to clear my head, time to grow accustomed to life amongst the Tribe, Utto had been drugging my tea so he could get into my head.

"I'm sorry," he says simply.

"Me too. I should have talked to you first." I should have done so many things differently. I should have fought for him.

He hugs me for a long minute before his body goes stiff. "We need to get back to the ship. I don't want to risk getting stuck outside at night."

He steps back, and I feel strangely shy after all the revelations as we finish packing up our things, but he seems brighter somehow, casting a warm smile my way. So much is out in the open now. So many things I should have said long ago.

I can't resist teasing him as I pick up his hat. "Don't forget this." I hold it out. "Remind me when we get back to find you a new ribbon to tie around it, so it doesn't blow away."

The smile fades noticeably from his face.

The fish is delicious. Flakey and salty.

Even better is sitting in the cradle of Ajax's arms as he leans against the rusty old ship later that evening. As the sun sets, low and gold on the horizon, the air cools. I'm grateful for his warmth at my back and the dancing fire on my face.

It's still too warm inside the ship, from a day spent baking in the sun, but hopefully it will cool down enough to sleep soon.

The last time I spent time like this outside was after the offworlders came to my planet and I entered a cryo pod to escape. That was before Ajax. Before Utto.

"So much time wasted," I murmur.

His arms around me tighten. I stretch a hand up and back to stroke his face.

"You mean with Utto. If we'd Bonded instead." His words, in his deep, husky voice, hit like a punch in the belly. How different would I be if we had Bonded immediately? I inhale sharply against a sudden flash of him moving inside me, filling me, claiming me as his.

He presses a kiss against my temple. "We'd be back on S-6. I'd be working in my healing bay. Maybe we'd be having a baby by now. You'd smell like flowers, and have the happiest laugh and the brightest eyes."

At the loss of that stupid, laughing girl, tears burn my eyes. "Do you wish I were still like that?"

The sky has darkened from a pale periwinkle to deep cerulean. Not a cloud in the sky. Stars peek through, bold already despite the lingering light. "I like you as you are."

Those are words I have never heard before. Simple. And more loving than a thousand other declarations.

Ajax presses a kiss to my shoulder, wrapping his arms around me more closely. "Sing for me."

I do, as night blackens the sky.

In the distance, a bird answers. A distant cooing hum.

The light wanes, and the singing bird is joined by another. They sing their song, and I sing mine.

Wings move against a darkling sky, small black dots flickering as they come closer.

The birds must be drawn by the song.

I stop singing.

Ajax stiffens.

The birds grow louder. Hundreds of them. Maybe thousands. Circling overhead. Black wings against a star-riddled sky.

"Move. Get inside the ship."

I make it two steps before the humming song shifts and becomes sharp caws.

Ajax curses, his body looming over mine, sheltering me as we move along the ship's hull toward the entrance.

He curses again. Wings flap against my skin, and Ajax lurches against me. "Birds," he mutters. "B is for birds."

CHAPTER TWENTY-FIVE

Close your eyes

FEOLA

Black feathers slap my face.

Ajax grunts behind me.

Shrieking caws fill the cooling night air. It's so dark I can barely see. Ajax's hands close around my upper arms, propelling me forward.

I curse again, and the birds scream louder. Hundreds, probably more, dive at us.

I throw my hands in front of my face. Talons—or are they beaks? —tear into the skin of my forearms.

He lifts me from the ground and tosses me through the hatch of the ship.

Black birds with wingspans the length of my arms crash against the walls, flapping and squawking. One dives at me, and I drop low, hiding my head with my arms, searching for something, anything to use as a shield or a weapon.

He shouts from the hatch, which he's struggling to wrestle closed. A bird dodges in. I slap at it, and it darts away, squawking.

Three more land on him. He twists, grabbing one from the air. Red streaks. Blood down the front of his shirt, vivid against the white.

He shouts at me again and points away, down the passageway.

I ignore him.

On the wall are a variety of tools. I twist the locking mechanism and pull out the first solid object my fingers close around.

A bird hits my back, digging into the skin. The pain is bad, but I am used to pain.

Vaguely I register that Ajax has finally sealed the hatch.

Black wings fly at my face, and I cover my eyes. My fingers close around a heavy wrench, longer than my forearm. Ajax shouts again. Massive birds slam and crash against the walls, screaming.

A bird lands on my shoulder, talons digging deep, beak pecking at my face. Squeezing my eyes shut to protect them, I swing around, roaring, wielding the wrench wildly, striking out.

A hand closes around my arm in an iron grip, stilling the motion. I open my eyes. Ajax stopped the arc of my wrench only a few inches from connecting with his head. His gaze is calm. No recrimination. Only concern in the depths of his vibrant eyes.

A pathetic whimper leaves my mouth.

An enormous black bird flops to the floor with a plop. Dead.

Five or six others litter the floor. Blood is everywhere. Pooling across the floor… just like…

He loosens his crushing grip on my arm. I'm breathing too hard. Too fast. I just keep on seeing Rennie's face. Grinning. Dead on the floor. Grinning. I drop the wrench.

It clatters to the floor, the noise echoing like a beating drum.

He wipes his mouth with the back of his arm, studying me with wary eyes. Blood drips down his temple. More streaks over his chest. His shirt is torn. Long gashes mar his beautiful, smooth skin.

He possesses rage, just like Utto, like all men and women do. I know that well. But from Ajax, somehow I just know it would never turn against me.

He squats in front of me, pressing a hand to my head, tilting back my neck. His turquoise gaze probes mine. He tilts my face to the side, eyeing my cuts and scrapes.my heart slows its panicked beats at his contact.

"Are you okay?" I ask with a glance at the sealed hatch, where the occasional slap or crash comes from the birds, still flinging their bodies against the hull, seeking entry.

He turns me away from him, pushes my hair over my shoulder, and hisses. "You're shaking." His hands close around my upper arms, pull me to my feet.

I look down at my hands. It's true.

"Come on," he says. "Let's get you cleaned up."

I almost laugh at that. "Me? Look at you. You're a mess."

"I'm fine. Come on."

He leads me down the passageway, where we strip off our clothes in the rusted bathroom, lit only by the low, lurid green emergency lights that line the edges.

The dark water ripples and steams. Argenti keep the sponge-like *stiranella* organism for a renewable water supply. The organism absorbs impurities from the water. A familiar joke among the Tribe's warriors is to say that someone's *stiranella* is thriving. The healthier the bathing pool dweller, the dirtier the warrior.

This one is quite healthy. The blackish-green organism hovers in the corner of the pool, large enough to make my nose wrinkle. Best not to linger on who else bathed in this water.

"What were those things?" I ask, to distract myself, and hopefully ease the tension in Ajax's shoulders.

"This was a resort planet. People came here for sport. But it hasn't been used in about three hundred years. Another planet, closer by with better weather, was found, and this one was abandoned. Who knows what sort of mutations the animals here have undergone."

"What do you think they wanted?" I wince as he runs a soft, soapy sponge over the scratches on my arms. The hot water burns.

"If I had to guess, I'd say us."

"To eat?"

He doesn't answer, just traces stinging soap over the cuts on my back.

Only when he's washed my entire body does he finally permit me to clean his cuts. I tried to be as gentle as he was with me, but the birds didn't just scratch at him as they had me. He protected me with his body as we ran for the ship, and the birds preyed on him. They carved deep welts into his back with their talons, punctured his skin with their beaks.

"Do we need to worry about infection?"

"I don't think so. The soap is strong. We'll apply balm that should help us heal faster." He lifts his shoulder carelessly. "We'll keep an eye on them."

It has to hurt, but he doesn't complain. The soap does its job, sizzling along his wounds, stopping the flow of blood.

"What happens now?"

He sits on a ledge in the bathing pool, and I kneel behind him, stroking my fingers through his hair. He tilts his head into my touch. "We need to talk about Utto and what he did … what happened back there."

My fingers freeze in the pale, thick strands of his hair. "Maybe, but not now."

"Soon. That drug…" His chest rises with his words, deep voice echoing around the chamber. He takes a long breath. "What Rennie did, whatever he did—"

"Please, Ajax. Not tonight."

He stiffens. "Bottling things up isn't healthy."

"I just… after today… it's been so perfect. Can

we just focus on us? On you and me. Here and now."

His shoulders relax, the tension easing. "It will get colder in here tonight. And we're too far from a water source. Heating and cooling will draw too much power, even with the solar absorbers working. We shouldn't risk losing what we need to keep the food fresh."

"So we'll keep each other warm." It would be easy to pretend Utto never happened. Bond with him tonight.

He nods vaguely.

"What else do you know about this planet?"

"Not enough. I should have looked it up."

"We were a little preoccupied."

He gives a short, breathy laugh. "Fair enough. What do I know about this planet? Nothing more than what we've seen. There's a hotel at the top of the hill, crumbling. We saw it. With waterfalls. There's water there. And presumably, some kind of roof to keep the birds out. There may be old communication systems too."

"So we'll go there tomorrow?"

He nods, and I wrap my legs around his waist, resting my cheek against the broad span of his back, letting my hands drift lower, down his smooth, coiled stomach. He's always hard. Always ready. I've never offered him half what he offers me.

I rise from the pool to stand above him.

He looks up at me, eyes rising from my toes, stopping briefly between my thighs, then higher, his gaze a hot caress, hotter than the steaming water of the pool. The air is already cool around us. It doesn't matter.

"I don't *need* you right now. It's important you know that." I swallow the thickness in my own through. "This isn't serum talking. It's just me. I want *you.*"

His brows draw together.

"Come." I hold my hand out to him.

A half smile lingers around his lips.

"I want you," I say again, only half certain I'm even talking to him anymore. I need those words as much as he does.

He hops from the tub in a lithe motion, a ripple of coiling muscles, too fast to see, and looms above me. Water sluices down his body, pools on the floor.

"What do you want from me?"

"I want to show you … What it means to me. Everything that you've done to keep me safe."

His finger pulls at my chin. "You don't have to show me anything."

He asks nothing from me, so I want to give him everything.

"That's the point, Ajax. I want to thank you."

His eyes narrow at that, and he turns toward the wall, snatches a couple towels from a shelf there.

He wipes his face, then thrusts a towel at me. "I don't want your gratitude."

"I know that." I wrap the towel around my body.

He turns away, running the towel through his hair. I step closer, wrapping my arms around him from behind. "I want to touch you. For me. I want to touch you because I want you."

He turns back.

My heart spikes. I've never done anything like this before. Utto took whatever he wanted or forced me to give. Ajax ... is so different.

"What do you want me to do?" he asks.

I drop my gaze to the thick erection that bobs between us and bite my lip. "I want you ..." I press my hands against his chest, and the muscles bounce under my palms. "To take a step backward."

His brow furrow and his lips quirk, but he doesn't say anything. Just takes a long, steady step back.

I have a sudden idea. "Close your eyes."

His jaw ticks a beat. After a moment, his eyelids drift shut.

"Take another step."

He does, arms loose at his sides. A man full of big, hard muscles, closing his eyes and walking backward, blind, into a dark passageway, for no other reason than that I asked. It might be a small thing on the surface, but a little piece of my heart melts. He trusts me. Enough to give himself to me, blinded and vulnerable. Some men don't need to hang on to the trappings of power; it comes from inside them.

"Stop," I say. And he does. My eyes burn, and confusing emotions clog my throat.

I walk around him, take his hand in mine, check

his eyes are still shut, and lead him down the passageway toward the pilot's seat.

That first time on his ship, before Pilan, he put me in the power seat, knelt before me. With his eyes shut, and the silent ship all around, nothing but darkness and dim blue emergency lights, I can do this. I will do this.

"Sit." After a quick tense second, he lowers himself to the seat. The material squeaks beneath his bare skin. His legs fall open. His stomach bunches, and the pale lights highlight all the crinkly hairs on his forearms, his calves, over the center of his chest, the thin line down his belly. The long, hard length of him, and the softer part beneath.

His arms drift to the armrests, lazy, relaxed.

Appearances can be deceiving. I know him well enough to recognize the fine lines around his lips. Heat coils low in my belly. It would be so easy to take him inside my body, bind him to me for all time.

A Bond with Ajax would be so different than with Utto. I'm already half-addicted to him as it is.

But forever? I'd be beholden to him for the rest of my life. Dependent on him. And if he died, what then?

His nostrils flare slightly, and his head tilts. What can he hear? My heart? The blood in my veins? Probably.

I close my hands around his shoulders, step closer to stand between his thighs. He lifts his hands and I cluck my tongue. "No, no, no, no. No touching for you. You stay still."

"Just feel," I whisper into the cold, empty flight deck.

He rests his head back against the seat. I trail a finger down his nose, over his lips, down his firm chin, over the sharp ridge of his Adam's apple. "You think all the time, Ajax. I see you. Your brain is always working. Analyzing. Evaluating. Stop it."

His breath comes fast. So much power in this man.

When I press my lips against his, he jerks, a tiny motion from him, eyelids tightening. And when I take his lower lip between my teeth, he sighs, leaning in. Because I want to, I climb astride him and take my time, trailing my tongue along his ear, the hollow of his neck, over his nipples, until his breaths come fast and his fists clench.

I drag my teeth down over his nipples and farther, until I'm on my knees before him. Not because he forced it, not because he asked for it, not because he expected it. Not because I need it. Because for once, I want to be here, for *him*.

His hips move, and his breath goes ragged when I close my mouth around the hard, velvet tip. I take him all the way into the back of my throat as deep as I can, until I gag and sputter and tears come to my eyes.

"Ah, fuck, Feola."

A hand touches my hair, and I look up to meet his intense turquoise gaze. When his eyes roll back, I shake my head back and forth, wriggling the massive length of him just a little deeper, laughing silently.

I pull out to take a breath, swirling my tongue around the tip, enjoying the guttural noises he makes, the way his hips jerk.

When I drift lower to trail my tongue over the soft sack between his legs, sucking half of into my mouth, his eyes burst open. The look on his face is… beyond words, and he makes a deep, hoarse sound that tells me he likes it.

His dark sounds grow even louder when I move back to his cock.

I love it when he's pliant, controlled, polite, but I love it more when he loses it. Controlled Ajax is sexy and powerful, but uncontrolled Ajax is wild and primal.

I can see it when it happens. His fists tighten on the armrests. His neck rolls back. His abs ripple. And in a flurry of motion, one massive hand finds my neck closing around it, the other palming the back of my head, holding me in place as he thrusts into my mouth, shoving into my throat, his gaze burning into me. In Utto it would have scared me. The blocking of my airwaves, the tightening of muscles so much stronger than mine, but in Ajax…

"Fuck. Oh, gods." His hips rock, in and out. "That's … oh, fuck."

I hold my breath and rake my nails up and down his thighs as he holds my head still and pumps his serum down my throat.

My body aches for him, throbbing in time with his movements, calling out to him, demanding I give him what we both want. A Bonding.

With him still in my mouth, I slide a hand down to touch myself, breathing heavily through my nose.

It doesn't take long but I drag it out, stroking him with my free hand, watching him, humming around him, and circling my slippery clit. Tribesmen can keep going. They can come over and over again. It was one of the things I hated most about Utto, but in Ajax— I just want more.

I set up a steady rhythm, swirling my tongue, stroking us both.

When he comes again, he shouts out, rough, throaty cries, thrusting. The sweet taste of his serum floods my mouth, and I swallow it down, riding out the orgasmic tide that sends my body bucking. His hands tighten in my hair, held me in place as his hips pump.

When it's over, he pulls me up into his lap. We sit there for a long moment, in the cooling blue air, just breathing together, letting our hearts slow. It doesn't matter how long we have together. It would be worth it.

"Ajax," I say sleepily, almost drooling against his shoulder, shifting so that my body presses close and the thick, still-hard ridge of him presses against me, where our bodies throb together like a pair of magnets.

"Yeah?"

"I want to Bond with you."

CHAPTER TWENTY-SIX

This ass is a thing to behold

AJAX

I freeze with Feola curled on my lap. My hand twists in her hair so tightly I have to remind myself not to tug. I carefully extricate my fingers, dropping my fist back to the armrest beside me.

I rest my head against the seatback. Hers rests on my shoulder. We sit frozen like that for a long time, like we're both afraid to move and break the spell.

Her words resonate across the silent cockpit. Low emergency lights reflecting off rapidly cooling metal surfaces leave us in little more than ghostlight.

Beyond the viewscreen, stars glimmer, and birds crash against the hull.

"Why?"

"Because," she says simply, shifting, trying to meet my eyes, but I hold her still, don't want to see the secrets in those eyes. "I trust you. We're almost there anyway. It's your body I crave, your serum I want."

I release the air I was holding. "And later?"

"If we aren't happy ... We can still see about breaking it if we want to, but at least it would be time together."

"A broken Bond is an ugly thing."

"I know," she says, voice muffled. "But I still want you."

"Out of gratitude?" The words catch in my throat.

She stiffens. "No, *Ay-shocks*, it's not like that. It's not like that at all. I just thought—" She breaks off.

I spent most of my life convinced I'd never see a single woman. And now one's on top of me, smelling like sex and like me and like every fucking thing I've ever wanted.

"And then you want to end it. You've seen what it does when you end it. It breaks people. It nearly killed Nissa and Tam. You want me to watch you go through that?"

Her head shakes.

"You want *me* to go through that?"

She sputters, but I cut her off, moving her off my lap to stand. "Let's go to sleep, Feola. We'll talk about it in the morning."

Her shoulders sag.

I take her hand, forcing my body to stay gentle despite the blood pumping furiously through my veins, and all of it surging at my cock, demanding that I just do it, now, before she has time to reconsider. Fuck her gratitude, and fuck her pity. And fuck her for offering up a Bond like it's something we can break at anytime.

She drifts in my wake. We were getting somewhere, or at least I thought so. But I was clearly wrong.

She doesn't trust me. Not really. Not with her secrets. And not with her future. Which is fine—she's been through enough to warrant mistrust and doubt, but what she just proposed is unreasonable. Insulting. A breach of ancient, sacred tradition. To me… the Bond is something beautiful, eternal, not something to be done for a month and broken at will. No, when I Bond, if I Bond, it will be forever.

We prepare for bed in silence but for the intermittent crash of the birds.

Cold air raises goosebumps on her skin, puckering her nipples to tight beads, and all I want is to climb on top of her and get them in my mouth. My balls tighten.

She shivers, teeth chattering as we climb into bed on icy sheets. "*Ay-shocks*, I know how you feel…"

No, she doesn't. If she knew, she'd shut up about gratitude or fear, and realize that Bonds are the only thing that matters to any man of Argentus, the only thing that matters to me. My people were dying off, fading out of existence, and the straight ones who are left are resigned to a fate without love or children or any hope of a future. There's no fucking medicine I can give them to fix that. So few of us even have the hope of a true Bonding.

Except me.

Except apparently not even me.

I snap. Lose control. Lunge forward, drag her across the bed, roll on top of her, silence her with a kiss. A long, hard one. When she tried to speak again, I fill her mouth with my tongue, thrusting the hard ridge of my rampant cock against the rise of her pelvic bone.

As the pleasure-pain reverberates from my dick across my entire abdomen, I hiss against her lips, drawing my hand down her hip, cupping the curve of her ass, pinching a peaked nipple with my other hand until she squeaks and shakes.

I trace my teeth along her ear, making her gasp, get my mouth around her breast, hungry, breathing fast.

"*Ay-shocks.*"

"Don't talk." My voice is harsh, and maybe even cold, but she doesn't withdraw, just presses harder against me.

"Ajax, I—"

"No words." I touch her lips, watching almost mesmerized as she opens her mouth for my fingers. I slide in one, then another, down along the velvet of her wet hot tongue, back, deeper, deeper into the place she just had my dick, all the way back to her uvula. "Good. It's okay. We don't need to talk right now. No more talk of Bonding. Or fucking gratitude. If we touch it's because we want to. Right?"

Eyes locked on me, mouth spread wide around my invading fingers, she nods.

"Good."

I pull my fingers from her throat, manhandle her onto her stomach, pull her up so she's on her hands and knees, so her pussy is spread before me. I'd love to jam my dick home, thrust inside her until she's mine for all time. No escape. No excuse. No remorse. No contention.

She's shaking so I pause. "You okay?"

"Yes."

"Good."

I'm shaking too, body vibrating, demanding the quick consummation we've been skirting since the first minute we met. My dick and my brain want exactly the same thing, so it is a mother of a bitch to ignore them.

"*Ay-shocks*, please," she says.

I don't want to hear, so I wrap my palm around the hair at the base of her neck and pull until her neck arches and her hands leave the bed and she's kneeling, neck bared. I scrape my teeth along her jaw and whisper darkly in her ear. "Shh. This isn't about gratitude, Feola. Your gratitude smacks of pity. And your pity makes me mad. But you know that no matter how angry I get, I will never hurt you, right?"

Neck still arched high, vulnerable, submissive. "Yes."

"You know I'll stop if you're scared. Just say the word."

"I'm fine."

I shift my hips, so I'm right behind her, my dick riding the valley between her perfect luscious ass. I drag my teeth over her carotid, releasing her hair to hold her tits in my hands.

She groans.

"We were made for each other," I hiss, letting my callused thumbs rasp over her nipples. "You just can't see it yet. Your ass is a work of art, and in my dreams, you take me inside it." I rock my hips, so my dick presses, just for a second against the puckered opening, then shift it lower, so it's against the slick entrance of her pussy.

It would be so easy. Just slide back a tiny bit, and press the head of his cock inside. But I hold back, dragging it forward her clit.

Her whole body shudders, and she groans low and deep.

"On your hands and knees," I whisper, letting her fall forward. She does, back arched, that ass pushed out. I slide a finger into her pussy, get it wet, move to her ass, press. "Anyone ever touch you here?"

"No."

I press harder, massaging the skin around it to relax the muscles, and they let me in. She groans, breathing hard, pushing back until my whole finger is deep inside. I kiss my way down her spine, swirl my tongue along the perfect pair of dimples at the base of her spine. "This ass is a thing to behold."

When I trail my mouth lower, over the rise of a full ass cheek, she sobs out a breathless complaint, trying to crawl away, roll over, get away from my lips, but I hold her still with an arm around her hips.

Finger still deep in her ass, I get my mouth at her pussy, fuck it with my tongue like I can't with my dick. She bucks her hips. I flutter my tongue on her clit.

She screams my name and my balls clench with glee. I ride it out, the bucking hips, her muscles clamping down on my finger in her ass.

When it's over, she sags forward on the bed, her face in the covers.

I stare down at her ass. I want to fuck and fuck and fuck until I'm not even me and she isn't her and we become something else entirely.

But not for fucking gratitude. I pull my finger out of her, and she whimpers. I use moisture from her wet pussy and wrap my palm around my dick, staring at her ass and imagining a world in which it's my ass to fuck whenever I want, imagine the tight clamp of those muscles around my dick, filling her full of my serum. My balls buzz and the head of my dick detonates, and serum blasts out, spraying over her ass in thick arcs, coating her back, pooling in the dip of her spine, drips down the seam of her ass, along the folds of her glorious, glistening pussy.

Unable to stop myself, I trail my fingers through a pool, glide them down to her ass, and push inside. Not a lot. Not enough for a Bond, but enough to make me feel … a sense of satisfaction. I push some more in. Then more. Feola will sleep tonight with my cum in her ass.

I don't deserve her gratitude. I'm not a good man. A good man wouldn't feel a surge of primitive anger. Wouldn't want so brutally to vent fury through fucking. And that's what I want to do, just fuck it all away, fuck her better, and end the sickening limbo of eternal serum-dispensing.

Gratitude.

I don't want it.

I want everything.

Always. Nothing less would do. Anything less is ointment on a severed artery.

I slide from the bed early the next morning, tucking the covers around her. She murmurs complaints, curling into the warm spot my body left on the sheets.

The ship cooled dramatically in the night, approaching freezing. She's still asleep, exhausted. I was too rough in the night, demanded too much from her.

My dick was incessant, and I didn't bother to say no to it. I woke her up multiple times in the night. She never pushed me away, just spread her thighs wide for my hands or my tongue. Something strange possessed me. A primal urge that spoke to something I've never felt before. Some unnatural need demanded I give her as much of myself as I could for the limited time we had.

She just kept asking for more. Even when I pulled her hand and wrapped her dainty fingers around the girth of my cock, or straddled her face, filling her mouth, when I pulled her atop to ride my tongue, when I pressed, not one, but two fingers deep into her ass, heedless of the serum I was pushing inside along with it.

She moaned, gasped against my neck, and panted my name in her musical voice. *Ay-shocks. Ay-shocks.*

She begged me for more. Ten times. A hundred. She moaned and pleaded and begged me to Bond with her. But always in the throes of passion.

I considered it, briefly, taking her. Just shoving my cock home, claiming her, Bonding her, and fuck reason or morals. Fuck integrity. Fuck it all. She asked for it. So why not? Just stake a claim and for once in my life do the dishonorable thing.

But I couldn't do it.

Instead, I took the coward's route. I fed her more serum, and shoved more in her ass, all the while daring the gods and playing a dangerous game with our chemistry. I rubbed it into the smooth skin of her neck and breasts until I couldn't tell their scents apart. I have no idea what will happen now.

A partial Bond? Is that a thing?

I yank on my boots and strap on my knives.

In the galley, I make a crappy mug of *eeffoc* and suck it down blistering hot. I smell like the inside of Feola's pussy.

I walk naked toward the hatch, mug in my hands, and peer through the porthole. An array of black feathers and spilled blood litters the ground near the ship, knocked unconscious perhaps, torn apart, cannibalized by their own kind.

The last of their thrashing against the ship's walls died at dawn.

Birds of the night, evidently.

Tam's message. B was for birds. A population of nocturnal blood-sucking birds, so vicious that an entire planet was deserted. In some ways it's better than wild boys or angry buffalo. But it does make moving dicey, since we can't be caught outside after dark.

It makes staying at the ship more desirable, but the last thing we want is to make daily treks to the river and back again just for drinking water. The flat plain we landed on seems ripe for flash-flooding, and judging by the lack of vegetation nearby, it seems like a reasonable assumption that it could happen. I have no idea what season it is. And no clue what other predators might exist.

It pisses me off all over again. I hate not knowing.

The hotel must have had protection from the birds at some point, whether in the form of technology, like a force field, or something more primitive like a simple roof, or a set of predatory domesticated animals. Unless the birds were a new adaptation. Three hundred years seems too short for that level of evolutionary adaptation.

I open the hatch.

The air has already warmed under the light of a still-weak and silvery sun.

I glare at the distant white ruins and columns of the hotel, nestled against its purple hills and glittering waterfalls.

Can't be more than four or five miles away.

We'll have to go early so we have time to explore and make it back before nightfall if need be. And hope there are no more surprises.

And no bounty hunters on our tail.

A footfall echoes down the passageway behind me.

Feola emerges.

I lift my chin at her.

She's pulled on her shoes and wrapped a blanket around her. It trails behind her. Her hair, a wild mass of pink-orange curls, skin pale, eyes bleary.

"Is that *eeffoc*?"

I nod.

"Is it hot?"

I lift it toward her.

She smiles sleepily, blinking those enormous yellow-green eyes, fringed in black, and yawns as she steps closer. She takes it, and I pull her to stand in front of me, wrapping my arms around her blanket-covered body.

"Are you always so warm?" She shivers. "I'd have frozen without you last night."

"You'd have *slept* without me last night."

"Maybe." There's a noncommittal tilt to her head.

I graze her cheek with my unshaven jaw.

"I liked it, though." Her voice goes straight to the base of my spine. "You're all bristly in the morning."

"And you're still all blinky."

She breathes out a sleepy laugh, and takes a long sip of the *eeffoc*.

"And pink." I twirl my finger through a curl of her hair, studying the different tones.

"I am me."

And I love her for it.

I can't tell her that, though. She'd just feel more gratitude.

So, I rest my chin on top of her head, and together we watch a sun spread its warmth and light across the plains of an alien land.

CHAPTER TWENTY-SEVEN

It's not enough

FEOLA

I tilt my hat back to see Ajax.

Something is wrong. It hangs in the air around him. It's in the way he looks at me. It's not anger. I know anger. This is different. Formal. Distanced. Like I failed him somehow.

He scans the grassy plain around us, moving with the same fluid, muscled grace as always.

He donned a new white shirt this morning, one that isn't bloodstained and tattered. It sticks to his skin. And he's wearing the silly hat, tied beneath his chin with a big, ridiculous bow of white fabric I tore from the dress the birds had destroyed.

On him, somehow, it's not as silly as it should be.

He did things to my body I never dreamed of. Whatever his medical training entailed, maybe it involved a more thorough and inventive analysis of the female body than Utto got and I'm super grateful for that. If Utto had found my ass as appealing as Ajax does, I don't want to imagine what he'd have done to it.

Last night was wonderful. And terrifying. When the memories crept in, I touched him, and his touch was enough. He soothed me. Ajax isn't Utto.

That, more than anything, filled me with a single bright hope. His healing touch chased away bad memories and hidden fears. Bonding with him would chase away the last breath of Utto from my skin, the last trace of him that invaded my body and lingers in my blood.

I hoped, repeatedly, every time he woke me in the dark, a hand parting my thighs, or cupping my breasts, that he'd Bond with me. I wanted it. I wanted him. I begged for it, sobbed, desperate for him to fill the growing void inside me. The shift began sometime in the cold and silent darkness; he took up a place in my chest beside Utto. I can feel them both there, now. Ajax, firm and stoic; Utto, angry and maybe desperate, vibrating like a livewire.

My nipples burn against the fabric of my dress, chafed from his tongue.

Ajax glances over at me, a question in his eyes. Maybe I'm in his chest too.

I lift a shoulder, unable to explain the growing frenzy in my blood. Something is different.

We've been walking all morning, so long my head is swimming by the time we get to the bottom of the hill under the hotel.

"Let's stop here for a few moments," he says. "I want you to know how to use a *rezal.*"

"Really?" I blink away the fog.

"You feel okay?" He tilts my chin up, presses a hand to my forehead.

I force myself to forget the awkwardness between us, the unspoken words, the fear that he doesn't really want me after all, at least not enough to Bond. "I'm fine." I swat his hand away. "Why the *rezal?*"

"If something happens to me, I don't want you to be defenseless. No reason you shouldn't know how to use every weapon available. This is a good spot."

He drops the pack to the ground against a nearby tree and tears off his hat, tossing it to the ground, then scrubs his hand through damp, sweaty hair. "You use your right hand." It isn't a question. He knows quite well I'm right-handed.

Another surge of heat blasts through me, making me flinch. I focus on his muscled forearms as he pulls one of the shiny, black-and-silver weapons from the harness around his waist. All bones and muscles and tendon. He's a work of art.

When he glances up at her, his eyes soften. "It's okay." He gestures me closer. "Come here."

I've never touched a *rezal* before. I force my feet to move over the blue star-shaped flowers and white leaves that carpet the sandy soil.

He points out the safety, the charger, the trigger, then shifts it to his left hand and offers it to her.

I hesitate, hand in midair. He brings it to my palm.

The surface is warmer than I expected, from contact with his body or maybe the sun. I don't know how to hold it, and for some weird reason, my knees hake.

Ajax steps behind me, keeping his hands loose outside mine. "It's okay." His voice is low and gentle. "First rule—only point it at someone if you're willing to kill them."

"Okay."

"See these two ridges? They're the sights." He touches his finger to a small raised fin at the back and another at the front.

He guides my hands higher, so I hold the weapon in front of me, arms partially extended. He shifted my grip. "Line the front sight up with the back one, and put them right on top of your target."

"What's my target?"

"Pick a tree."

There aren't a whole lot. Three silvery purple trees. I choose the one in the center.

When his lips graze against my outer ear, my belly hitches. "You're allowed to breathe."

"Okay."

"I'm going to let go now and step back. Okay?"

"Okay." My arms shake. He drops his hands, and the *rezal* is a thick, sullen weight without him there helping support it. There's an intensity to the weapon, more a weight than a darkness, that speaks to all inherent potential it carries, the infinite ways it could change the future, the lives it could save, the lives it could take. It's like holding one of the threads of the Fates.

It takes several breaths to stop the tremors, to control my breathing, until the nose of the *rezal* stops shaking.

A few birds twittered. Minutes pass.

"You can pull the trigger," Ajax says, voice containing a single note of humor. "It will be loud. Your hands will want to kick up toward the sky. Let your arms take the motion."

I slide my finger from the barrel to the trigger.

Deep breaths.

The little ridges form a line.

I tighten my finger. It's harder to squeeze than I expected. And he's right—it was loud. My eyes squeeze shut against the noise, and my hands fly up against the recoil. A blast of light flares at the edge.

Where did it even hit? It's too fast.

"Did I hit it?"

"Hit what?"

"My tree."

His eyes get squinty at the corners. "Not yet. Spread your legs a little wider. Lean forward. Arch your back. Try again."

He keeps me shooting, offering corrections between shots, until the *rezal* runs out of power and my finger hurts. The sun is high in the sky when we finally stop, and my belly is empty, but at least my knees no longer shake, and I've learned to control the recoil.

"You did well," he says.

"Really?"

He nods, and I feel about as tall as he is. Like I could take over the galaxy, all on my own.

We eat lunch fast. Rations from the ship that leave me full but unsatisfied.

Something is different today. My body pulses hotly, in tandem with my steps.

I shift uncomfortably, with another flashback from last night. It hits like a punch to my low belly. I hiss against pleasure and need that broaches painful. And the burning memories of Utto's flinty eyes and Rennie's grasping, clammy hands seem … lesser somehow. Like Ajax chased some of the darkness away. Instead of their mean glares, I see only Ajax's shadowed face as he stroked my breasts, pushed my thighs wide. His growls as he spurted serum over my breasts.

Another burst of desire flares low.

"What's wrong?" he asks.

My chest tightens against a blast of Utto across the Bond, and I've never wanted him gone so badly.

"I think I need—" I break off, irritated with my own constant neediness. "I need you."

A muscle in his jaw tightens under the sun's harsh, beating rays.

I fucking hate this. I drop my gaze.

"We need to go another half mile maybe. About ten minutes at the most to get up this hill. See that clearing, up ahead? Those dark trees?"

A look up, pressing a hand where the heat pools.

"I can make it."

Maybe he can feel me; he certainly seemed able to read me closer than ever. I take a step and stumble when a stab of need courses wet heat between my thighs. Arousal flares in his turquoise gaze.

His hand wraps around mine and he pulls me into the shade under a copse of trees.

We barely make it before he tugs at the ribbons of his hat. I twist in his arms, pressing him back against the smooth silver bark of a tree. My legs wrap around his waist. I struggle to get higher, wanting to feel his cock against me, needing it.

I wrap my fingers around him through his thin khaki pants.

"Shit. Slow down," he hisses through gritted teeth. I bat at his hands, pushing away from him, struggling out of his grip, until he finally let's go. I drop to my knees. With a snarl, I get his cock free, and swallow it. He grunts. I sucked harder.

I look up to see him arch his neck against the tree.

His hands fist in my hair, drawing me closer up, pushing into my throat. I bob my head up and down, hollowing out my cheeks.

"Gods, you look beautiful when you do that."

I'd smile but I can't, so I stroke my hands up his muscled legs, over the springy hairs that covered them, to the heavy sack that hangs between his legs. The cords of his neck strain, and he fists my hair tighter, moving my head back and forth, thrusting his hips, fucking my face in a steady rhythm, using my mouth for his pleasure so he can give me what I need all the faster.

Even when he's greedy, it's for me. Even in the dominance of the position, his concern is evident. I squeeze a little harder.

He comes fast, thick and long, pulsing down my throat, holding me still, pumping his hips. It settles my stomach and stills some of the burn coursing slick between my thighs, but it isn't enough.

Utto thrashes against the Bond, wilder than ever, beside the seething intensity of Ajax's climax, two men fighting an invisible war inside my chest.

I pull away. "It's not enough," I growl irritably, my voice hoarse and shaking.

"What?" He lifts his head slowly. Brows drawing together, breathing hard. How can he not feel it?

"It's not enough. Something's wrong."

He straightens, bends over me, presses a hand against my cheek. "How so?"

"I don't know. Utto feels stronger in my chest. I can feel him more."

"Is he closer?"

"I don't think it's about proximity. I think he's angrier or scared or something."

Ajax frowns. "He can feel you with me? That'd piss him off for sure."

"But not like he normally can. It's almost like, I don't know, like he's afraid of something. And I need more from you. That didn't fix the problem. You're in my chest too." I press my hands over my heated face. Embarrassed to the depths of my being, loathing the addiction that rules my body. "I need more serum."

His eyes close briefly and he curses. "I gave you too much last night. It must have affected the Bond. That explains why you're feverish and your pupils are dilated."

"You mean it's shifting to you?"

His head makes a part nod, part shake. "Maybe. I can feel you in my chest too. I feel your emotions. I thought I was imagining it. It must be a partial Bond."

"A partial Bond?"

He lifts a shoulder. "I don't know any more than that. It's possible to have a connection without a Bonding, but it's unhealthy."

"Good. Then finish it. Right now. I want it."

"For a few weeks," he says, words so bitter they sting.

I surge to my feet. "What do you want from me?"

His brows rise.

I step closer to him. I swore I'd never need anyone like this again, but it doesn't matter. Something was off with Utto from day one—he poisoned and manipulated me, drugged, abused and victimized me.

Well, no more.

Never again. I ended that along with Rennie. The thought brings a fresh surge of anger. Maybe I needed Ajax all along. He won't hurt me, and like he said, if he needs me equally, at least I won't be alone.

I shove my hand against his chest, breaking the

silence, refusing to be pathetic for one moment longer. "I won't beg you again, Ajax. I swore I wouldn't beg. Not for anything. Everything he did to me, I never once begged Utto for anything. I begged for you last night. I could hate you for that alone."

He doesn't move a muscle.

"I've made it clear what I want." My voice rises. "I thought you wanted me."

"I do." He pushes away from me so fast I nearly fall in the vacuum of his wake.

"Then what is it? I'm right here, Ajax." Have I ever shouted at anyone before in my life? Probably not. It feels good. I shout again, just because I can. "What do you want? You want me one minute, and the next you say no. I can't keep up."

He rounds on me, muscles tight, head and shoulders above her, a quivering mass of furious man. "I want you." He storms closer, eyes angry, motions fast and jerky, breathing hard. A big, hard, angry man, and I will not back down. "All of you," he snarls, nostrils flaring, body vibrating and enraged.

I catch myself, foot threatening to retreat, and clench my fists and instead step closer so we are scant inches apart. "I refuse to be afraid of you."

He backs up a step, breathing with effort. "You shouldn't be afraid of me."

"Answer me, then! What the hell do you want?"

"You."

"I'm right here."

"For a few weeks or a month. You're asking me

to take you now and give you up later."

I swallow. "Do you think it will be easier to let me go if we never Bond at all?"

His gaze drops down to his hands. "You saw how Nissa cried, and how sick she got. She nearly died. I swore I'd never let that happen to me, let alone a woman I was lucky enough to Bond with. And that was before I—"

He scrubs his hands through his hair, jaw flexing.

"She survived. So did Tam. So would we." I touch his shoulder, but he pushes me away. "I do want you, Ajax. Now. Why can't that be enough?"

"I don't want a few weeks. I want forever."

All my anger drains away, faster than it came. I close my hands around the large fist hanging at his side. So much power right there, in the sinews and bones of his hand. "I'll try."

He nods tightly, not exactly as happy as I'd hoped, staring into the distance. Why does this have to be so hard?

"Let's get to the hotel." His face stays unreadable, but his voice softens. "If we're going to Bond, we need a safe place to stay. It could take days."

He snatches the pack off the ground and hefts it onto his back. "As soon as we have ten minutes to think, we're getting rid of that bastard's serum. I'll make you a stockpile of my own. One thing I won't tolerate is my mate taking some other man's serum. Ever." He says it like he expects me to argue.

I don't. "I'll wash the vials out for you."

He adjusts his pants, checks his straps, pulls his hat on his head, and ties the white length of fabric into a big jaunty bow under his chin.

He tosses my hat through the air like a disc. I catch it.

"Come on."

He's not happy. No problem. I'll be happy enough for both of us. I'll make him happy.

CHAPTER TWENTY-EIGHT

Before everything changes

AJAX

I meet her yellow-green gaze.

The prairie spreads behind her, lavender and white. Groves of pale blue flowering plants broke clusters of silvery-violet trees, matching the sky stretching overhead, endless and cloudless.

And then there's her, face flushed pink, hair a brilliant fiery mass. And those eyes, vivid and as piercing as a knife to the gut. Nothing on the horizon has half her brilliance or a quarter of her color.

I should be happy. I am happy. She wants me. I want her. We'll be together. Bonded. A few months of glory to remember on my deathbed. If I have to survive the breaking of a Bond for her, then so be it. Harder will be watching her do it, but I can. For her. If I have to.

And in the meantime, maybe I can change her mind.

I *will* change her mind.

And if not? I've seen a man after breaking a

Bond—Tam. He was broken. Weak. Sick. Without regrets.

Feola moves to stand beside me. Closes her hand around mine. Smiling that glorious wide smile, white teeth, full lips, and all the air leaves my lungs. She'll be mine, to claim, to love, to protect. The Bonding would change the metabolic pathways of our cells. We will be different people after it's over.

Everything will be different.

We climb the hill. The foliage is sparse everywhere on the plain, but it's thicker here on the hillside, and damn near full beside the winding river, and the remnants of an old rutted and dusty white road that must lead up the mountain to the hotel.

Feola's slippers are too thin for the pitted path, and it makes me want to kill Utto for giving her such stupid useless footwear. He wanted her helpless. Weak. I'll make sure she's stronger than she's ever been. Healthier. Happier.

As it grows steeper, I move so she's in front, where I can keep an eye on her footing. The last thing we need is a twisted ankle.

The Bonding ceremony will lay us down for a while. It varies depending on the couple. Tam's took three days. Feola's with Utto took hours, she said. We have rations in the pack, and there's fresh running water in the river near the top of the hotel. The biggest question is the blood-sucking birds off and how we keep them off our backs at night.

"I need to ask you for something, Feola."

She nods.

"Give us a chance."

She's quiet for a while as we climb.

Then she pauses, looks over shoulder to me. "I just need to know that I won't be trapped again, *Ay-shocks*. I need to know that if it's not working, you'll let me go."

"If you are unhappy, we will sever the Bond. But woman, I swear by all the fucking gods, you won't be unhappy."

She chews that full pink lip and turns away, stepping up the white road.

"I don't think I'll be unhappy, *Ay-shocks*. We should have done this earlier. I'm just scared. He had total power over me."

I'm about to open my mouth, to insist I'm not Utto, but she stops me.

"We've never talked about it. About what it was like with him."

As we climb, she pulls a long, feathery leaf from a tree and trails it through her fingers. And I listen.

"At first, I was so confused, I think because of the *septusine*, and I wanted so badly to love him. To forget about you. But then, it just… I couldn't. And I think he knew it. Living with him—with Utto, I had no privacy. He tried to make me disappear. I shrank every day, became less me and more him. The physical part wasn't the worst of it. It was being trapped. No escape. I was stuck on an alien base with no one to turn to, no hope of getting away, ever. He had total control over me."

Familiar anger boils in my heart. I want to ask

about Rennie... but this is her story. I'll find out during the Bonding anyway, when our memories pass back and forth.

Her back is rigid, like she's fighting off memories even as she speaks.

"It shouldn't have been like that," I say, hoping she believes me. "That's not who we are. That's not what Argentus is supposed to be. My father and my mother loved each other. He survived her death and my sister's, but barely. I think he only managed because of my brother and me.

"He used to come home from work for lunch some days, just to surprise us. He loved us kids, but it was my mom he really wanted to see. It was as if they were on a positive feedback cycle, like contact with each other recharged them. I wish you could have met her. She smiled a lot, like you. And she sang too. My father would have died rather than see her hurt, and she for him. It was a partnership, Feola. I don't really want to think about the serum thing with them, but my dad needed her every bit as much as she needed him."

When she doesn't respond, I add, "You'll have equal power over me."

"Okay."

We climb the rest of the way in silence and stop before the crumbling entrance of the old hotel.

"It must have been so beautiful," she says, eyes shining.

In the merciful shade of a grove of trees, I pull off the wretched hat and shove it into my pack.

White stones and blue glass tiles. No mildew or cracks or decay. It's in good shape, like it was cleaned and locked up for safe-keeping and simply abandoned. A few windows are broken, and white soil covers most of the surfaces. Silvery, white, pale blue, and bold purple vines climb walls. Here and there, trees broke through cracks and upset tiles, but for the most part, it's shockingly pristine.

I close the massive, cracked blue doors behind us. There's no evidence of animal inhabitants. My boot steps echo. Feola's slippered feet barely make a sound.

"Look at these tiles," she says, in the hushed whisper people automatically take on in large spaces.

I tear my eyes from the enormous blue glass sculpture hanging from the ceiling, pulling her with me so we don't stand below it. She brushes white dust from the floor to reveal ornate abstract floral patterns in cobalt and cerulean.

A large staircase stretches before us, spiraling up to the second floor. The walls are all white but covered in fine blue paintings depicting hunters with birds, stars and moons, mountains, streams with fish.

"Where do you think the birds live?" Feola asks.

"Hopefully not here."

"We'd see poop," she says.

I grin at the way that sounds in her singsong voice.

"I think so. Let's keep looking around. I'd like to find a room where we know they can't get in."

We move through space after space, past blue and white wooden furniture that has barely crumbled despite the centuries passing, even fabric draperies that are mostly intact. A massive hearth sits in the center of one space, circular, under an opening in the ceiling.

That makes me uneasy. Did the birds answer Feola's song the night before? Did they smell us? Sense us?

The hotel is big and built into the side of the mountains, so the windows all face out over the plains and the river and the small bursts of trees. The waterfall cascades down one side, near a massive terrace with dining tables and chairs.

But no evidence or birds or other wildlife. Maybe the hotel has some natural deterrent. Or perhaps some kind of invisible laser technology that keeps them away.

We searched all seventy-five guest suites, and the service halls, the main restaurants and meeting areas. Not so much as footprints in the dust.

I haven't spent any time thinking about creating a space for a Bonding ceremony. But I guess it's time.

"Let's pick a room with a fireplace. Maybe we can even remove the dust from the bed." She flushes violently. "I liked the one with the blue ceiling. Can we take that one?"

"Whatever you want."

The room has an enormous fireplace and an even bigger bed. We spend a while cleaning out the dust and pulling the covers from the bed. I check the doors. The locks hold. And the windows have shutters and dusty drapes we can pull at night.

We gather wood for the fireplace, stockpiling.

There's a bathroom nearby. We clean the tub and fill it with fresh water from the falls using a bucket. Then take a long soapy shower under the falls. And when we're done ...

I stand facing the windows. Naked. I deposit my weapons around the room so I can get them easily. The chamber is clean. We've eaten. Food and water are on the bedside tables within easy reach.

We're ready. The door snicks, and I turn around.

Feola steps out of the bathroom, naked, hair damp. I let my gaze roam down her body, over the beautiful, smooth skin of her neck, and her perfect little breasts, nipples hard and tight, over her small waist and the flare of her hips. The patch of dark curls between her legs. We move at the same time, crossing the chamber. Inches apart, we both paused.

"You're beautiful."

Her lips part, shaking.

I don't need to ask why. "I won't hurt you. I promise."

"I know you won't. I was just thinking that it should have been like this the first time. It should have been you. I'm so sorry for—"

"I should have stopped you."

"You should have," she whispers.

I pull her close.

It doesn't take much, just a hand beneath her ass, and her legs wrap around my waist, all that warm skin, mine for the touching. "I used to dream about this."

She stares at me, eyes level with mine.

"Well, okay, if I'm honest, I used to think about this and jerk off."

"About Bonding?"

I carry her to the bed, lower her to the mattress. "I used to stay up late at night, imagining how it would be. Where I would touch you, how I would touch you. I didn't know it was you. Not until I met you." I shake my head. "You don't know your own power."

Her smile stretches, her teeth touch against her bottom lip, her foot strokes my calf, and my cock twitches against her.

"Okay. Maybe you do."

She laughs as I stretched her arms up over her head, holding her wrists in place with one hand, so I can let my mouth drift down her neck, over her ears. Graze along her collarbone.

"The Bonding works by changing us. Your body will crave my serum aggressively early on. Later it will steady out. And my body will need proximity to yours." I trail my nose through her hair. "I'll just need to smell you to want you, which is pretty much how it is now anyway."

"And you'll just need to exist for me to want you," she breathes, lifting her hips off the bed. "It doesn't sound all that different from now. Y-you smile at me, and I get all stupid."

"Oh, it'll be different. Trust me." I slide my hand down her belly, between her thighs, pressing her legs wide open. "Gods, you're so wet."

She arches into me and moans, "*Ay-shocks.*"

"You know the first thing I thought about you?" I bite down on her earlobe.

She shivers. "N-n-no."

"I loved the way you say my name." I trace my nose behind her ear, lapping at her skin right over a spot near her jaw I fully intended to bite later, right when she's in the throes of an orgasm. "Like a song." I cup my hand over her pussy. Her heat, her pulse radiates outward.

She whimpers and pushes against me, my fingertips resting just over her slick opening. When I slip a finger inside, she sighs with relief.

"I want to hear you sing it when I'm inside you, all the way."

She nods, making strangled sobs as I trailed my thumb in tight circles around her clit. I've been learning her body in the days since our escape. I suck her nipple between my teeth, dragging my tongue along the surface until her pants become sobs and she thrusts her hips wildly. I know how to make her scream too, but that will have to wait.

She fidgets and fusses, writhing beneath me. "Please, *Ay-shocks* … Just do it. I want you inside me."

I laugh, and even to me it sounds a little evil. "I hate to deny you anything, Feola. But there isn't a chance in hell that I'm rushing this."

I catch her mouth in a rough kiss, and her nails rake along my back, tugging at my hair.

I smile against her fevered skin and trail slow

kisses down her neck, across her breasts, down, down, down.

"Spread your legs." I sit up, looking at her flushed face and beautiful body. Her nipples puckered tight, her thighs scissoring, her hands fisting by her sides.

She blinks at the sunlight streaming in the windows, back at me.

"Open for me."

She parts her thighs a few scant inches.

"Wider."

She does.

"Even wider."

She rolls her eyes but does, until she is spread open. Her cunt, her ass, all fucking mine.

With a growl, I drop my face between her thighs, suck at her clit, reveling in the way her hands tug at my hair, the soft guttural cries, the way she rubs her smooth thighs against my face. She tastes like heaven, sweet and a little salty on my tongue.

She chants my name, and when she screams, I feel like a fucking god. Her thighs clamp down, her fingers dig into my scalp. I ride out her bucking hips, my tongue fluttering in a steady beat until her screams turn to whimpers and the whimpers become pleas.

"Please, *Ay-shocks*. Please fuck me."

I settle my knees between her thighs. Trace the thick head of my cock against her warm, pink entrance.

We both gasp as I push inside her slick heat. I keep on pushing until she winces and wiggles her hips, and my balls press against her ass, and nothing in the universe has ever felt better. Almost painfully tight, slippery hot, and silky smooth.

I stroke a hand down her cheek, tracing her jaw, holding that yellow-green gaze. "There's something I want you to know, now before everything changes."

She stares back at me.

"I love you."

CHAPTER TWENTY-NINE

Someday, woman

FEOLA

Parts of this are familiar, if I'm honest. Ajax isn't touching me anywhere I haven't been touched before. But the way my body reacts, the way my lungs shudder against the onslaught of burning physical need, is something else entirely. Ajax's touch sears far deeper than skin, to that innermost place that has always belonged to me alone.

Not anymore. He shoves aside all the layers of protection that allowed me to survive Utto, that I relied on in the days following my escape, leaving me open, defenseless and bare.

He sees the parts that are ugly and dark. The scared places, the selfish places, the broken places. My darkest deeds.

The guilt and the shame, the anguished fear, and the self-loathing... all of it fades away. Ajax fills me so completely there is no room for anything else. The thrashing in my chest recedes.

Inhaling sharply, I force myself to focus on this man inside me. On this moment with him.

The vibrant turquoise of his eyes steadies me, reassuring and familiar, but dark too, revealing the person within him, beneath the layers of civilization, respectful manners, and gentle motions. There is a dark, selfish place inside Ajax too. And it only wants one thing.

Me.

I squeeze my eyes tightly shut, breathe in deeply, tighten the grip of my legs wrapped around his waist, the muscles of my sex contracting around him.

Thick and full, stretched to aching.

I love you.

His words echo across the room, as he pulls back and shoves in deeper.

I can't say it back.

I try but he lowers his mouth to mine and fills my mouth with his tongue and his kisses. Every breath smells like him, overpowering me. I writhe you with my hips, slamming up and into him.

I dig in my claws, drag my teeth over the skin of his chest until he curses, and his control snaps. He thrusts his hips so hard I wince. He fists my hair in a rough hand, baring my throat to him. Shoves deeper, pulls tighter, fucks me harder until my brain shuts down.

Growling, his other hand moves down to hold my hips in place so he can shift the angle, plunge his cock in deeper, matching the beat with his thrusting tongue.

It stings, the hand in my hair, but it stings in a good way. It doen't sting because he wants to hurt me; it stings because he's forgotten to treat me like I might splinter into a thousand fragmented pieces.

He snarls against my lips, hips growing erratic.

I've never felt stronger as I lift my hips to meet the powerful trusts of his driving cock.

His face contorts, lower lip jutting out, a vein standing out on his forehead, and when he explodes, and his serum hits me, hot and powerful, as I tighten around him, spiraling beyond reason, and out of control. Our gazes lock, his irises darken, and the pupils tighten to sharp pinpoints.

It's strange … reliving my life through another person's eyes. Our bodies dissipate under the onslaught of memories, neurons firing.

Images cross before my eyes on a loop. My childhood and my parents and friends and the Green Sea outside Trian. Me skipping through the Red Gardens, over lush red ferns, singing and laughing with Mamma.

And Ajax's life too. At the same time, simultaneous like twin holo-vids in fast-forward, as he toddled on bandy legs across a mossy blue yard to pick up a yellow ball, which he threw at another boy, older, but clearly his brother. The other boy laughed, and somewhere in the distance an infant cried.

We speed through our childhoods, superimposed across one another. I feel Ajax's pain when his mother died, and then his sister. The horrible burial. His father withdrew into himself, leaving Ajax even more confused. We pass through my teenage years. Finally, Mamma's face as I entered the cryo pod.

Tears burn at the last glimpse I'll ever have of Mamma's face. We speed through Ajax's schooling, and his decision to join the Tribe, to become a warrior.

Through the time when the Vestige came to my planet, and finally, we arrive in a dark cave, where I hesitate, staring down at an orb-shaped preservation pod, desperate to escape Triannon at whatever cost, desperate to find a place where I belong.

And then we're in a room I recognize. The white-and-silver room on Sierra-Six where Ajax found me, where I woke up to his handsome, gentle face for the first time.

He strokes a strand of hair back from my forehead. The healing bay is empty and quiet. He doesn't need to be there. The look on his face, the way he studies me—I belonged with him the first minute he found me.

This time, maybe because I'm prepared for it, I can feel the Bonding changing me. I know the exact moment Utto's furious, rearing Bond vanishes from my chest and Ajax takes up residence there, firm and gentle.

It isn't a massive physical sensation like an ache; this feels more like a spring, attached on one side to him, and on another to me. Binding. Reassuring.

Warm and light.

When his body shudders out a climax, gushing more serum into me, I feel his pleasure.

He knows my secret. He knows I killed Rennie. Stabbed him right in the back as he walked away.

I wake at some point. On the third day? Maybe the fourth? I'm collapsed atop his chest, my face pressed against the smooth skin and prickly hairs over his steadily beating heart. Is he awake? I glance up. He isn't.

He sleeps with his face turned away, and as I shift, he stirs and murmurs but doesn't open his eyes. Exhausted.

He looks like he lost weight. I probably did as well. If we ate more than three meals in all that time, I'd be surprised. Mostly we fucked, and moved serum around like it was some kind of magic-Bond affirming spell, rubbing it into my skin, scooping it between my lips.

He smells … about like one would expect… after three or four days of fucking. So, do I. Like him. Like me. Like sex.

We need to bathe.

A thin crack of light visible through the drawn, faded curtains says it's day.

Moving slowly, scarcely breathing, I shift my weight to lift my leg off his.

His eyelids flutter. "Feola?"

"Hush. Go back to sleep. I'm just going to get some water and use the bathroom."

His brows lower, and he's back to sleep before I even draw the blankets over his chest.

I can't resist pressing a kiss to his forehead. A fleeting smile crosses his face.

"Let's go hunting," he says later that day from the window as he leans against the frame, looking out over the plains. Bracing his hands on the frame, he stretches, sleek muscles rippling. "I'm so hungry. And those things have to be edible."

He tips his chin toward the pale gray animals with long, slender legs roaming the plains below.

"You can hunt?"

He looks affronted. "Of course, I can hunt."

"Why?" They spend their lives in space, on ships, with nothing to hunt.

"I'm an Argenti. We can all hunt."

"Why?"

"Why would I not? I'm a healer, but I still went through all the normal manhood rituals."

So many memories transferred through their Bonding, but there's still so much we don't know about one another.

"When I met you, you lived on a ship in the middle of nowhere. What reason would you have to learn to hunt?"

His eyes trace over my legs, bare beneath the hem of his shirt I put on. "Did you not hunt on Triannon?"

"Me?" I grin. "No. There were lots of women who did, I suppose, but mostly we ate animals that came from farms."

"It was an important part of the manhood ritual on Argentus." He turns back toward the window, watching the grazers, and I step in beside him.

"What is the ritual like?"

A half smile lights his face. "The manhood one? There's a big hunt. A celebration. And then time with a dominess. By the time I came of age, there were far too few dominesses and too many males. Years ago, the rituals took a full week. But for me, it was only three days."

A burst of jealousy spikes through my belly. I should be grateful. Whoever she was, she was nice to Ajax. Instead, it makes me feel mildly cranky.

I press my face in the hollow between his shoulder blades. Press a kiss to his freshly washed skin, wrapping my arms around his waist, careful not to spill *eeffoc* on him.

He takes my mug, places it on the sill, and pulls me around to stand in front of him, facing away. He tugs the shirt over my head in an easy motion, and cool morning air puckers my nipples. "Put your hands on the glass."

"Wha..." I fall silent when he takes my hands in his. His motions are gentle but firm. I don't resist, don't want to, as he places my hands in front so I'm leaning forward, bent slightly at the waist.

"You just got jealous," he says, a grin in his voice.

"Maybe a little."

"For some reason, I find that hot." He tugs my hips, so I take a couple steps backward until I'm leaning forward, forced to take more weight on my palms.

A finger traces down my spine, and has me arching my back for him, pressing out with my ass. "Spread your legs wider."

A rush of liquid heat courses through me, but I do it. He spends a long minute behind me, and I can only assume he's staring at my pussy and probably my ass. It's both … uncomfortable and hot.

When he's ready, he walks around to stand beside me to cup my breasts, pull at my nipples. "When I first saw you, I thought you were the most beautiful person I'd ever seen in my entire life."

I felt that in the Bonding.

"I was wrong."

I glance at him sharply.

"You're so much more beautiful now that you're mine."

I don't have a response, can't think past the delicious husky whisper of his voice.

His fingers trail, feather-light along my neck, turning my chin toward him. "Am I scaring you?" he whispers.

I shake my head. Ajax has never scared me.

His hand trails over my hip to palm my ass. He groans, his lips against my ear, bristle scraping, breath sending shivers down my spine. "This ass... Gods, this ass is perfect."

He unbuckles his pants, and thwacks the rock-solid length of his cock against me. Traces the broad head along my slit, gathering fluid, running it to the tender bead of my clit, and back across the folds, then higher. The blunt head presses in.

I freeze, tightening my fingers on the glass, fear, arousal, curiosity roiling within me.

"Did he touch you here?"

"No."

Moving slowly, he traces his cock back down to my pussy, and I relax as he eases inside.

A hand on the small of my back holds me bent forward as he presses his hips in close, the hairs on his thighs tickling me. A finger traces over my ass again, finding that spot, slippery and wet from earlier. I flinch as he presses his finger inside. It doesn't hurt, but I've never felt so tight.

When he wiggles his finger, I groan a deep, primitive sound.

"Someday, woman," he says in my ear, his voice hoarse, "I'm going to fuck this ass."

On a deep primal level, I love the idea of him being inside me in a way Utto never was. On another, the idea terrifies me. Ajax is huge. He'd never fit. But right now, his finger there, it feels good.

"Do you want me to take you there?"

"I don't know."

"Why not?" His teeth stroke over the thin skin of my neck.

I'm shaking, shuddering as if I were freezing. "I'm scared."

"Do you think I'd hurt you?"

"I know you won't."

"Then it will be fine."

"Okay." It comes out long and high pitched.

"That's right. We'll work up to it. It won't hurt. I'm going to fuck you here and you'll sing for me as I do." He thrust his hips again, driving the thick length of him inside me, his free hand coming up to knead my breasts, holding me steady for the violence of his thrusts.

I can't do anything but brace myself against the window and enjoy the knife's edge of pleasure as his heavy sack smacks against my clit, hot and prickly with hair, his finger in my ass moves, stretching me, driving me insane

A second finger probes against my opening, pushing inward, and it triggers an orgasm so strong I'd probably fall over as my hips buck and thrust against him. He holds me steady, pumping out his own erratic orgasm while he grunts and curses and floods me with serum.

CHAPTER THIRTY

A dark figure moving on two legs

AJAX

In the end, it's a joke how easy it is for me to hunt.

The animals clearly haven't been exposed to people before. They eyed Feola and me suspiciously as we approach, scenting the air, gathering tighter in their herd, but ultimately, they don't seem to recognize the danger until after I've fired my first blast. And by then it's too late.

The animal isn't very big. It probably weighs about half as much as Feola. A took a smaller one on purpose. It will be more than enough meat for us.

Not knowing what attracted the birds, though, we can't bring the carcass back to the hotel.

So we build a fire right there in the plain, and I gut and skin it, cutting the meat into strips beneath the wide periwinkle sky. Not a cloud on the horizon.

I test the meat using the same reader I used on the

water and the fish. It's fine. Untainted.

The shadows grow longer, and we pack up the meat, now smoked and preserved.

"We should get back."

"Can it wait about ten minutes?" She makes a face. "Sorry."

"Don't be. I was distracted. Sorry." The unease is in my chest. I just took it for my own doubts about the birds.

With a smile, she presses me down to sit on the ground, reaching to unbuckle my belt. My dick responds instantly to her smile. And—*oh fuck*—when she wraps her lips around it, my head dropped back.

I lean back on one elbow, stroking her orange-pink curls with my other hand. "As soon as we get back, I'll return the favor."

She purrs, a low hum that vibrates through my balls.

She sucks harder, bobbing her head up and down and when she looks up at me, eyes wide and beseeching, I come hard down the back of her throat.

She smiles with her eyes, swallowing me down greedily.

I flop onto my back when it's over, dropping my arm over my eyes to block out the sun, shaking as she continues milking me for more.

Just kill me. I'm too happy to fight.

"That was... perfect."

She crawls over my body to straddle my waist, cuddling in. I wrap an arm around her, get a grip on her ass, my fingers curling around her hip.

I close my eyes. "Just give me a minute. Then we'll go back."

She sighs against my neck. I drop my arm back over my eyes, keeping a firm grip on her.

Five minutes.

It was maybe ten before I stand, exhausted and hungry again, pulling Feola to her feet, and scan the horizon, wondering if it'll ever rain. It must rain here sometimes.

Something dark catches my eye. High contrast against an eternity of pale soil.

A dark figure, moving on two legs.

Shit.

CHAPTER THIRTY-ONE

Somewhere they can't follow

AJAX

I duck low, pulling Feola with me. It's a stupid, wasted effort.

We have a fire burning hot and pumping dark clouds into a flawless sky. We may as well have sent out smoke signals for anyone on the planet looking for us.

And there I was, lying around in post-blowjob bliss, feeling smug and untouchable.

We even fired off a great big echoing *rezal* blast.

I wrap my hand around Feola's.

"What is it?"

"Someone's here."

She stiffens, crouching low, scanning the horizon, following my gaze. "I don't see anyone."

"Trust me, they're there."

"Come on." I drag Feola with me, backing toward the stand of trees behind us. We're about half a mile down a sharp and treacherous hill from the hotel, and the figure in the distance is about a mile and a half away.

Hidden in the tree line, I unstrap a couple of knives from my chest. She sputters when I press her back against the tree and drape the straps over her shoulder. Two of my best knives, and a *rezal*.

It's not nearly enough. I'm about to break my very first promise to her. "No goodbyes, okay?"

I yank her into a run, and she pushes hard. We sprint for the hill, and the road. If we can get there first, I'll have the advantage of windows to hide from, high visibility, but up the hill, in her slippers, Feola just can't move as fast as whoever is following us.

I lift her up, throw her over my shoulder, taking a quick look behind us, running as fast as I can up the hill.

I can't see anything, but they're there. We have no chance of outrunning them, and even if we could, then what? A showdown up at the hotel? Maybe possible if I had enough head start to get Feola somewhere safe and find a vantage point, but they'll be on us before then for sure.

It's not possible.

There's a strand of trees by the river that runs along the side of the path. Not too far away. It's the only hope we have. The rest is nothing more than low, scrubby gray plants. I drop her to the ground just inside the fronds.

I shove a bottle of water into her hands, walk to the edge of the curtain of willowy purple leaves, and part them slightly to peek through along the horizon.

The black figure has been joined by another. And then another. They're not even pretending to hide now. Openly approaching.

Three men—no, four—fan out. They've closed distance by now. Wearing black, with long black hair, they are clearly Vestige.

Whatever they want, there's almost no chance they mean to help. Vestige don't help Argenti. And they're fast, far faster than I can move with Feola. The uphill climb makes us too slow.

Six, maybe seven more minutes before they're on us.

My stomach tightens.

We need to separate. It's the only way she'll have a chance of getting away. And there isn't much time.

I cross to where she's leaning against the tree's trunk, watching me. I bury my nose in her hair. Let myself breathe her in. A large part of the Bonding relied on the pheromones her body releases. And I breathe hers in.

In typical Feola fashion, she isn't panicked. Just calm. Stoic and ready to face whatever she needs to face. This is a woman whose planet was invaded, her people slaughtered, who got into a cryo pod and woke up half a millennium later on an alien military base surrounded by men. She was drugged into marrying a bad one, abused, and she claimed her freedom. Panicky, weak are not words she knows.

"What are you going to do?"

No clue. I can't admit it. Won't admit it.

Instead, I stroke her cheek. "I'm just going to try to get a closer look at them."

Her eyes are hard. "You are *not* leaving me, *Ay-shocks*." Her voice is harder.

"It will be okay. Take the food." I hand the bag to her. It has water that could last her through the night if she's careful, and meat from the grazer. "Go up to the hotel and get the bag of serum." Still Utto's... "You'll need it."

She opens her mouth, ready to argue, but I cut her off, wishing I'd made time to refill those vials. "It's okay. Just go up the hill to the hotel. Float down the river, somewhere downstream. Hide somewhere near the ship during the day. Sleep in the bathing chamber at night to stay warm if you have to. But don't stay there during the day. They'll look for you."

Her brows lower mutinously.

"I need to be able to move fast. I can do this faster without you. I need to know you're safe."

She bites her lip, but nods, thousands of questions flickering through the layers of yellow-green in her eyes.

I grab her up for a quick hug, take a last breath of her, and then turn her so she's facing away from me.

"Go." I give her a gentle shove between the shoulder blades to get her moving. "Go."

CHAPTER THIRTY-TWO

let the current take me

FEOLA

I run as hard and as fast as I can. I don't turn around and look behind me. I don't pause to listen. Just block sound from my mind. Denied the noises that invaded my ears.

Blasts? Absolutely. If there's one thing I knew, however, it's that I'll do Ajax no favors by getting myself captured.

Run. I do, and take comfort in the steady pulse of him in my chest. I can feel him there. Alive and fighting. As long as we're alive and fighting, we'll be okay.

So I run, pushing my body to move faster until my stomach aches and the hot, dry air gushing through my lungs burns. It isn't until my feet hit the smooth, dusty tiles of the old hotel that I stop. I spin a circle on the terrace at the top of the plains, overlooking the dry expanse below. Man-sized blurs moved in the distance, but I can't make out which black blurs are which.

I can't stay here at the hotel. Even if they didn't actually see me run, it's too obvious a place to look. Footprints and fresh evidence of fire will show them everything they needed to know about where me and Ajax have been staying.

I rummage through our items with shaking hands.

Vaguely, a distant portion of my brain recognizes my own pounding heart, my gasping breath, my stinging eyes.

Calm down.

I glance out the window. The blurs are gone. He hasn't been shot, or I'd feel his pain through the Bond. Oh, fuck. Where is he?

Think. It can't be a coincidence that they're here. They must be here looking for us. Either Guarda or someone working for Utto's family.

I blow out air slowly.

They can't leave this planet without me. It doesn't make sense to kill Ajax until they find me.

Okay. So, they can't find me.

Breathe. Okay. I can do this. I. Will. Do. This.

With a canteen loaded, rations and the dreaded vials tied up in the corner of an old sheet, I do exactly what Ajax told me to do.

I jump into the river and let the current pull me over the falls.

CHAPTER THIRTY-THREE

Wharr is the woman?

AJAX

I've always held my own in spars, took pride in practicing, honing my body and my skills. But that was in simulated tests, on training mats, with brothers in arms. Even during on-ground operations on foreign planets they were training ops.

None of my opponents were ever trying to kill me. There is big fucking difference between fighting an opponent for training purposes, and fighting one for real. One who wants to kill.

The men crossing the plain are not Argenti. They're Vestige, and whatever the Tribesmen liked to say in locker rooms and when they drank, the Vestige are fierce in a fight.

They move with precision. With the same speed I expected.

It doesn't take long.

I lead them away from Feola to a copse of shimmering lavender trees, where I take careful aim and squeeze off several blasts. Catch one of them squarely in the chest. No chance of recovery. Another, I get right between the eyes.

The third and fourth circling behind me. I barely even have time to draw my blade before they're there.

The sinuous silvery leaves part and I'm face to face with Vestige warriors. One holds his own weapon, sights centered squarely on my chest.

I lift my hands up. There's no point fighting or resisting.

"Raise your hands," says a man in heavily accented Argenti.

For some reason it surprises me that he speaks Argenti? Argenti kids are taught Vestigi in school. The politicians back home believe firmly in knowing our enemy. Apparently, the Vestige either feel the same, or this man has experience with Argenti.

I raise my hands over my head. Stark tattoos spread over the exposed skin of the neck and forearms of the man facing me. They can't be active Vestige military. They're not dressed for that. They wear civilian clothes, but they are fully armed.

The tattooed man jerks his head in my direction, and the other man approaches and unhooks my straps in deft, swift motions, then shoves my chest, hard enough to force me to take a step back.

Without my weapons, I feel lighter and far more vulnerable.

"You killt two offf my men."

"That appears to be correct." It's true and I'm not sorry.

Tattoo narrows glittering eyes as dark as the massive tattoo swirling up his neck. "Wharr is she?"

"Who?"

Tattoo jerks his head again, and a blow to the side of my face has me staggering to the side to keep my balance. Shake my head to clear my swimming vision.

"Wharr is she?"

"Who?" I ask again.

This time, I know it's coming, so I duck, swinging my elbow out to catch my would-be-puncher in the jaw.

The blow comes from the other side. Tattoo has crossed the copse and lands a hard punch right in the corner of my temple. The pain bursts bright, exploding behind my eyes. At least that had to hurt Tattoo's knuckles too, but I can't see because my vision's gone black.

Shit. I shake my head harder.

Slowly, it comes back, hazy, in white powdery splotches and smoky black blurs.

Tattoo studies me, impassive. He speaks in Vestigi, too fast for me to understand, and the other one backs away. Which made me instantly uneasy.

Tattoo's *rezal* clicks as he adjusts some setting along its barrel, raises his weapon and takes careful aim. "Wharr is the woman?"

I ignore him. Make him repeat it three or four times just because I can.

Finally, Tattoo comes closer, though still not in range. "I saw the woman. I know you sent her somewharr. I will torture you if I need to. I will find her. Might as well make it easier on us. And on her. I'll punish her for every delay you cause."

"Who do you work for?" It has to be Upranimus.

"Wharr is she?"

I don't even blink.

Neither does Tattoo. "I'll kill you if I have to ask again."

"You can't kill me. She'll need serum or she'll die."

"I can provide Vestige equivalent."

I have no idea if that's true or not. I don't know what comes out of these guys dicks, but I keep my face neutral. "It wouldn't work."

Tattoo blinks slowly, almost as if he's bored. He glances at the other one, chewing on the inside of his cheek.

After a moment, he nods. And pulls the trigger.

The blast hits me in the chest. Knocks me off my feet. Cold spreads through my limbs.

This time, my vision stays black.

CHAPTER THIRTY-FOUR

What about the birds?

FEOLA

I paddle to shore and the grove of willowy lavender trees.

I have no idea how far I floated, but the hotel is beyond sight, over the horizon's curve. I floated a long way. Hopefully, it's far enough.

A bloom of pain bursts in my chest. Ajax.

But he's alive.

I drag myself out of the water, over the soft sand. My dress is waterlogged, tangling around my legs, and now it sticks to the beach.

Eventually, they'll decide to search the river. It's the most practical choice.

Another burst of pain beat in my chest. He's been caught, then. I suck in a long, deep breath, willing him to be okay and rummage through the bag.

How long before I need serum again?

My fingers close around one of the vials of Utto's serum.

We didn't have a chance to replace it with Ajax's. It feels especially heinous now.

If those men were Argenti Guarda, I'd happily turn myself in. We can fight all of Argentus, and Utto's family, legally. Together. If we have to.

But if they aren't Tribe, if they work for Utto or his uncle, they'll use Ajax to capture me, then kill him and take me straight back to Utto.

Another blinding stab coils in my chest. *Ajax.* What are they doing to him? Torturing him?

Abruptly, the Bond goes slack. Empty.

Nothing comes from his side but stillness. Silence. A sob catches in my throat. *Is he—?* I refuse to finish the thought.

I need to find him. Come up with a plan. My eyes burn and the pressure at the back of my throat brings back memories of the early days with Utto. Panic.

Ajax is fine. Ajax is fine. Ajax is fine.

I repeat it like an incantation. Until I believe it. Until my throat relaxes.

Now, I need to plan.

I yank off my dress and spread it on a stone in the beating sun to dry. I'll freeze at night in a wet dress.

Naked, drying my hair in the sunshine, I trace my fingers along the leather of the weapon holsters, feeling the reassuringly hard weight of the knives and the *rezal* there. It reminds me of him. It smells like him and feels like him.

I have one advantage. Ajax said so. They don't know I have weapons and they'll assume I have no clue how to use them.

No sense roaming around with the weapons strapped visibly across my chest.

Where else can I keep the weapons? My dress doesn't hide much, and it clings to my torso.

But not my legs. It will hang loosely around my legs when it dries.

Carefully, using the knife, I tighten the leather harness so it fits around my thigh. I can wear the knives on one thigh and the *rezal* on the other. It isn't perfect. The *rezal* will be lumpy. But maybe they won't look. Maybe they won't notice

I'll have to cut the dress short, above my knees, so I can get my hands on the weapons when I need them.

It makes sense anyway. The dress caught around my legs as I ran earlier.

I stuff one of the rations down my throat and swallow a canteen full of water.

Where is Ajax? Where would they take him?

They captured him. I have to believe that. They wouldn't kill him, would they? It wouldn't make sense.

Their smartest play would be to keep him alive and use him to find me.

I need to trust him. And have hope. Still, I keep finding my hand coming up to rest where the Bond feels empty and flat.

The birds. What about the birds? And how will I stay warm without a fire? Ajax said I should go back to the ship, but I have no idea where the ship is. It twisted and turned, and for I know, I came out miles farther down than where we fished that day.

The sun sits, opalescent and shimmering, above the mirage of the horizon.

Night will fall soon, comes cold solitude, and flesh-hungry black birds.

CHAPTER THIRTY-FIVE

Facts I've been told from birth

AJAX

I stare at the men who captured me, wincing against the ache in my abdomen where the stun blast hit me.

I'm probably purple-black from bellybutton to pectorals, but with my hands bound behind my back, I can't look. Bruising and tenderness for certain, but I doubt any serious damage. I'll feel like shit for a week though.

They set up a force field that deters the birds. They squawk and dive at the invisible barrier relentlessly, circling in the night sky, a deafening cacophony.

My captors aren't bothered in the slightest.

They move about their tasks, bagging up the bodies of their fallen comrades and digging graves with an efficiency that speaks of old association.

Comfortable with one another's motions. Comfortable enough with death that the loss of men they knew and clearly respected doesn't stop them from completing their mission.

Grief is evident in the lines of their faces, the gravity with which they handle the bodies, but it doesn't change anything.

Professionals. That much is clear. And friends, if I had to guess. There's no sense of formality or ceremony between them. Tattoo is thicker, taller, the harder of the two. The other one was wiry, with solid strength and a face rimmed in laugh lines, he looked like a hard man in a fight, but probably a fun one over a drink.

They're not a pair I can fight. Not alone. Not with my hands tied behind my back.

Feola thumps in my chest, the sweet weight a steady comfort. She's safe, somewhere. Planning something. Hopefully at the ship, safe from the birds, warm and curled up in a corner of the bathing chamber. She'll have to take Utto's serum soon if she hasn't already. I flex my palms behind my back where my wrists are bound, itching to feel her body against mine, smell her hair.

I try to send messages over the bond but get nothing back except low-key anxiety.

They speak in Vestigi occasionally, and I understand enough to know they're bounty hunters.

Former soldiers.

So they were sent by Utto. Or maybe his uncle. Probably both.

They wear thick coats against the cold, implying they had better information about the state of the planet than we did. They wrapped a blanket haphazardly around my back, shoving me to the ground beside the fire.

The light bounces off their skin, making them stand out like ghosts against the inky sky and landscape beyond.

I tilt my head back and roll my shoulders.

Stars spatter across the sky, swirling like snowflakes as the massive wings of the great black birds black them out.

The smoke disappears, thick and gray.

Squatting down in front of me, Tattoo takes a long sip from his canteen. "Water."

I nod. "Please." My mouth tastes like smoke and dust.

Tattoo jerks his head, and I get it. It isn't exactly how I helped the sick men in my healing bay to drink, but it is kind, nonetheless. Kinder than he has to be, to offer me water.

I open my mouth and tilt my head back.

Studying me like a lab rat, Tattoo pauses to let me swallow a few times.

"Thank you."

They could have left she me here, thirsty as hell, and ignored me entirely.

It's eerie. I can't always tell where those pitch-black eyes are looking, though when the firelight hits them right, his eyes gleam amber with tapetum lucidum, like a nocturnal animal.

He nods slowly and walks away, the firelight reflecting off the thick mane of black hair that falls down his back.

"I'm Ajax," I say to his back.

A grunt is the only response.

They mostly ignore me for the rest of the night.

It's unnerving. I've spent my whole life hating them. They killed my mother. And Clari. Every man, woman, and child of the Tribe knows the Vestige are evil. I've heard stories. The atrocities, barbarism, lack of empathy for the plight of others. Only monsters would murder women and children.

They tried to annihilate Argentus.

And yet these two men behave for all the world like any member of the Tribe. Just soldiers. In the dark, if it weren't for their eyes, they could be Tribe warriors. What stories did they grow up hearing about Argentus?

"How much Argenti do you speak?" I ask in Vestigi, partly because I'm curious, but partly because they don't seem like monsters, maybe they won't kill me if they get to know me.

They ignore me.

I speak in Argenti. "I have a horrible illness. I shit blood and piss bile. It's highly contagious. Travels in the air."

The laughing one chews on the inside of his lip like he's hiding a smile, but otherwise, neither reacts.

"I'd like to kill you. Eat your bones and shit on the

grave."

The smile breaks free, and laughing one laughs, earning a dark glare from Tattoo.

"I hear all Vestigi jerk off into their *eeffoc* before they drink it. Or do you jerk off into each other's?"

Laugher laughs again. No poker face. In a different scenario, I might have liked him.

They return to their meal.

"I grew up hearing that you guys slaughtered children and ate each other. I've never thought about it before, but growing up, what did you hear about Argentus?"

Two heads swivel at that. Leaving the fire, and locking on me. Two pairs of black eyes glitter in the night. A long moment passes. "We learned you sent the Dark Death that nearly destroyed our people two centuries ago," Tattoo says, in a voice low and gravelly deep.

The hairs on the back of my neck rise.

"We learnt that you tie your women to you with addictive chemicals so that they are forced to fuck you or die. It's the only way you can keep them. We learnt that you spread through space like a virus, destroying every land you touch, taking everything you can get your hands on. We learnt that you come from the pits of hell."

I flex my neck. "So you do hurt children for fun."

Laugher isn't laughing anymore. He rises half to his knees, but Tattoo smacks him back down.

"Truth in every rumor," Tattoo says. "There was

a time when our planet starved. We were near to death from your disease. A few resorted to cannibalism. No one escaped unharmt. Your Dark Death murdert ninety-five percent of our population."

I frown. That plague was brutal, decimating the population of Vesta, but it hadn't come from Argentus. "We didn't send that plague."

"A lie."

"No."

Tattoo traces his knife across the fruit in his hands. "We are a population of warriors. Yours is the population of doctors and scientists. Do you think it is likely that we coult develop such a thing?"

I shiver against the ring of truth in his voice.

"Or do you think it's more likely that we simply altered the one that had already been sent to us?"

My stomach twists. *Altered?* He means the Plague of Days. My mother and sister. A plague the Vestige unleashed on Argentus. "So it would kill Argenti women?"

"It was supposed to only kill men. It backfired."

Facts I've been told from birth, or a fiction developed by a desperate class of rulers determined to keep the peace on Argentus? Where had the Plague of Days come from? The Vestige sent it. Our oldest enemy. I know it as surely as I know that water is hydrogen and oxygen. I've always known it. Never questioned it.

And before that? Three thousand years ago? The first plague to ravage Argentus?

Who started that one? The very first one?

Three thousand years ago, a plague came that lasted years. They called it the Blood Sickness for the way the victims bled from every orifice, dying slowly and painfully, with recoveries and relapses ensuring the illness spread like wildfire. How could you quarantine people for years?

It killed in droves, moving in cycles for centuries. A thousand years of death. That's when serum evolved. So men could save their women. It took hundreds of years for it to develop into its modern concentration. For the Bond to become so strong it could heal someone even from the Blood Sickness.

I wrote a thesis in school positing that the serum was actually a concentrated form of the original virus, and my instructor ripped it to shreds.

What if the remnants of that virus were used to create a new plague two hundred years ago? What if the Tribe had engaged in bioengineering weapons and had indeed sent the virus to the Vestige home world, Vesta, and nearly wiped them out?

Then the good were not so good. Maybe the bad were not so bad?

It makes more sense that the Vestige manipulated an existing virus, the Dark Death on Vesta from two hundred years ago, and sent it back to Argentus in the form of the Plague of Days. Can you even blame them?

I see my mother's face. And Clari's.

Laugher spits into the fire. "If I had the chance, I'd send a new plague to your people. And watch you all suffer."

Tattoo hisses, and the sound blends with the crackling flames.

I close my eyes. In the morning, I'll keep trying to piss them off. Maybe they'll make a mistake and give me an opening. Or at a minimum stall them.

CHAPTER THIRTY-SIX

Strike twist pull

FEOLA

Night comes cold but dry, the darkness fast on its heels, bringing desert gusts and a glorious surprise.

The lavender trees with fronds that reached high into the sky into mammoth arches before returning to the powdery white terra. All along the fronds, night-blooming blue blossoms as big as my palms spring forth. They glow in the night and make my head spin with their heady perfume.

I have a lighter. I could build a fire … but the birds.

Glancing furiously around for something to use as a blanket, or shelter, my gaze lands on the great trees. On the long, feathery fronds.

Using one of the knives, I cut away great handfuls, weaving them into loosely braided coils, like the baskets and mats I made on Triannon.

It doesn't take long. The fronds are so thick and soft that in almost no time, I have a shapeless tunic with a hole in the center for my head. It hangs to the floor, thick and plush, fragrant and cozy warm.

And best of all, Ajax beats warm and soft in my chest. He's alive.

The birds came to us that night on the plain… maybe because of my song or the fire. Maybe it was our smell or sound. But now maybe if I stay quiet and wait, they'll leave me alone.

Draping the bag with her belongings over my shoulder, I climb into a notch at the base of a branch, and gather up more fronds to cover myself.

I tuck my feet beneath me, and with my knife in my hand, rest my head. I doubt I'll sleep, but at least here, like this I'm somewhat safe, thanks to this tree.

Night passes quietly. No birds. Just the cold, the dark, and the silence. The morning brings light and heat. The blue night blossoms close their petals and I drop to the floor, a cloud of soil bursting around me as my feet touch down. I squash the tunic into a ball and tie it off with more fronds. I'm not leaving it.

Need for Ajax burns but I ignore it, refusing to acknowledge Utto's gross vials. I drink water, stuffed provisions down my throat and try to pretend my head isn't pounding, that my hands aren't shaking, that my vision isn't blurring.

Today, I'll cover my hair and hope that in my white dress I blend in with the landscape. And I will find them. They have to be staying somewhere near the river. They, too, need to drink and wash. They have to sleep. I'll follow the river back to the hotel.

I walk in the slight depression of the beach, between the water and the rising land, sticking to the copses of trees for shade and camouflage. It's cooler there. It takes all morning and part of the afternoon to find them. But I do.

They have a fire. A slim column of black smoke rising to the sky.

Waves of chills break across my skin. My blood thrums, hot and angry. I need Ajax. But no fucking Utto. Never again.

They have a crude camp set up beneath a scramble of trees a few yards from the river. I want to run straight to Ajax, but instead, I back away, into the shade of a tree, and lift myself up high, parting silvery branches so I can see them. Surprise. That's my advantage.

The only reason I survived Rennie was instinct and impulse. There'd been no time to plan, just sheer blinding panic.

This time, I have a chance to plan.

I'll find my opening.

I watch all day as they stride from the shade in their black clothes, to splash water on their faces, refill their canteens from the river… and that's when an idea takes hold. The Vestige holding Ajax are men, just like any other.

All men must pee. Fact of nature.

And these men peed in the same spot. They even

brought Ajax there twice so he, too, could empty his bladder. They had a designated pee spot.

It was slightly downriver from where they refilled their canteens, beneath the base of another tree, in the shade. I wait until the sun hangs low in the distance, and their pissoir is vacant. Then I run across the tiny blue flowers and the dusty white soil, and climb the tree right over their spot to wait.

Night will come. And at some point, one of them will come alone to pee beneath my tree. I don't want to think too close about the monster inside me capable of planning like this. I know what will happen when the man comes beneath my tree. I'll do what Ajax told me to. I'll strike hard, in a soft fleshy spot when he least expects it. Twist. Pull.

I close my burning eyes and finally give in to the constant, aching pull in my mind. Like a headache, it beckons, summoning me to the darkest place and time.

Rennie's voice in the bathroom of Utto's chambers on Romeo-Two. Cold and thick. Brittle. He pressed his gross penis against me, his hands drifting over the bare skin of my thighs. *I'm going to lay down on your bed. Take off my clothes. I'm nice and hard for you. Feel that?*

He met my eyes in the mirror. I wrapped my fingers around the pillowcase that held all my hopes and dreams. And a knife.

Feel it? I'm big and hard, little doll.

I nodded, throat convulsing as he butted his hips against me.

*You're going to fuck me. And you're going to smile while
you do it. And when I'm done, you're going to walk around all
day with my cum oozing out of your cunt, and when your mate
returns, he'll get a nice, creamy reminder of who owns him.*

He'll kill me. Please, don't do this. I begged. I pleaded.
He didn't care. My hands shook. My head spun. The
fine hairs on my body rose.

Not my problem.

His fingers drifted higher. Nausea curled in my
belly, and sirens blared, whirring in my ears. My
vision darkened, and all I saw were the darks of his
eyes, tight at the ends in a mirthless smile. A wide,
toothy grin stretched across his face.

Smile, he said.

And I did. I smiled, big and dazzling and wide,
sneaking my hand inside the pillowcase.

That's a good girl. Smart girl.

*He straightened, adjusting his pants. Come when you've got
your cunt wet and ready.*

Something snapped inside. All the terror and rage
of months under Utto's hands boiled up, filling my
face with hot pressure, my eyes pulsing, and the sirens
blared again, blocking out all sound. All I saw was
Rennie's broad back as he sauntered away.

I didn't even think. I didn't hesitate. Not so much
as a breath between the second my fingers closed
around the bare handle of the blade, and the minute
it plunged into his back. Whatever vital organs I
managed to hit, he fell to the floor almost
immediately.

A pool of blood oozed from between his lips to

spread across the floor. More blood spread beneath him. The handle of the knife. Sticking up from his back like a lurid flag.

Him or me. Him or me. Him or me.

He was an evil man.

And so are these men who kidnapped my mate and will return me to Utto.

Them or Ajax. Them or Ajax. Them or Ajax.

I wrap my fingers around the knife in my hand, breathing silently in the night air, surrounded by the fragrant, glowing blue blossoms. Draped in feathered fronds, covered from head to toe, I blend in. I wait right above their pee spot.

All I have to do is drop down and strike, twist, pull.

A shiver of serum sickness runs along my spine. Or maybe it's fear of this new Feola. They'll never see me until it*'s too late.*

CHAPTER THIRTY-SEVEN

The little monster

AJAX

The metal device they used to shackle me, whatever it is, isn't budging, no matter how hard I struggle with it. And I struggle until the muscles in my arms burn and my wrists chafe.

They've only removed them three times and only then so I can piss. They keep their *rezals* trained on me the entire time. Always watching. They take no chances. Didn't even remove them so I could eat. Just poured a protein drink down my throat so I wouldn't starve.

I need them to make a mistake. Anything to give me an opening, but so far they've proved efficient and intelligent. Apparently, their plan is to wait Feola out. They figure she'll run out of serum eventually and come find us when she gets desperate enough.

They sit facing outward, scanning the horizon, searching for her until night falls, the temperature plummets, and the crazy black birds return, thumping against the invisible force field with bursts of blue flashing grids.

Then they relax visibly, and I watch them even more closely for any opening.

I haven't felt any burst of serum-induced pleasure across the Bond, which means she didn't take Utto's serum and probably also means she's fevered, weak and turned on as hell.

Which makes me worry they might be right.

Laugher stands, clipping on a portable force-field backpack, and walks into the darkness.

With the fire at my back, I'm warm enough, but what about Feola? It's freezing. I keep imagining her curled up in a ball, shaking and scared. Through the Bond, I feel anxiety, fear.

Something feels wrong.

Tattoo notices it too. He shifts to the edge of the circle.

Laugher's been gone too long.

I lumber awkwardly to my feet. With my hands behind my back, my balance is off and I have to shift to my knees first.

Tattoo barks something in fast Vestigi and, moving quickly, crosses to me. A hard shove in the shoulder, coupled with a hook behind the knee, and I hit the ground. I scrabble back up to my knees, searching the darkness beyond. They chose a piss spot not far from the camp. If a bird got Laugher we'd have heard something.

But maybe there are other predators than just the

birds? Fuck, Feola's out there. What if they find her too? I yank at the shackles fruitlessly.

Another pang of activity pours across the Bond. Grief or guilt or anguish. And my whole body goes still. Anger, fear, and shame pours through me.

She didn't follow my advice. She came for me. *Fuck.* What the hell is she thinking? I suck in air and wriggle myself to my feet.

Tattoo curses and stalks to the edge of the force-field clearing. At his approach, the blue grid glows like fine netting. I can barely hear beneath the clamor of the birds.

Tattoo shouts into the darkness.

I scan the shadows.

No response from Laugher.

Tattoo rounds on me, eyes glinting dangerously. "Is that her? Is she here?"

There's no way to answer that question.

Tattoo turns back toward where Laugher disappeared. "I'll kill your man," he shouts. "Show your face."

"He's lying," I shout. I may or may not be. It doesn't matter. "If you're out there, don't listen to him."

Tattoo raises his eyebrows, lifting his *rezal* to level it at my chest.

There's nothing to hear but the birds.

"You think I'm lying?" He cocks the weapon. "I will count to ten."

"Don't do it, Feola. Run away. If he kills me—"

Tattoo circles the fire. "You don't fear bullets? Fine." His boot kicks out, fast.

I try to dodge it, but it still connects. A hard, blinding glance off my temple that sends me back to the ground, taking the bulk of my weight on one shoulder.

"Five seconds," Tattoo roars at the sky.

A blast echoes across the desert night, scattering birds.

Tattoo hisses and drops to the ground. "Fuck," he shouts in hoarse Vestigi.

And there she is, like an angel materializing out of thin black air, wearing a furry, gray sack. A *rezal* held high in her hands, just like I taught her.

"Drop your *rezal*," she says evenly.

Tattoo laughs. "Fuck you." He aims his *rezal* at her face. "Drop *your rezal*."

She doesn't move.

"Drop your fucking *rezal*." Tattoo fires, and the blast flies just over her shoulder.

I hiss, scrambling across the dust like a crab, trying to block her.

"Drop. It. Now." Tattoo's voice is even and controlled.

She glances at me and slowly lowers her *rezal* to the ground.

"Arms up high."

Her gaze never leaves mine. It's good to see her. Better than it should be, considering the circumstances. The boiling pit in my stomach, the blurring focus recedes at her sheer proximity. Her eyes glitter in the firelight.

"What the hell are you wearing?" Tattoo asks. "Take it off."

She pulls the gray sack over her head, revealing her bare, slender legs, the sheer white dress.

Tattoo stalks across the camp and runs his hands along her shoulder blades, down her chest, between her breasts, up her thighs beneath the dress, ignoring the building furious growls leaving my throat.

She lifts her chin. Her lips wobble.

Tattoo's jaw ticks, but he jerks his head toward me. "Go to your man."

She takes off at a run to tackle me to the ground and wraps her arms and legs around me.

I topple back, landing on my shoulders, wishing like hell I could hug her. "Take off these shackles," I growl.

"No."

Feola's crying. Fat tears drip down her cheeks. I manage to sit back up, with her straddling my lap. I can't wipe her tears away, so I use my own cheeks, tracing them along her hot skin.

Her face crumples.

"It's okay," I whispered awkwardly.

"I n-need serum."

Her pulse is fast. Her skin fever hot.

"Take off these shackles, so I can help her."

Tattoo shrugs impassively. "I'll turn my back

when the time comes."

"Fuck you."

Tattoo laughs darkly. "Fuck me? Fuck *me?* You're lucky I'm letting you help her. If I couldn't smell how sick she is from here, I'd tie the little monster up and go find out what the hell she did to Jasto."

Feola shudders against me, breath hitching.

"You didn't use Utto's?" I whisper into her hair, feeling mingled frustration, elation, and fury.

"No. I couldn't ..."

"Shh." I curl my neck around hers, breathing her in. "It's okay. Shh. I'd have done the same thing. You did nothing wrong, baby."

"I'm sorry. I'm so sorry. I couldn't do it." She keeps breathing it out. Over and over and over. "I just couldn't."

Her legs tighten around my waist, arms around my back. She lifts her lips to mine. Shame spears through me. This is so fucked up.

Panting, moving awkwardly, I scuttle across the dusty earth, closer to the fire to warm her. Her hands tug at my clothes. She's shaking, her skin blazing hot.

"I need you," she whispers, a mess of tears and snot and need.

CHAPTER THIRTY-EIGHT

An elaborate pantomime

FEOLA

Another lesson from Utto—enjoy the good moments. I lived for the first beautiful, hot sip of *eeffoc* in the morning, or the feel of sliding into cool sheets after a long day, a long soak in the bath while Utto was gone. I learned to linger on the pleasure of those little moments, because far too often, when they were over, Utto brought bad moments.

Eeffoc, cool sheets, hot baths—none of them account for a speck of a glimmer of an inkling of the sheer pleasure I feel as I wrap my arms around Ajax's big, warm body. I bury my face in his neck and breathe him in and don't let the shame of my failure to kill the laughing guy get to me.

I press wet, open-mouthed kisses against his skin. Salty and sweet and perfect. Ajax. He always smells like heaven.

"These fucking shackles." He squirms under me,

but his deep rumbling voice ripples down my spine, swallowing up the tremors and the violence and the fear.

His lips drag along my neck, and I burn for him.

I'm panting like a rabid animal in his ear, too confused with lust to do anything but writhe atop him. I need more. Have to get closer. My gaze lands on the Vestige man, with his black eyes glittering in the firelight.

I know those eyes. I've seen him before.

Ajax's teeth graze my neck, and rational thought flees.

I shove my hands under his shirt, shuddering when I feel the skin of his chest.

Vaguely I'm aware of the Vestige man turning around.

I slide my hands lower, unbuckle his belt, and there it is. Hard and solid as steel. I circle my thumb over the bead of moisture on the head and bring it to my lips, hungry noises leaving my lips.

I lift my hips, line up his shaft, press into it, and take him deep inside in a single thick shove.

Our lips find each other again, but I'm too far gone to focus. Mostly we just breathed together, mouths open, gasping as I move my hips over his. *I love you.* I want to say it. But can't somehow.

His eyes flash open, gleaming. Maybe he hears me anyway. "These fucking shackles."

I rise up and crash down. *I love you.*

"Again."

I love you.

I slam down, and my tired serum-withdrawn body spirals out toward climax.

He stops talking after that. We both do.

The big Vestige man Ajax calls Tattoo watches as I lay my feather leaf tunic on the ground. When I point at the blankets, he shrugs, a strange look lingering in the shape of his dark eyes.

I drape the blankets over Ajax's body, trying to help him get as comfortable as he can with his arms behind his back.

"Can you not at least move them to be in front?" I ask Tattoo.

"No."

He crosses to crouch in front of me. "Hands."

I sigh but hold my hands forward. He drops new shackles around my wrists. They're unmovable. I can't imagine how Ajax must feel, stuck like this all this time. He ties our legs then too.

Ajax doesn't complain.

Tattoo then stomps away from camp, down to the river. From his shouts, I can tell he's found his partner. They return a few moments later, the partner red in the face, a blood gash on his forehead, furious and shouting. But he doesn't touch us. They speak in Vestigi for a while.

He points at his head, gesturing and talking wildly,

and Tattoo takes a look.

Whatever he says, I can't make out. But the other guy barks out a laugh, and then they're both laughing hard. The Laughing guy does an elaborate pantomime of himself taking a piss and then suddenly something falling down from above. Me clearly.

I just couldn't do the stab twist pull. So I launched myself out of the tree and swung the butt of the rifle at his head with every ounce of muscle I possess.

They look at me now and laugh some more.

I should have stab twist pulled.

I wiggle back so my body presses closer to Ajax. I'm warm, his legs spooning me, and the fire against my front, the blankets around us, but I keep feeling the dark eyes across the dancing flames. And every time I shut my eyes, I relive it. Falling through the night air, the rezal in my hand. The thud as I brought it down on his face. I should have stabbed him. If I had, we'd be two against one. I just … somehow, I couldn't do it.

In the morning, the two Vestige give us some privacy, and I get serum from Ajax, which is awkward with both of us cuffed.

While we're pressed together, I bring my lips to his ear. "I have an idea."

His eyes cloud, clearly about to argue so I rush through. "He still doesn't see me as a threat. Not like he sees you, or he'd have tied my hands behind my back."

His face bumps against my cheeks as his head shakes.

"Just follow my lead, okay?" I struggle to my feet with no hands.

"Feola, wait."

"Hey! Where are you? M—M—Mr. Vestige?" I whirl toward the pee spot, not wanting to look too closely in the direction of the men who… And I come face to face with Tattoo.

He raises a thick, black brow.

"I have to pee."

The brow doesn't move, and neither did he.

I lift my hands. "Can you uncuff me so I can pee?"

Nothing.

"Do you want me to pee on my dress?"

He stares for a long minute.

"I'll smell if I do."

His jaw hardens, but he presses his thumb to a flat, black square on the top of my shackles, which glow blue for a second before the metal circles that wrap my wrists pop open. Interesting.

"Thank you, er… what is your name?"

"Torum." The way he says it, the *r* rolls together in a thick, viscous sound.

"Torrrrum. Thank you." I turn to the other one, the one I hit. "And yours?"

He laughs but doesn't answer.

Torum jerks his chin in the direction of the trees. "Stay in sight."

I do my business in the partial cover of a small tree, with my back to Torum's glowering face.

When I'm done, I come right back, presenting my hands for the shackles like an ideal prisoner. "Thank you, Torum. Ajax needs to pee now."

Their eyes narrow. I smile brightly as Ajax lumbers to his feet. When the shackles loosen, he winces, rolling his shoulders, but doesn't comment.

CHAPTER THIRTY-NINE

The fifth time I stumble

AJAX

Torum mixes another of his vile protein drinks and stomps over. I know the drill. I tilt my head back and open wide so he can dump the crap down my gullet.

It's disgusting, but my stomach is hungry, and I have a feeling I'll need the energy.

Feola eyes the concoction with narrowed eyes.

Torum pours another batch, and holds it out to Feola's face. "Open."

She wrinkles her nose and shakes her head.

"Open."

With a morose glare, she opens her mouth.

Torum pours some in, and she promptly coughs it up, spitting it out onto Torum's boots.

Torum hops backward looking affronted and

disgusted. Laugher, busy packing up the force field, laughs uproariously.

Feola keeps gagging. "It's this pregnancy," she pants, raising her shackled hands to wipe her mouth. "I'm sick all the time."

I spit some of my own gross shake out over the blue flowers on the powdery ground in front of me.

Torum cocks his head.

"You're what?" I can't clear my head.

Feola sits up on her heels. "Oh, *Ay-shocks*. What a terrible way for you to find out. I'm pregnant."

I should be a better man. I should feel elated, joyous. Instead, the first numbing thought to cross my mind is to wonder if the baby is Utto's. "How far along are you?"

"Not far. I only just missed my cycle."

I know her well by now. The way her eyes widen, and she freezes for a split second before speaking. She's lying. "Aren't you happy?"

I cough and nod and try to look overjoyed.

She chatters with Torum as he finishes packing up supplies. Or rather, she chatters *at* Torum. He ignores her.

She goes on about baby names and the advantages of girls over boys, as Torum and Laugher herd us into an awkward march.

First, we need to take Torum and Laugher out. Use one of their thumbs to remove the shackles. Take Torum's ship. Contact Tam. Get off this miserable planet.

I study Torum and Laugher when they're not looking. Laugher has a slight limp, like an old injury. It might be a weakness. If Torum has any, I can't find it.

My dad used to to say the same thing over and over, when we struggled in school or with friends. *Be weak when you're strong. And strong when you're weak.*

About two miles into their walk, I stumble over a thick ridge of the little blue flowers, dropping to his knees.

Feola runs over to help.

I shake it off, make a big show of reassuring her, under the watchful eye of Torum and the amused one of Laugher.

I stumble again a few yards later.

Again, Feola helps me rise.

The fifth time I stumble, I don't rise, not even with Feola's help. Torum curses. "Stand up. Or I kill you. I don't need you."

I pant and drool pathetically into the dust.

Laugher, predictably, laughs.

Torum rotates his *rezal* on its strap, so it hangs behind his back, and walks over. I screw my face up like I'm in horrible pain. Out of the corner of my eye, I watch him hesitate. He places his hand under my elbow and pulls. I let him pull me up to kneel.

Then I collapse back to the ground.

"What's wrong with him?" Laugher calls.

Torum just shoves me in the shoulder, hauling me back to my knees, where I sag, limp in his grip.

Irritably, Laugher tosses his gun over his shoulder and stomps over to stand beside Torum. "What's his problem?"

Torum shrugs and reaches for his canteen, leaning forward, finally within range. It's the closest he's let his face get.

I slam my head forward. The hardest part, the solid knot at the top of my forehead. It connects with the softest part of Torum's nose.

He flies back, hands flying instinctively up to cover his nose, and I'm on my feet. I slam my foot forward, connecting first with Laugher's groin. A second hard kick to Torum's temple, and the man's eyes shut.

Laugher falls forward, and I kick him in the face. It all happened fast.

Feola scrambles forward, grabbing Torum's *rezal*. Laugher bucks, rising to his feet with a shout.

Three things happen all at once. Feola shouts. Laugher lunges. And the *rezal* fires.

It echoed long and loud.

Laugher falls to the ground, eyes wide with shock, hands coming up to press over the bleeding hole in the center of his chest. He barely even makes a sound before he falls to the ground.

Dead.

Feola drops the *rezal* to the dust. A cloud rises up around it.

Her lips shake. "I'm sorry. I didn't mean to... I didn't mean to kill him." Her face contorts, going so pale for a second, I worry she might faint.

"It's okay." I jog toward her. "We need to get out of here."

"No, we need to get these cuffs off and him tied up." She tugs away, shaking her head, mouth a tight line, drops to her knees, and presses Torum's thumb against the top of her wrist shackles.

The metal springs break free.

"Hurry, *Ay-shocks*. Bend down so we can get yours off."

CHAPTER FORTY

Open

FEOLA

Torum's sleeping. His eyelids flutter for the barest flicker of a second, and then his shoulders buck, his eyes snap open, and he roars, body twisting, thrashing, trying to pull his arms out of the shackles.

I stand over him, using my body to shade him. "I'm sorry. I really am. You've actually been fairly kind to us. And I ..." My throat tightens and a rush of shame and guilt and sorrow slices through me. I killed a man he cares about. "I'm sorry."

He whips a partial circle on the dusty ground, sweeping out with his foot to knock me over, and I hop out of his path. He launches himself up to his knees, glaring around until he sees Laugher, slumped over and covered in blood. Then he goes still, brows drawing together, lips parting, and I swear, the light in his eyes dims.

"I am. I'm so sorry," I say, and his eyes drift closed. It does nothing to help the discomfort, the knowledge that a man was alive with hopes and dreams and now he's dead. That man wasn't like Rennie. He didn't take pleasure in killing.

Ajax pulls me back and asks Torum, "Can you stand?"

Torum's eyes flash open and he snarls, a steady stream of spitting curses erupting from his mouth. His face is bruised across his temple, and dried blood mats his hair.

"Are you nauseated? Is your vision clear?"

"Fuck you," Torum grunts.

"Get up," Ajax says. "And I'll give you some water."

Torum's nostrils flare, and his mouth turns down, but he staggers awkwardly to his feet, his big shoulders arched back.

"It's uncomfortable, isn't it?"

"Fuck you."

"You want water or not?"

"Fuck you."

A smile spreads across Ajax's cheeks. "Open."

Torum lashes out with a leg, but Ajax dodges it and they play out the same routine a few more times until Torum either gets tired or bored, and I just slump against a tree, trying to sort out my feelings. I felt a lot after Rennie, but guilt wasn't really there. He was a bad man who wanted to hurt me, but Laugher

…?

Ajax pours water into Torum's open mouth while I scan the horizon. Nothing in sight for miles. We've left the grove of trees and the river behind, and the plain with its clusters of white leaves and blue flowers have given way to hard, cracked soil. I don't want to spend the night out here, so far from the river.

"Where's your ship?" Ajax's voice is as calm as ever. He's unflappable.

"Fuck you."

"Okay. So, we'll kill you now. We can live here for as long as we need to until our people come for us. Your ship can help us get them here faster, but if you won't help, we might as well kill you and look for it on our own."

"You won't kill me." Torum's gaze settles on me. "She likes me."

It's not entirely untrue. He could have been far crueler.

I squat down beside him. Ajax's hand on my shoulder keeps me from getting closer.

"I don't like you. But I'd hate to see you hurt. You were kind to us, sort of. Or you could have been less kind." I tilt my head, studying his sparkling eyes. "You were there."

The lights were dark, but he was at the performance at the club on Pilan.

Ajax makes a weird noise in his throat.

"You were following us even then. You saw what we did on Pilan to get away. I'd perform naked before a thousand men again if it guaranteed I'd never have to go near Utto again. I…" My throat closes up, memories of Utto, of Rennie, and now this new dead man we left behind in a grove of silver trees. "Do you know what my mate did to me?"

He freezes, his eyes slipping past my face, settling in the distance.

"Did anyone tell you why I ran away? Probably not. I ran because Utto used to hurt me. He's a big man. Like you. He didn't usually leave marks, at least not where anyone could see, but he knew how to hurt me. And I was stuck there, alone and scared, because I needed his serum. I was his slave."

Torum's eyes don't change at the word *slave*. If he were deeply involved in the business on Pilan, he'd know about the slaves. He'd react somehow. But his face doesn't move, which makes me think he doesn't actually work for the Upranimus family, that he's a mercenary.

"And then his cousin came to visit."

Ajax's fingers tighten on my shoulder.

"And Utto let him touch me. He didn't want to, but Rennie had power over him. Rennie found me in the bathroom the day I planned to escape. He—he wanted me because it was a way to show his power over Utto. Like I wasn't even a person. Just another slave to be used by them."

Torum looks away, his jaw tightening.

"He touched me—he told me to get myself ready for him and come into the bedroom naked so he could have sex with my body. He was bigger, and if I resisted, he'd have beaten me. So I killed him."

A hot gust of air lifts my hair, and the sun burns my back.

"I saw the way you acted when you thought I was pregnant and sick. You're not a man who likes to see women hurt. Please. Don't make me go back to a man who hates me." I swallow against the thickness in my throat. "I'm sorry about your partner … I can tell you cared for him. And I can tell he wasn't like Rennie. He wasn't cruel or malicious. I didn't …" My eyes well up and I look down at my hands. "I'm sorry."

Torum lumbers to his feet, big body swaying. "He was my bestfrient. But he knew the risks." He looks off and into the distance. "We always expect to die far from home."

For some reason, that makes the tears bubble over and I turn away, into Ajax's chest.

CHAPTER FORTY-ONE

Get your stinky shit off me

AJAX

Torum's ship is nothing like the Tribe's spacecraft. I've seen a few Vestigi ships but never this close before.

A fresh wave of boyish wonder has me reaching out to stroke a hand along its sleek, black hull. Their ships are rounder, and unlike the Argenti ships, they aren't reflective. The Vestige don't have camouflage capabilities—at least not in wide use. So their ships are dull and dark to blend in with space. It's beautiful, though, slim and flat, like a massive disk.

I widen my eyes at Torum and mimic his accent, "Open."

The corner of his lips twitch, but he stares at me like he's trying to decide if he can murder me with the power of his eyes alone.

"Excuse me," Feola's accented, musical voice trills

out. "Do you two plan to stare into each other's eyes all day? Because I'd like to know now. I could just go find a seat in the shade on the other side of the ship and wait."

Torum glances at her, and I don't care for the gleam in his eyes when his gaze lands on my mate.

My mate. The thought makes me smile. She's mine.

"Don't look at her like that," I say, and the warmth in his eyes fades. "Not unless you want me to break your nose again?"

He rotates his jaw a few times, but finally steps toward the ship and presses his thumb over a small pad on the side. A hatch opens, metal grinding against metal.

I've never been inside a Vestigi ship.

It's … cool.

A gust of cold air rushes through the open circular hatch. I gesture for Feola to go first and then Torum so I can keep an eye on him.

Icy air blasts against my face. With awkward two-handed motions of his still-shackled hands, Torum shoves his thumb into a pad inset into the wall.

The hatch slides shut.

"Where's your communication device?" I ask.

Torum does the staring thing again, and Feola sighs, wandering off down the halls, poking her head around corners. Eventually she calls out, "I found the bathroom. There's a bathing chamber."

I need a shower and she needs me, and I need to

know she's okay after killing Laugher, so I study Torum, then the shackles. The ship has two vertical support bars at the rear of the hull. I reject those. Loops hang from the ceiling, handles for a crew waiting to deploy.

I pull my *rezal* from its holster. "On the deck."

"What?"

"On the deck."

"Why?"

"I'm not leaving you out here unsupervised, and I'm going to join my mate in the bathroom."

"What are you going to do? Blindfold me? Hogtie me?"

"Unless I cut off your thumb."

Torum's black eyes narrow. "You wouldn't."

"You'd be surprised what I'd do for one minute alone with her that I didn't have to worry about someone interrupting."

Torum lowers himself to his knees slowly.

"Face down."

"This hurts."

"You'll live." I roll my still-stiff shoulders. There's no way laying on top of his hands for a minute can hurt as much as having my arms cuffed behind my back overnight.

I find rope in a closet off the main passageway and knots his ankles, crossing and double-crossing. If he struggles, they'll get tighter. Then I blindfold him with a strip of fabric from my own stained, filthy shirt.

"This fucking smells, *migane*. Get your sweaty shit off me." The curse reminds me of my childhood. My brother, Spiro used to call people that. There's no direct translation in Argenti. It means the hairs around an asshole.

"You'll get used to it."

I use one of his straps and loop it behind his arms and haul him to his feet.

"Where's your brig?"

"Fuck you."

"You've got a great vocabulary, you know that?"

Torum scowls, but says nothing.

It takes a few minutes, but I find the entrance to the brig. No lights. Whatever. He won't die, though it rankles locking a man in his own brig, even with his hands tied behind his back.

I slam the hatch and double-check the lock, check the room for hidden weapons, and go find my mate.

CHAPTER FORTY-TWO

I think we need a ... longer instrument

FEOLA

I float on the surface of the water. It's warm and smells clean, like the fresh breezes in the forests of Triannon after the rain.

Stretching my arms over the water's surface, I comb my hands across the bubbles, gathering them closer. The room is dark; not much more than a dull gleam of pinkish-purple light glows across the ceiling.

Peaceful.

More peaceful than I deserve.

That man must have washed in this tub. Not Torum. The other one. The one I killed. The one with a flashing white smile. The one who laughed even after I hit him in the head and knocked him unconscious beneath the trees by the river.

My eyes burn, and I clench them shut, tightening my hands into fists until my nails bite deep. Who have I become? Ruthless. Heartless. A killer. What would Mamma say?

My throat tightens.

I sink beneath the surface.

Underwater, I open my eyes, watch the purple lights dance overhead. Ajax's head moves into view, and I pop up.

He drops to a squat, looming over me. Whatever he sees in my face, it tightens his jaw, firms up the line along his lips.

He tosses his boots to the side. Rises briefly to tug his pants down. The hard planes of his body shift and move with each economical movement. Familiar, predictable even, in a safe and comfortable sort of way.

He steps into the pool. He doesn't reach for me, though. Instead, he leans against the ledge. "I'm sorry, Feola."

I blink. "For what?"

"I shouldn't have let that happen. I should have protected y—"

"You don't have to protect me, Ajax."

"I'm your mate. I do."

"Y—"

"That's who I am, and I'm not going to change. Don't want to."

"B—"

"No buts. It's a fact. You've proven you can take care of yourself. But you shouldn't have had to kill that man. It should have been me. That's on me. That's not your fault. I'm trained to handle this. You aren't. It was my job to protect you. It's my shame to bear that you were forced to protect me."

"Shame? What do you think you should have done?"

"Something. Anything. I failed you."

"You were tied down. You didn't fail me. I don't blame you." The water laps against the tiled edges of the pool as I slice my hand out hard, emphasizing my point. "And why should you have to kill everyone and bear the guilt. I don't blame you."

"You should. Because then you wouldn't blame yourself."

"I don't blame myself." I don't. It was him or Ajax. If I hadn't killed him he'd have shot Ajax and Torum would still have us in cuffs

He cocked his head, a knowing smile lurking at the corner of his lips.

"You did that on purpose."

He picks up soap.

"You manipulated me?" I splash water at him.

"You needed manipulating."

I glance down to my shaking hands. "That man…."

"It was him or us, Feola. He was going to take you to Utto. They'd kill me and … You made a decision that saved our lives. Would you blame me, if I had killed him?"

No. I wouldn't.

"Then why are you harder on yourself than you would be on me?"

I don't have an answer for that, but my heart feels lighter, so I swim into the circle of his open arms.

His grip is hard as he pulls me into him. I sigh as my legs wrap around his waist, bouncing against him in the water.

He cradles my head in his palm. "I'm going to make you talk to me about Rennie. You need to talk about it with me. You can't push it aside."

"Yes, Healer Willo." My words are mocking but my tone isn't. He's right.

His eyes flare with something. Lust? A small smile appears at the corner of his lips. "It's very important, Feola, that as your *professional* medical practitioner, you submit to my regular evaluations."

I bite my lip. "Does that include physical examinations?"

He nods solemnly. "Is something troubling you?"

"Something doesn't feel right. I think I need you to touch me and make sure everything is okay."

He laughs. "What seems to be the problem?"

"Well. I'm all hot. And ummm…" I push my hips against him. "Sort of achy. Throbbing."

His brows tighten and he releases a protracted sigh as I trace my hand up the silky skin of his cock, squeezing until a low grumbling purr leaves his lips. "That doesn't sound good."

"It doesn't feel good," I whisper against his lips.

"Oh, yeah it does." He bucks against my hands.

"No, it feels like I need something." I stroke my thumb over the head, slippery with serum. "I need—I don't know. I think I need…"

His grip on my hips tightens.

"Healer Willo, I think I need your help. Can I show you where I need you?"

"Mmmm. Yes. I think that would be wise."

I take his hand and drag up to my breasts. His rough callused thumb grazes my nipple.

"It hurts here?"

"Not hurts, but they feel hot. Tingly. But that's not where I really need you."

"Oh?" His eyes are purple in the light, and hooded by half lowered eyelids.

I drag his hand lower, letting his fingers tickle my skin, under the surface of the water, down, down, down.

"Here? This is where you feel uncomfortable?" His fingers slide inward.

"Uhhhuh."

He finds my clit, brushes past to press inside, teasing against the entrance.

"You do feel hot," he whispers. "And so soft." The word is the barest of caresses, drifting across my skin.

"The real problem is inside. Deeper."

He slides a finger in. "Deeper?"

"Yes?"

A smile dances across his lips. "Hmmm…. I think I need to use a… longer"—he laughs—"instrument to evaluate properly."

"Yes, please, Healer Willo." I look down at the massive penis in my hands. "This would work."

He grins. "Good idea."

I lift my hips up and shift so our bodies line up. "This should work."

His hands wrap around my ass, and pull me against him, so he fills me all the way full. I drop my forehead against his.

God, I love him.

"Well, healer?" I ask, when he's all the way inside me.

"Huh?" He opens unfocused eyes.

"Is it serious?"

A ghost of a smile passed his lips. "I think it will require frequent internal penetration. But you should be" —I pull out and push back— "fine."

"So I'll live?"

His hand snakes up my spine to grip my neck, arching me back so he can get my breast to his mouth.

There's no more talking after that.

About an hour later—with hair still damp from the bath, feeling cleaner than I have in days—I pull on a loose black shirt and pants I find in the lockers. I have to roll up the waist, sleeves, and legs, but they are clean.

Ajax is wearing them too, but on him they fit like

a second skin. He's been talking to Torum.

"Show me how to use the communication system."

"Take off these cuffs."

"No."

"Then I won't show you the comm system."

Ajax runs a frustrated hand along the back of his neck. "No problem. No comm system. No water. No food."

Torum shrugs. "*Migane*."

In the end, Torum does show us the comm, but in exchange for new shackles, and a chair in the brig.

So while Ajax enters in the codes to reach Tam, Torum settles into his new chair, watching us through the open doorway of the brig, and I chew my fingernails.

It takes a while, but when Tam's grinning face fills the flat screen, my knees wobble.

Nissa shoves him aside, smiling. "Feola. Thank the gods, you're okay. Come home. We have a place ready for you."

Tears burns at the back of my eyes.

"We've been in contact with Argentus," Nissa continues. "We've formally claimed Feola as our own, and you, Ajax, as her mate."

"How did they respond?" Ajax asks.

Tam shrugs. "Doesn't matter. They can go to war with us, or they can let us keep you legally. They won't go to war with us."

"But," Nissa says, "they can keep our courts locked up for years. Senator Upranimus isn't giving up."

"Our ship is no longer flyable." Ajax explains briefly how we crashed.

"I'll contact your brother. He's on his way here now. He'll come pick you up and bring you here. He's got a woman with him."

"A woman?"

"Yeah. Your father made a political alliance. She's the daughter of some senator, some big opponent of Upranimus. They're engaged in exchange for his support."

"I can't let Spiro do that."

Tam smirks. "You really think he minds?"

Ajax looks uncomfortable at that, so I ask, "So what happens next?"

"We start working on a case against Utto's family." Tam's voice is hard and dead even. "You have any information?"

Ajax raises a brow.

I squeeze his shoulder. "Yes. He used a drug on me called *septusine*. That's how he coerced me into marrying him in the first place."

Tam's eyes darken. "Is that what I think it is?"

"Basically. It's a serum-based, mind-altering drug that was made during the Plague of Days when all our women fell ill," Ajax explains.

I can do this. I will do this. I will face Utto again, and when I do, I will bring his family to their knees.

"And there's more."

Everyone looks surprised, even Torum sitting smugly in his seal, hands cuffed in his lap.

"They're kidnapping women. They're selling them as slaves. Rennie was one of the kings of Pilan."

"A scum-king?" Ajax mutters.

"Yes."

"What's a scum king?" Tam asks, and Ajax explains about the politics on Pilan.

Tam puffs out his cheeks. "So now we build our case."

CHAPTER FORTY-THREE

Truly, the sun shines upon us

FEOLA

The next five days are the happiest of my life. Most of my time is spent wrapped around Ajax. We have plenty of problems. The threat of a showdown with Utto's uncle looming, a grumpy prisoner, but all of it fades away.

Torum dismantles the brig. Headbutts the camera, kicks apart the bed (but not the chair), floods the toilet, and generally makes so much noise that we let him out of his brig and tie him down to a cot in the passageway where he glares and shouts insults in Vestigi, demands food or water or a toilet, and watches us the rest. It doesn't matter.

We are too happy to mind.

It's the first time since childhood that I've been able to open up, without limitations, to another person. There's no doubt with Ajax. No hesitation. He gives, and if I offer, he takes with unabashed joy.

There was no sense that if I withdraw or resist, he'll use his superior strength against me. No sense that if I were to offend him by disagreeing, he'd exact vengeance. If anything, I know it's virtually impossible for me to displease him.

He treats me like I'm something rare, and profound and beautiful. The memories of Utto's hands and Rennie's blood slowly recede. We talk about it constantly, about the man we left behind in the copse of lavender trees, the ones he shot the day before, and Rennie.

Ajax is determined. Gentle, but implacable. He makes me repeat over and over that I defended myself, defended him, saved their lives, that I made the only possible choice in an impossible situation.

After days of periwinkle sky and endless sun, the world erupts in stormless thunder, and a great white ship descends from above to settle on the powdery dust beside Torum's ship.

"Bring me. I'm fucking bored!" Tor shouts and Ajax and I shrug and roll the cot he's tied on out to stand beside the newly arrived spaceship.

The hatch opens as the dust settles and a man pauses, looking so much like Ajax that I gasp.

His hair is darker, not the pale blond I've come to love, but more a burnished gold. But he moves with the same cool grace and carries his head with the same proud ease. Spiro. Ajax's older brother.

A woman steps out behind him, as though she's

not entirely sure where to stand. Tall, with warm blond hair and rich honey-colored skin.

Ajax wraps his arm around me and pulls me forward to meet them.

"Ajax. *Insuffairtus shanumay,*" Spiro says, pulling him into a gruff hug. It's a greeting I know but have never heard said aloud. It translates roughly to *Truly, the sun shines upon us,* an old Argenti expression of joy at meeting.

"Spiro." Ajax returns the greeting as they smack each other's backs. "This is my mate, Feola."

I take Spiro's outstretched arm and grasp his forearm as I learned on Romeo-Two.

A vague tremor dance across the back of my neck at the proximity to another man, but I force it away, turning to smile at the woman beside him. Spiro smiles warmly, his eyes crinkling in the corners just like Ajax.

"This is Klymeni, my future-mate," he gestures proudly at the woman, who inclines her head, a reserved smile flickering across her lips. "Klymeni, this is Feola, mate of my brother."

I haven't met any Argenti women, but Klymeni seems more formal than anyone I've met, almost prissy. Her gaze drifts over Torum, hulking on his cot and he shouts a string of wild insults. Not at her specifically but at all of Argentus in general.

Spiro laughs. "What the hell are we going to do with him?"

It's something we've discussed at length.

"We have to bring him to Triannon for now."

Spiro scowls. Klymeni doesn't speak.

Torum grunts. "Stupid fucking *migane.*"

Ajax sends him a filthy glare. I can't stop the bubble of nervous laughter in the back of my throat.

"I can't see any way around it. I don't want to kill him. And we can't leave him here. He'll just follow us."

"I would not follow you. I want to get as far away from the pair of you as I can. Trust me."

Ajax smiles at that. "We'll take him with us. It's the only option. We'll figure out safe passage for him some other way."

Spiro's brow furrows, and after a moment, his teeth flash in a white grin that makes me love him just a little. He looks so much like Ajax. "I doubt they'll let him go. We'll have to turn him in on Triannon. Argentus will intervene. We're already asking enough trying to get you two asylum."

Torum is not a fan of this plan.

And so it goes.

An hour later, I'm buckled in a ship, wedged between Ajax and Klymeni as the ship gears up for takeoff, thrilled beyond reason to leave Araa-Ara behind.

"It will take about four days to get to Triannon," Spiro says, in a voice so similar to Ajax's that I shiver.

CHAPTER FORTY-FOUR

A blurble

AJAX

For two days, everything goes smoothly. Mostly. Spiro's mate sulks in one corner while Torum hulks and shouts in another, but that does nothing to quash my happiness.

Spiro seems to be at a total loss for how to handle his future-mate and essentially ignores the woman, leaving them locked in inimical détente.

Spiro claims to be giving her the space and time she needs to grow comfortable with their future Bonding, but I'm not sure about that tactic.

Klymeni, for her part, rarely speaks and occasionally goes so far as to say, "I do not condone this Bonding."

Feola has tried speaking to her repeatedly but hasn't any luck in softening her feelings for Spiro.

Klymeni stares into her food morosely and lists

about.

And Torum never lets up. Every waking minute, he filled the air with shouts for freedom.

Feola and I spend most of our time in the chambers, with me balls deep inside of her, and I'm perfectly fine with that. Her orgasms are stronger with something in her ass and I can't wait to get to a place that has anal plugs. Just imagining it, I tease her ass and manage to work a second finger in, triggering an orgasm so strong her pussy clamps down and my orgasm follows almost instantly, leaving us both sweaty and drained.

When I catch my breath, I press a kiss between her shoulder blades. "I should go check on Spiro. We left him alone for hours."

She nods sleepily as I slide from the bed, tugging on my pants, and pad toward the flight deck.

Spiro glances up from the pilot's seat, a mug of *eeffoc* in his hands. "We're good here. Go back to your mate."

I hesitate. It's been a long time since I saw Spiro.

He slants me a look. "We can catch up later. I get it. You two seem like a good match."

"Yeah." I'm unsure what to say. It means something to me, having his brother's approval.

So I squeeze his shoulder and leave to give the rest of the ship a quick patrol.

Klymeni's in the galley, washing dishes. When I poke my head in the room, she ignores me. I offer what I hope is a non-threatening smile and duck back out.

Torum, tied up to the wall, doesn't waste the chance to bargain for his freedom, swearing not to come after us, rattling his bed, shouting threats, growling false promises.

We removed his shackles a few days ago, preferring to stick to the ropes, since there was lingering concern, he'd figure out how to break his thumb off and use it to open them.

It hasn't stopped him from trying to break out of the ropes, but his struggles have only tightened them so dangerously that his hands turned purple, and we had to retie them.

He's thankfully stopped twisting them lately and instead resorted to verbal assaults and general noise pollution.

I ignore him and head back to Feola.

She's asleep, a small smile on her perfect pouty lips. I slide onto the bed beside her, wrapping my body around her soft, naked skin.

And wake sometime later.

There's no siren. But something is off. I strain my ears but hear nothing. I scent the air.

Something's wrong.

I creep off the bed and slide the hatch open a crack.

Still nothing.

Feola sits up in bed.

A muffled grumble. A man's voice.

Then another. I'd recognize Spiro's voice anywhere. Especially the dark and steady tone it took on when he's deadly serious.

But whatever he's saying, it's muffled.

As is Torum's answer.

Feola's gaze locks on mine, her eyes full of questions.

She rises, setting her feet silently on the floor, pulling on my shirt.

I slide my blade from a sheath and lift a smaller one to my left hand.

She slides one of the smaller blades out as well, tucking it into her palm exactly as I taught her.

When I open our hatch to exit, not a single noise comes from the passageway, save the standard whir of the ship's operating systems.

I turn to check on Feola. She frowns.

Something is seriously wrong. I gesture for her to stop and wait.

Her frown deepens, and she mouths, "No."

Stubborn.

We walk on padded feet down the passageway.

Feola barely breathes behind me.

The passageway opens to the main flight deck, with the pilot's seat and passenger strap-ins. I pause a few steps from the end of it, straining my ears, but picking up on nothing more than three people in the main body of the cockpit. And something burbling. Two on the right, and one near the pilot's seat, where Torum shouldn't be. Which means either Torum is near Klymeni, or he's somehow taken Spiro's seat.

I gesture more emphatically. This time she only nods tightly back.

I shift the knife to my right hand, my better throwing arm, and flexed my left-handed grip on the blade, so the butt rests in the base of my palm. I slow my breathing.

Several feet back, Feola sinks to her haunches against the wall, watching me. Pale cheeks and blazing yellow-green eyes.

I creep to the edge of the passageway again and glance around the corner.

Just a flash.

It's enough.

Shit. Blood. A lot of it. What happened to Spiro? That burble means blood in the lungs.

Torum's holding Klymeni with a knife at her throat. "Ajax," he bellows. "I see you, you *migane*. I don't need any trouble. But I do need the code to your brother's escape pod. Tell me the digits, and I'll leave you all in peace."

"Ask him yourself."

"He's unavailable."

I slam my shoulders back against the wall. "What did you do to him?"

"He's bleeding. I'm no healer. But it looks bad. A knife to the gut. And I sliced his neck. If I so much as catch a glimpse of your blond head again, I'll kill the woman."

There's an answering gurgle.

Spiro. My big brother.

"The codes, healer. I need the codes."

"I don't know them. Let me go to him. Let me stop the bleeding. Please." His voice echoes down the passageway. Vaguely, my brain registers Feola's steady palm sliding across my shoulders.

"Think. Give me the codes, and we'll go."

"I don't know the fucking codes. Just turn the damned ship around. Take us wherever you want to go, but let me help him."

I lean around the edge of the corner, trying to see Spiro, to find out bad it is. In that split second, a blade flies toward me. I manage to duck, barely. It lodges in the wall where my face was, with the sharp twang of vibrating metals.

"I've got every last one of your brother's knives. You do the math. We can do this all day. And in the meantime, Spiro will die. Neither of us wants that. Codes." Torum's voice is empty. Void of compassion, urgency, or sympathy.

Ajax's heart plummeted. The metallic scent of blood fills the air.

"Codes. Take a guess if you don't know. We can keep on trying."

What would Spiro have used? I shout out my own birthday, Spiro's birthday. Our father's. Or maybe some version of his name.

In the end, out of sheer desperation, I shout out the date of our mother's death. The escape pod hisses open.

"See to your brother, healer. Be fast."

I don't even hear Torum enter the escape pod or its departure from the ship. I've already crossed the deck to find Spiro, face down in a pool of blood.

Trying to staunch the flow, I roll Spiro to his back.

Fuck. Even with every machine in the Argenti fleet, it still might not be enough but this ship doesn't have anything but a box of medical supplies that thumps to the deck beside me.

Feola. "Thanks."

I run a tube into his lungs and set him up with a balloon Feola bumps for me. I staunch the wounds to stop the flow, but it's not enough.

Blood. He needs blood.

Rummaging through the crate, I fashion a line to transfuse blood.

Time slows to a crawl.

I sway on my knees, as blood flows down the slender tube.

My vision blurs.

"Ay-shocks?" Soft at first. Then more insistent, *"Ay-shocks!"*

I disconnect the line, motions slow and blurry.

Feola's over me, eyes wide and sad, blood staining her cheeks and matting her hair. "You need to change the ship's trajectory, *Ay-shocks*. We need to go to the nearest Argenti base."

I fall forward, rest my head on the deck beside Spiro. My brother's skin is pale. His breathing shallow. His heartbeat so faint.

I lift sluggish eyes back toward her. "We can't—"

"We *can*. We have to." Her eyes are bright, and her voice doesn't waver. "Do it. I can face Utto. We'll face him together. But we can't let your brother die."

I swallow the shame and nausea roiling in my throat and stagger to my feet. The ship spins around me, and if it weren't for the surprising strength of Feola's shoulder bearing up beneath my arm, I'd fall. "I'll drop you somewhere safe first. You can't go back. What if they make you return to Utto?"

"I survived him once, Ajax. I'll do it again. We are not letting Spiro die."

My throat convulses. I look down at Spiro. Skin white as death. Spiro has a mate now. He can't die. I'll find a way to keep Feola from Utto, but first, we need to get Spiro to safety. "You're sure?"

"Yes."

CHAPTER FORTY-FIVE

Blast into space with morbid glee

FEOLA

I clutch my hands in my lap. It's the only way to stop them from shaking. Spiro is in Torum's cot. Ajax managed to lift him.

I'm in the cockpit, staring out at the darkness, absorbing the quiet in the aftermath of the frenzy. I'm still wired, hands shaking.

Klymeni's gone. Taken by Torum. Maybe. Either that or she helped him escape? Helped him attack Spiro? She'd seemed suspicious, scared, overwhelmed, but not heartless enough to betray a good man.

But who am I to judge? I'd have done worse to escape an unwanted pairing.

And I can't regret what we're about to do. Not for a second. Ajax gave up everything for me. His position as a healer, his reputation and good standing among the Argenti. I can do this.

It means facing Utto, facing probable arrest, but I'll fight.

The communication system dings. A pinging chirp.

I look around. If Ajax managed to somehow fall asleep, after giving away way too much blood. I won't wake him for anything. With a tentative hand, I press the button. A bluish holo of a man's head appears over the button. He looks surprised to see me.

"Hello?"

"This is Communications Captain Simoline from base Foxtrot-Thirteen responding to an emergency request for docking."

Here we go. "My name is Feola from Triannon."

Simoline's face changes, slides along my hair and eyes. He knows my name.

I brazen on. "We have a wounded Argenti named Spiro Willo with us. He needs emergency medical treatment. Please let me know where we should dock."

He nods. "Please stand by."

I have no choice. Torum took the escape pod. I'll have to face the Argenti openly. Honestly. And the only thing that matters now was that Ajax can't be arrested along with me. I write down his instructions and follow them to the letter.

My next call is to Triannon.

When Nissa and Tam finally come on the holo,

they don't look happy.

Tam argues. Nissa watches it all with shrewd eyes, and mutters about reporters, Tam grumbles about assholes, and Reyback, the shifty man who always seems to be in the background, grunts something about Pilan. But hopefully, they will help.

When it's done, I creep down the passageway, hoping not to disturb Ajax, but mostly to avoid his notice. We've never addressed the vials. I gather them now—every last one and creep back down the passageway to the bathroom with the toilet waste ejector. I drop the vials in one by one, hit the evacuation button and watch them blast out into space with morbid glee. I'll never take Utto's serum again—never.

Beyond that… I don't have much of a plan but to lie through my teeth and make it clear that whatever we did, I was the evil mastermind who duped Ajax and he is innocent.

I'll do whatever I have to do to protect him. Ajax will not be punished for helping me.

It seems like no time at all before the hulking concrete bulk of the base spreads before us, wide and studded with tiny rectangular windows of light. My heart rises in my throat, and my stomach does jumping jacks but I'm determined.

Ajax, pale and irritable, sits beside me, moving the controls with ease. He keeps sputtering like he wants to speak but can't find the right words.

I know the feeling.

Our future is... undefined and turbulent. The possibilities are too dim to consider. Imprisonment. A return to Utto. Death? Is that even an option? It's hard to imagine a race on the brink of distinction would actually sentence a woman to death, but who knows. I killed the son of a senator.

I watch Ajax's hands on the controls. Memorizing them. Just in case. They're beautiful things. Long and elegant, with a fine dusting of pale hairs. I feel a familiar stirring in my lower belly. We've deliberately abstained, hoping to force the hands of the officials on the base. They'll have to let us see each other once we become too ill.

The alternatives are inhumane. And precedents are well established for criminals with mates. Spiro did the research.

"Whatever happens, Feola, just tell them the truth. There's nothing to hide. You didn't break any of our laws. You did nothing wrong. Tell them everything you know about what Rennie and Utto were doing."

"What if they work for Utto's uncle?"

Ajax's eyebrows rise, but I can tell thought isn't a new one to him. He isn't that naïve.

I've learned the hard way not everyone can be trusted. He's just had a crash course.

"This would be a strange place for him to have spies," he says. "This base is far away from his usual operations. But I'm sure he knows by now. They'll have started reporting up the chains of command by now. Calling in favors, maybe making bribes"

"Yeah."

Tam and Nissa will help. Spiro will live.

The desire to run the second they unload Spiro and Ajax is real. I kind of know how to fly this thing. I could go back to Ara-Araa or Pilan. It's the fear talking. I know it is. "Do you know how they'll proceed?"

Ajax tugs on his ear. "I think they'll separate us, almost immediately, for questioning. Look for any differences in our stories. They'll ask for specifics. We certainly made an impact on Pilan, so we'll have the same, verifiable story there. And they'll contact Tam for corroboration. They'll look into the details of Rennie's death. And they'll look at the details I found in the healing bay on Romeo-Two. They'll see the fracture and the contraceptives. They'll see the truth there. You did nothing wrong."

I'm not sure I agree.

Ajax is underestimating Utto. And his uncle. Ajax is tough, capable, strong—he's proven it—but he's never seen the ugliness of life. Not like I have. No one has ever hurt him on purpose, just for fun, for no other reason than that they could. That changes a person.

CHAPTER FORTY-SIX

An unhealthy look in his eyes

FEOLA

Foxtrot-Thirteen looks enough like Romeo-Two to bring back memories of the first and only time I docked there as Utto's new bride, dewy and bright, gazing with vapid wonder at the exotic base, hulking in clear black space, the windows glittering like neon squares, the glowing dome in the distance.

I should have seen it even then, Utto's darkness. There were clues. He looked at me with a simmering possession. Ajax looks at me with desire and hunger, but there is a gentleness there too. A sense of restraint.

Hindsight is so much clearer, though. And the clock doesn't go backward.

The hatch doors open.

I unclip my seat buckles and surge to my feet.

Healers rush in wearing medical garb, holding IV packs and pushing a gurney.

Ajax rushes to help them.

Spiro's skin has turned almost gray, his lips flaking and dry.

Ajax joins me at the hatch as they roll Spiro out. He takes my hand. His is shaking.

There are Guarda waiting for me. They wait a few yards out, giving us space, I guess. Or waiting.

I step into him, wrap my arms around him. The warm weight of his arm settles along my shoulders, like it belongs there. His perfect Ajax smell, the calm he always wears wrapping me up tight. My heart slows at the contact. This is what a Bond should be. What it should always be.

I look up at him. "I love you, Ajax. Whatever happens. I love you."

His warm, turquoise eyes crinkle at the corners, and a half smile stretches one side of his mouth. "Crappy timing," he whispers and drops a kiss to my temple. "I love you."

I disagree. It's perfect timing. We have no idea what's about to happen.

"You ready?" he asks.

I nod and we turn to the dozen stern-faced Guarda, *rezals* held firmly across their chests, staring back at us. An older man, with the tired, world-weary eyes of an official, steps forward, his face a tangle of hard lines.

"Ajax Willo and Feola Upranimus?"

I shake my head. So does Ajax. "Ajax Willo of Argentus and Feola Willo of Triannon. We've Bonded." Ajax's voice is firm.

I get a little thrill hearing his formal name attached to mine.

His arm stays around me, but it drifts down from my shoulders to rest in the small of my back.

A familiar blue head shines under the harsh overhead lights of the docking chamber. Utto. I move closer to Ajax. I'd hoped there'd be more time. But so be it.

He bursts out of the crowd, elbowing his way past people. "Feola," he shouts. "Thank the gods! You're alive. I couldn't feel you anymore. I thought you were dead. What does he mean, 'Willo'?"

It makes my stomach clench, seeing his snub nose and dark eyes; the bright, shiny white teeth; and his hard, brutal jaw. He looks genuinely concerned.

Ajax slips his arm from around me and steps in front of me, but I keep my gaze leveled on Utto. His hands fist at his sides. There it is, a tell I recognize so well. The slight pull of his upper lip. Rage, barely controlled, simmering beneath the surface.

"Hands up, Willo," the older Argenti official says.

"Get him back. He nearly killed my mate. We aren't moving until Upranimus is gone."

The official pauses, face conflicted.

I slide my fingers into Ajax. "Ajax is my mate now. We *Bonded* under a bright blue dome on a planet covered in purple flowers beside a waterfall for *three days*." I purr out the three days because the shortness of our Bonding was always a sore subject for Utto. I look up at Ajax and bat my eyelashes. "It was beautiful. I've never known such ecstasy."

Utto's nostrils flare. The muscles in his neck bulge. "Get the fuck off her, Willo." He storms forward, shoulders tight.

Ajax steps between me and that blotchy red face and shimmering blue hair.

The official does too. He jerks his chin at one of the Guarda, who steps in Utto's path. Utto is escorted away, thrashing and cursing.

Ajax raises his brows at me, mouth turning down in a wry expression of approval. "Not bad."

"You did the same thing at Romeo-Two," I whisper back.

"Arms up." The official's voice echoes, and we no longer have a choice.

Ajax lifts his hands up in surrender, and I do the same.

We are immediately removed and separated. A knot of panic rises in my throat as a man takes me by a firm hand on my upper arm and guides me down a hall.

I will not cry.

A man with a kind smile and skin and hair and eyes the same warm brown introduces himself as Inspector Miles. He takes me to a small, dark room with a big, uncomfortable chair. "Are you thirsty?"

"No."

He brings me water anyway.

It happens pretty much exactly as Ajax said. They ask me questions. Over and over again. And I answer until my mouth runs dry and I drink the water.

They draw blood. Ostensibly to confirm the existence of my Bond with Ajax.

They make me talk until I can't talk anymore. Until my stomach knots and sweat drips down my cheeks. When I couldn't answer questions anymore because my stomach convulses, vision darkening, hands shaking, and the heat that floods between my thighs makes them all too uncomfortable to be in the same room with me, they leave me alone.

Finally, they bring Ajax back. He comes in furious, veins bulging on his forehead, shouting about rights and illnesses and maltreatment. He's angrier than I've ever seen him, shoulders bucking against the shackles they put him in.

The Guarda shove him in, and he stumbles, still shouting.

This is not cool, calm Ajax. This is a madman with an unhealthy look in his eyes.

Until he looks at me.

Then the anger slips away.

Still breathing sharply through pinched nostrils, he freezes, hands locked together in front of him. I pick my head up off the cold metal surface of the table and push to my feet, staggering over to him like a woman possessed, dropping to my knees, almost inhuman. Jerky and sharp and fast, I pull his cock from his flight suit.

Every muscle relaxes when the first drops of his

serum hit the back of my throat. I'm making noises. Weird moaning zombie noises as I gobble him down like a woman possessed. The shakes and the fever and the nausea recede. Eyes wide, I stare up at him, his beautiful turquoise eyes staring down at me, cleared of the manic frenzy. "I thought you were dying," he says, voice gritty and dark. "I need to be inside you." He says it like he might die if it doesn't happen fast.

"Me too."

I back up to the table, pulling my dress up around my hips so he can step between my thighs.

Since his hands are stuck behind his back again, I have to guide him inside.

We come together, fast and sharp, the serum bursting hot and wet, pumping deep inside me, our moans echoing off the room's walls.

How many Guarda are listening outside the room? Or even watching? A flush breaks across my skin. I scan the room's four corners but don't see a camera. Which doesn't necessarily mean one isn't there.

Ajax's head drops back. "Someday, we're going to spend a month in bed. We won't move. No one will bother us. We won't have any handcuffs. No one will be able to hear us." His voice rises to a bellow. "Or fucking see us."

I can't help but laugh. His cock flexes inside me as he shouts.

"I'm going to pull out because I'm pretty sure they won't give us much more time."

I pout. "Okay."

"Cover up, okay?"

I hate when the warm thickness of his body leaves mine.

A smile tugs at the corner of his mouth. "Will you do me a favor and put my cock away?"

CHAPTER FORTY-SEVEN

Enough to hold majority

AJAX

A week passes.

A week on a hard cot in an interrogation room.

A week of soggy food and stale water.

A week of visits with Feola scheduled like clockwork for every three hours. At least they stop cuffing me for those.

I'm not allowed to see anyone. No one will tell me how Spiro is, and I can't get a straight answer as to whether or not anyone has tried to find Klymeni. Her father has to be terrified that his daughter is stuck in the hands of a Vestige bounty hunter. With Spiro unconscious, I feel responsible for her.

It's illegal to deny me access to a solicitor, but they haven't technically charged me with anything yet. Nor Feola.

They claim to be holding us. For our own *protection.*

The Bond is the only blessing in a load of crap. Because of it, I can feel Feola, sweet and light on the other side. I never feel fear or hurt from her end. At any second of the day, I know she's okay. It's the only thing that makes this tolerable.

Finally, on the eighth day, a Guarda opens the door. I slit open an eyelid.

Tam saunters in, looking smug in a tunic the color of blood, with great big silly epaulets. He also has on tights, or something that looks a hell of a lot like tights, and great big shiny boots.

"What the fuck are you wearing?"

Tam cocks a shoulder with a big easy grin, his hands spreading wide. "It's the royal dress. I'm here on official business."

"You look stupid."

The Guarda shut the door.

Tam's grin spreads. "Nissa likes it. I don't give a fuck what I wear."

"She here too?" I sit up on his cot.

"Yes." Tam leans against the wall, crossing his booted feet at the ankles.

"Good news?"

Tam clucks his tongue a few times. "Yes and no."

I wait.

"Spiro will be fine. He's being kept sedated and probably won't wake up for a while, but he'll recover. No word on the woman yet, but they are looking into it."

I drop my head back for a second, letting my eyes drift shut. A big piece of me relaxes. I'd never have forgiven myself if Spiro had died because of me. I can only imagine how panicked he'll be when he wakes up to find that a woman who'd been in his care has been kidnapped.

Tam gives me a minute before he starts talking again. "Utto's no problem. He's a sure thing to go down. He keeps losing control. The senator basically dropped him. Utto's got no case. The evidence is clear, corroborated by you and the healer from R-2. But the charges against Feola, and against you for abetting her, are more serious."

I lean forward. "Okay."

"The senator's throwing a lot of money at this. His reelection is up in a year and a half, and he doesn't want this besmirching his name."

"That makes sense. So he's trying to get her declared a murderer and get us both shipped off and out of sight."

"Basically. But the people are on your side. I mean, you look at a picture of Feola and a picture of Rennie, and it's just almost impossible to believe she could actually kill him." Tam pushes off the wall and walks across the room, his boots clipping on the floors. "Nissa's got Childers, the reporter for the big news network, plastering Feola's photo up day and night, with commentary about how she weighs a third of what he does, and how she's head and shoulders smaller, untrained. People on Argentus are furious, and they hate the senator by default. Nissa goes on the holo-vids every day, crying about how the people of Triannon miss Feola and want her returned, threatening to sever ties with Argentus if they don't free you immediately." He grins. "She's so good on camera, man. It's uncanny."

He drops to a seat at the foot of the cot. "They think you're a big golden hero. Rescuing the maiden and all that."

"That all sounds like good news."

"It is, and it isn't. Because public opinion only counts for so much. But the reporter has basically made sure that there's no way in hell you stand an unbiased trial."

"So what's the bad news?"

"The DNA on the knife, the angle of attack, the fibers on his clothes. There's no chance Feola didn't do it."

"She did. It was self-defense."

He takes a deep breath and stretches back to rest his head against the concrete wall behind him. "She stabbed him in the back."

"So?"

"The senator's lawyers will fight light hell to make yours prove innocence on that one. And that's harder."

I tug on my jaw. I haven't shaved since we got here and my growing beard itches. Argenti culture is deeply rooted in the Tribe's military procedures. Stabbing someone in the back is considered pretty low and dishonorable. Convincing the court that she had no choice would be a matter of personal opinion, and subverting subconscious values. But the weaker person is almost always given the benefit of the doubt.

"But she's a woman."

Tam tugs on his ear. "Which helps. The problem is, though, that no woman has been tried in a court for so long, no one really knows how to handle it. The lawyers say the judges are looking at old trials ... but this is new territory."

"She's so little. All they have to do is look at her. She wouldn't have had a chance if she attacked him face to face. He's trained. Three times her weight."

"That's what your solicitors will argue. But the senator is throwing the full force of his money and power against it, and honestly, man, the solicitors are saying he's been greasing wheels left and right. I'm not sure I trust the High Convene."

"You think he'd bribe the High Adjudicators? That's a criminal offense."

"Only if he loses. And he doesn't need them all. Just enough to hold the majority. He walks free, and you and Feola are found guilty."

CHAPTER FORTY-EIGHT

The scum who?

FEOLA

The door to my cell opens only an hour after Ajax left me, so the second the hinge creaks, I know it isn't him. But no one ever comes, except to bring food or take it away, and dinner is still a long way off.

I jump to my feet.

The red fabric of a gown rounds the door a split second before Nissa's face appears around the doorway. She's holding a small wrapped package.

I pause, unsure how to greet the Queen Designate of my planet. We knew each other long ago, and once, I wouldn't have hesitated to hug her. But now, I'm prisoner and she's a queen.

Nissa doesn't hesitate, though. She crosses the room on quick feet and pulls me close, in a tight, warm hug that smells like home. Like warm vines and plant life. I find my breath catching.

A tear escapes, and I slap it away fast before Nissa can see it. I've never wanted to go home so badly. Back to where the ferns are red and the sea is green, and the terra is warm and wet and filled with life, back to where I belong. I want Ajax by my side, and I don't ever want to leave again.

"Do you need anything?" Nissa asks, her hair trailing down to her waist, a crimson fall.

A million things. "No, not really. They're treating me well, considering..."

Nissa studies the room with wide green eyes. The bed, the chair in the corner, the dining table, the alcove with a toilet, shower, and sink. She frowns but doesn't argue.

We sit side by side on the cot, and Nissa fills me in on all I've missed.

Chewing on my thumbnail, I think it all out. "There's only one thing to do."

"What's that?"

"We need the trial to be made public. We need your reporter in that room so every Argenti in the galaxy can decide for themselves. That way if they find me guilty of murder, the people know the evidence."

Nissa tilts her head.

"What if you said since it's an interplanetary issue involving a citizen from Triannon and her mate, that it needs to be treated as an international incident? There's no precedent for this with a Trianni."

"Especially in light of all the corruption, I could get my father to petition the Premier of Argentus directly." She stands and paces, the dress moving around her feet like mist. "I like it. We demand a fair trial for our citizen on foreign territory, and the only way to guarantee that is to have it broadcast live so all the people of our two great nations can bear witness."

"There's one more thing."

Nissa spins around, brows raised.

"What about *septusine?*"

"No one has been able to find any connection so far to Utto or Rennie or the senator. But we haven't stopped looking. Reyback went to Pilan looking for evidence."

"Tell him to talk to Shepherd. Rennie was the third scum-king. I just know it."

"The scum who?"

It's my turn to fill Nissa in. So finally, in the company of one of very few people in the world I trust other than Ajax, I give voice to the thousand suspicions lurking in my mind.

It was too early for hope. But maybe soon.

Just before she leaves, Nissa sets the package down on the bed. "Appearance matters in these types of situations."

CHAPTER FORTY-NINE

A murderess

AJAX

"Are you ready?"

I look up at our solicitor, Jamione, the man who will represent Feola and me before the High Convene today.

Nissa and Tam were able to force the base to grant us a solicitor. We've been working together for so long now that I can read the stress in the lines around the man's mouth, the worry in his eyes.

He isn't the only solicitor working on our case, but he is the lead. There's a whole team of them with dedicated duties, seeking evidence of corruption and fraud in the Argenti government, of connections to mafias on Pilan and several other off-shoot, ungoverned crime beds, but so far, they've found minimal proof. Nothing of substance. A bulk of our defense rests on Feola being short and small, our ability to convince the court she's telling the truth and Nissa and Tam's pleas on behalf of Triannon.

Feola and I have become beacons of hope to the Argenti people. An ideal. A Bonded pair is a sacred thing, and there are far too few of us in the Argenti world. Civilian hearts bleed for us.

The reporter, Childers, has done everything he can to support that image, painted us as a pair of lovers on the run from the evil and corrupted senator, but none of that will hold sway with the High Convene.

Feola stiffens beside me on the sofa in the quarters we've been assigned while on base. We've been treated far better since Tam and Nissa arrived waving Triannon bureaucracy in everyone's face.

"Could we have a moment?" I ask.

Jamione nods and backs slowly from the room.

Feola is wearing a red dress, the traditional garb of women of Trianon. Nissa brought it to remind everyone watching that Feola is, first and foremost, a daughter of Triannon and therefore not subject to the laws of Argentus. But beyond that, she looks like a wet dream, like a queen from a fairytale. Her pink-orange hair piled up in an ornate bun, the dress revealing the sides of her breasts, the long column of her throat, her bare arms. She looks tiny in it.

She presses her nose into my neck. I pull her in to straddle my lap, just to feel her close. We already satisfied the demands of the Bond. This is just for comfort.

This is it. At the end of the day, the fifty elders,

the High Adjudicators will gather together in the room that serves as High Convene on Foxtrot-Thirteen. Fifty strangers will hear our case and decide our fates.

Feola and I will either exit the massive rulings chamber, free to take up our lives anywhere in the universe, or I will be sentenced to Insuractius for aiding and abetting a murder, and she will be held for who knows what. Their Bond would be broken while she waits sentencing for her crimes.

She shivers and I press a kiss against her temple.

Combat would feel better. This trial, though, and trusting solicitors to fight for us, sucks. It's unnatural. I'd rather face Utto one on one. Man against man.

There's nothing to say. We've already said it all. So I wrap her up tight and try to memorize the feel of her, the smell of her, the sounds. My eyes drifted shut. I squeeze tighter, and she squeaks. A tiny musical squeak.

And squeezes me back.

Ten minutes later, the solicitor knocks again and leads us into the darkened Rulings Chamber of the High Convene. I feel naked. No weapons. Not for anyone but the guards.

Our steps echo off the polished concrete floors like a funeral dirge. Feola's hand clings to mine. Utto and the senator are already there, dressed in the formal wear of Argentus, simple, somber black suits.

The Tribe has already dismissed Utto from service, so he's dressed like a civilian. I'm in my military finery, stark gray jacket with polished silver buttons. Spiro retrieved it for me with the help of the chiefs on S-6. A subtle showing of support.

Reporters line the back wall of the chamber, recording the proceedings for all of Argentus.

Feola lifts her chin and stares at Utto. His face reddens, mottling, muscles twitching. She holds his gaze like a queen staring down the length of her nose. I've never been so proud of her. I stare too, letting all the disgust in my heart burn in my eyes.

It may be a small victory, but from the resolve and hope pouring across our Bond, it feels like a major one. If nothing else, it's a personal victory of Feola. She's stronger than ever and letting him see that.

We wait in silence, on hard, black chairs, only to lurch to our feet when the adjudicators file in with somber dignity. The entire High Convene of old men who will decide their fate.

Shadowed beneath dark hoods, their weathered, wrinkled faces peer curiously, a rainbow of shades, sporting a wide array of facial hair. One woman stands out from the pack, face softer, eyes warmer. She looks to be about the age my mother would be now, were she alive. One of the rare women to survive the Plague of Days.

Who is honest?

Who is not?

That's really what it comes down to now.

Who will listen and side with Senator Upranimus? Will they do so for cred or favors? Who will side with Feola and me? For decency and honesty?

I try to glean evidence of corruption or dignity

from their faces and came up blank. This one has laugh lines and that one scowl lines, but what does any of that mean? It speaks to temperament rather than morality.

Tam and Nissa file in, and Spiro, recovered from his wounds. Spiro holds his hand up in a tight fist, a gesture of solidarity. Our father stands behind him, and for just a minute, I hold my breath.

I haven't seen him in nearly a year. He's a touch grayer, and the wrinkles slightly more pronounced around his mouth. There's nothing but love and support in his face. I bow my head in respect, all too aware of the embarrassing tightening in my throat.

Finally, the admirals and chiefs walk in, and last, the High Adjudicator of Argentus. Wizened and hunched, with white hair pulled back in a bun, dark, angular eyes and a cane made of polished *yibani* wood. The silken fabric of his robes shines under the light as he bows his head. Everyone takes their seats.

The High Adjudicator is over a hundred years of age. He's presided over the High Convene for longer than I've been alive. His weathered gaze wanders the chamber, lingering on Utto and the senator beside him, traveling over our team of solicitors, to me and Feola.

I don't flinch under the weight of that steady perusal. I don't look away. I hold the old man's gaze. Feola does the same, her hand tightening on mine.

"These proceedings are highly unusual," the High Adjudicator says. "This is the first time in nearly three centuries that media has been permitted within these chambers. Our proceedings are usually conducted in private. Today, we welcome our entire civilization, from vast places, far reaching and remote, to help us see justice served. To my fellow adjudicators, I offer the same simple comment as always. Today we seek the truth. And we seek to honor it. Nothing more."

Silence reigns. A hundred bodies in a single room barely dare to breathe or shift in their seats. Someone coughs. One of the solicitors drops his stylus.

Utto's solicitor speaks first. Followed by Feola's. Then the senator's. Finally, mine. Round and round it goes.

Witnesses are called. The Guarda were present at their initial showdown at the docking bay before we fled R-2 testify that we broke the law. Samila, a friend of Feola's from her time with Utto, testifies to Feola's strange behavior. She mentions Feola's fear of her mate, unexplained absences, stray bruises she didn't manage to hide, marks she never had a good explanation for. Healer Rillard, who had helped me back on R-2, testifies on classic behavior of the abused.

Tam and Nissa speak in our favor, speaking of our character, and our welcome on Triannon, the support of the people there.

Expert witnesses are called to support Utto's claim that Feola is a chronic liar.

A team of doctors speak about the dangers of *septusine*, and its potential uses in the slave trade, but there is no proof. Evidence of the senator's or Rennie's involvement is widely discounted as unsubstantiated.

The adjudicators listen without affect.

When Feola takes the stand, it takes everything I have to stay in my seat and not barge up to the stand to hold her hand.

"It started almost immediately," she says in her softly accented voice. She doesn't cower or mumble. She speaks clearly, with her head held high. Beautiful beyond belief. "Maybe a week after the end of our Bonding, he grew... critical. He didn't like my hair or the way I dressed. I thought that was normal, for Argentus. I didn't know. Bonds on Triannon are more formal. Less emotional. Less personal. So I tried to change, to fit in with the Argenti. I wanted to make a home with him."

Those big, yellow-green eyes, clear and bright, fix on Utto. A wealth of questions in them. I hate that the fucker ever even got to look at her, let alone touch her. He left a mark on her soul.

"It was maybe two weeks before he hit me the first time. Not too hard. He just lost control. I could see it on his face. It surprised him. He slapped me. Hard enough for the spot to be tender and a little red." She gestures at her cheekbone. "But nothing anyone else would notice." Her gaze wanders the room, and I follow it. She looks at Nissa and Tam. She looks at the solicitors and the adjudicators, and the reporters.

I try to send support across the Bond. Her gaze shifts to me, and she smiles. Reassurance wafts my way. In the middle of all this ugliness, she's trying to comfort me.

I've never loved her more.

"After that," she says, "it became more frequent. His demands grew more difficult to satisfy. He didn't want me to interact with anyone who might see the bruises. It was my fault I had them, he'd say. He didn't like me to wear anything but white so he could tell if I got my clothes dirty. I think he started looking for reasons to hurt me. New ways to control me."

My throat tightens. The power behind a single blow from an Argenti male, against a Trianni female makes it all the more gruesome.

"To punish me, sometimes he withheld serum. And then Rennie came to visit. Utto let him touch me. Touch my breasts, and…"

A hiss reverberates around the room.

"I don't know what happened. It's blurry in my mind. Utto went to training, but Rennie came back. He said he was going to spend all day with me. He touched me … everywhere. I'm not sure. It just happened. He said … he said he'd fuck me and leave me with his serum in me for Utto to find later. Those were his words."

There's a wave of shifting and murmuring around the courtroom.

"I just … I knew Utto would kill me if that happened. I just … I didn't even think. I had the knife in the pillowcase I'd taken to hold everything … I just … I grabbed it because I didn't want to ever be weak anymore, and then Rennie turned away. He told me to take off all my clothes, get my pussy ready for him, those were *his words*, not mine, and meet him in the bedroom, and I… I just snapped. I don't even remember moving, but suddenly the knife was there. Right in his back. He fell to the ground." Her eyes burn into mine, imploring, asking for me to understand. I do.

"I killed him. I think I even meant to do it."

The silence stretches, winding across the room.

Feola closes her eyes.

Utto shifts in his chair, leaning forward to rest his blue-haired head in his hands, big fists clenched tight, beefy shoulders hunched. Even he looks appalled.

I take a long, slow breath and return my gaze to Feola.

When it's over, she walks back to me calmer in the Bond than I've ever felt her.

Her hand slides into mine, cool and dry, right where it belongs.

The High Adjudicator clears his throat. "Simundo Upranimus."

The senator glances around the room, face stolid and unperturbed, a gentle politician's smile firmly in place as he rises to his feet. In tidy civilian's clothes, a neat foppish necktie, and a jacket emblazoned with all the insignia of his public office, he looks like nothing more than a high-ranking official with a warm heart and an honest dedication to his office.

What would possess him to delve into shady, illegal activities? Hubris? Greed? No, he'd been born to a wealthy family. The man hasn't needed anything, ever, in his whole life. It isn't money that drives him.

The spectators in the darkened room shift in their seats.

The senator's polished shoes echo on the floor as he marches up to the seat.

The senator's solicitor rises, his robes swirling under the overhead lights. "Senator," he begins, voice wavering slightly. "Would you please tell us what you know of the activities of your son, Rennie Upranimus, on Pilan?"

The senator flinches before patting his gray-blue hair. "Of course. Rennie and I weren't as close as I'd have liked." He glances around the room, gaze moving steadily over the spectators, settling on the cameras at the back of the room.

The guy is good.

"I'm sure many of you can relate to having a child who isn't... receptive... to one's efforts." He glances down at his lap. "Nonetheless, I loved my son. Very much. There's probably nothing he could have done that would have changed that. Not that I support or respect everything he did. He was always difficult. Strong willed, and opinionated. I don't know if what this young lady says is true or not, but it's possible. I won't pretend to have known my son well enough to speak to his character. He may have tried to touch her. He may have been involved in any number of illegal activities on Pilan or the gods only know where." The senator shook his head tightly. "But he didn't deserve to be murdered—stabbed in the back. No one deserves that."

The solicitor paces back and forth, looking thoughtful. "Have you ever heard of Pilan?"

"Of course, I have. Everyone has heard of Pilan. It's all over the holo-vids, and in the news. It's a constant problem for the government. A hotbed of crime. But I've never been there. Never had a single interaction with anyone there."

I frown. What the hell is their plan? Push all the blame onto Rennie? Establish that Rennie and Utto are guilty, but the senator is innocent?

"Had you heard of Feola before your son died?"

"No." The senator glares at her. "But I certainly have since the day she murdered him."

"Did you know," the senator says, glancing around the room again, a picture of innocence. "Did you know he's not the only man she's killed?"

All around the room, people inhale sharply. Sucking in breaths.

The senator nods. "She murdered a man on Pilan, and then later, a bounty hunter on Araa-Ara, the planet they absconded to after they escaped Pilan. They've left a trail of death and destruction everywhere they went."

I nearly rise off my chair. My legs strain against the effort to stay seated. Whispered conversation flutters across the court. The adjudicators glace at one another.

The High Adjudicator shambles to his feet, back stooped. "Silence." He doesn't have to shout. The court silences. "Why are you only sharing this information now?"

"The transmissions from the bounty hunter only just arrived. They nearly killed him too. His name is Torum. He and his partner were able to track their ship to Pilan. They followed them there, learned of their murder of one Argenti expatriate, Quasilliaro, and then followed them to Araa-Ara, where she killed one of them, and they took Torum hostage."

Solicitor Jamione gives me a tight nod. He knows the story. We've hidden nothing. Been honest with the officials, who were unable to prove any of this and left it out of their reports, since it was all beyond their jurisdiction. This is nothing more than a backdoor attempt to pollute the case.

Solicitor Jamione clears his throat. Waiting until the senator has his say. This is all part of the plan. Let the senator spin his lies and establish his web. None of it matters. "This is all gossip, from a *Vestige* bounty hunter. The Guarda inspectors didn't include this in their reports because all of it fell outside Argenti legal jurisdiction."

The senator's solicitor cocks his skinny head. "It establishes her propensity for violence. She is a murderess."

Jamione objects. "Actually, it was Healer Willo who killed Quasilliaro, as well as several of his *Vestige* guards while trying to escape him after Quasilliaro decided to sell Feola into slavery. And it was also Healer Willo who killed the *Vestige* bounty hunter on Araa-Ara. We should be asking the senator how he has the connections to hire bounty hunters from the Vestige in the first place."

The senator smiles. "Of course, I know many intergalactic bounty hunters. Please. I'm no fool, and at the time I hired them, I believed I was rescuing my nephew's mate from a kidnapper. Little did I know they were *both* murderers."

Feola over her shoulder. I follow her gaze to see it lock on Nissa. She nods, and Nissa returns the gesture, with a tight nod and a devious glimmer in her green eyes.

Nissa rises calmly and walks out of the room.

I lean in toward Feola's ear. "What the hell is going on?"

She squeezes my hand. "You'll see."

CHAPTER FIFTY

Nothing can stop the frenzy

FEOLA

I take a deep breath, my pulse staccato in my throat. All around the room, Argenti crane their necks, trying to get a better view of me after the senator's allegations. Heat rises up my neck. I turn into Ajax, denying them a view of my face.

He wraps an arm around me.

The gaze of the High Adjudicator settles upon me, as does those of all the other adjudicators. My skin prickles. All I want to do is run away as far as I can, but it's too late.

The senator's iron-gray lizard eyes, so similar to Rennie's, fix on me. His hair is duller, iron mixed in with the blue, but he has the same charismatic tilt to his head, the same ability to make his eyes twinkle and his mouth smile, commanding trust and feigning intimacy. His brow shifts, the barest hint of a twitch.

A shiver rises up my spine. I grip my fingers and push it away. I am no longer that sad, cowed woman. Not anymore. Never again.

I turn toward them all, let them see my naked face, red as it is. Let them look at me. Let them see me.

The doors at the back of the chamber open again, and this time, Nissa walks in, Reyback on her heels. They walk down the center aisle.

Nissa boldly shrugs away the reprimands of the solicitors, raises her voice. "High Adjudicator, I request, in my status as formal Ambassador from Triannon and representative of one of our daughters lost in your realm, the ability to call another witness. But it requires the media to turn off their cameras. Voice recording is fine, but the identity of this new witness must remain a secret."

Here we go.

Ajax stares at me.

I chew my lips.

Tam walks to the back of the room to stand beside the doors.

The High Adjudicator is silent for a long moment, just studying the people in the High Convene. After a time, he inclines his head. "I will permit this."

The rustle at the back announces that the reporters have hustled to stop their visual recordings.

Nissa nods, and Tam opens the door.

I suck in a breath. Hold it.

Shepherd walks into the High Convene.

He isn't wearing the same slick, shiny suit he wore

on Pilan. Instead, he's in a dark-gray, official uniform, emblazoned with medals and insignia. Gone is the swagger and affectation. In their place are shrewd, hard eyes. He even walks differently. More controlled. He prowls.

Ajax squeezes my leg.

Shepherd stalks down the aisle to stand before the High Adjudicator. Tucked under his arm is a digi. He bows stiffly before the old man and hands over a slip of paper, an introduction perhaps.

The High Adjudicator clears his throat. "This man wishes to stay anonymous for the purposes of this High Convene, but he is Guarda. From the Department of Sex Trafficking."

The senator's smile doesn't fade. Not even a flicker.

I just watch. Waiting. Looking forward to the minute it starts to dawn on him. The façade will crack. It's just a matter of time. How many women has he helped destroy? Utto hasn't moved much since my testimony. I refuse to look his way, refuse to feel anything for him besides contempt.

"With your permission, High Adjudicator," Shepherd says, indicating the digi in his hand.

The old man accepts it, his black robes glinting with the motion. He pulls a small pair of half-moon glasses from his robes and perches them on his nose. After a long minute of reading, his head snaps up.

He hands the digi back to Shepherd with a tight nod. Shepherd places it on a table and presses a few buttons. Holo feeds rise up, glimmering frosty blue.

The senator and Rennie walk side by side down a dark, squalid hallway. They're smiling and chatting, their words too quiet to be heard, but looking like birds of a feather, with matching blue plumage.

"I'm working undercover." Shepherd's voice is cold as ice, and his face gives nothing away. "I've been looking for hard evidence of the sex-trafficking crew and have only recently managed to infiltrate their inner circles. We know the Upranimus family is involved in trading women as sex slaves. But we don't know where they are finding them. What they are doing with them next. Where they go." He indicates the screen. "This is Pilan. That's Senator Upranimus and his son, Rennie."

Only moments before, the senator testified that he'd never been to Pilan. The chamber explodes with whispered conversation.

Strike one. Proof the senator is a liar.

I keep my gaze on the senator. His smile fades slightly. The lines around his eyes tighten. But the mask stays firmly in place. He works his face into dubious lines.

Shepherd surveys the room. "We know, for example, that nineteen women were sold last year. Fifteen the year before. Twenty-one the year before that. They disappeared after they were auctioned. Where did they go? I've been searching for that answer for five years." Shepherd's voice echoes across the chamber.

On the holo, the senator and Rennie shake hands with a man wearing a familiar metallic plate over his nose and cheeks. Quasilliaro. All three men laugh uproariously at something the senator says. Ajax flinches.

The senator's smile disappears. "This is ridiculous. These holos are false."

"This man," Shepherd says over him, "the one they are meeting with, went by the name 'Quasilliaro.' He worked for Senator Upranimus. He's the one who received the shipments of women. We aren't sure where they came from, but we suspect a variety of planets. Some of the women were Vestige. Most were women of Argentus. Recently, we've been seeing arrivals from Triannon."

Another angry hiss rises around the chamber.

The holo changes. A woman stands alone on a stage. Her hair cascades down her back, long and rippling and black. Her skin gleamed, oiled and slicked a warm honey brown. The senator sits beside his son in the audience.

"They're auctioning her off to the highest bidder," Shepherd says.

No one moves in the audience. My heart aches for her. What had happened to her? Where is she now?

The senator's brow furrows.

Shepherd clears his throat, gaze never leaving the holo. "The senator made frequent visits to Pilan. I have a record. He came once or twice a year for the last several years. Met with Quasilliaro. Rennie played a vital role in the trade there. There were three major figureheads on Pilan. We each had our roles to play. Quasilliaro, Rennie, and I. But we all took our orders indirectly from one man. Senator Upranimus."

This time, the noise that rises around the chamber swells to a cacophony. People surge to their feet. Even reprimands by the High Adjudicator don't stop the frenzy.

Strike two. Proof of the senator's guilt.

I rise, craning my neck to see what's going on. In his seat atop the dais, even the High Adjudicator looks surprised. People are shouting. At the very least, they would have a fair trial now.

Ajax lets out a happy whoop from beside me. His turquoise eyes blaze warm and hot. His hand closes around my neck, pulling me forward. When his lips touch mine, I melt into him. Our teeth bump because we're smiling so wide.

Laughing. Overjoyed for once. Full of hope.

The final strike against the senator will come when the adjudicators cast their stones. White for innocent.

"We did it," I whisper against his smiling lips. "This is what you wanted. Now it's just us. No past. Just now. Nothing between us."

Our lips meet and I feel—peace, for the first time since my bond with Utto.

The blow comes from behind. So hard, and so fast, it knocks the air from my lungs.

I land on top of Ajax as we hit the floor, tossed forward from the force of the impact.

His eyes flash wide with surprise, his hands coming up to catch me, but it's too late.

The air leaves my lungs, and I can't get it back.

Someone shouts behind me. All I can do is fight

to inhale air that won't come.

Hard arms close around me from behind, fingers threading through my hair, pulling it tight, lifting me up.

I lurch under the pull of my burning scalp.

I'm barely on my feet before I'm wrenched backwards, toppled off balance, still frantically trying to suck in air.

I close my fingers around the hard hand in my hair, my gaze locked on Ajax as he surges to his feet, wild-eyed, staring just over the top of my head. My chest heaves, but no air will come.

Something sharp and cold digs into my throat.

Ajax goes still, crouching low like an animal coiling to spring, hand drifting up to his waist, reaching for a weapon that isn't there.

No one is allowed to be armed in the chambers but for the Guarda.

The crowd seethes around us, a hundred Argenti shouting about the senator's lies. No one even notices us.

I can't breathe. My vision spots. My knees wobble, and surely if it weren't for whoever it is behind me pulling my hair, I'd fall over.

CHAPTER FIFTY-ONE

An armpit bath

AJAX

I don't move a muscle. My body tenses, coiling in preparation for … what?

I have no weapon.

Utto knocked the wind out of her when he hit us. She can't breathe. Her face turns deep red, her chest lurching with the effort to suck in air, eyes wide and terrified, mouth working hard, but in a minute, her body will override the fear and panic and she'll either pass out or breathe.

She'll be fine. Assuming nothing changes in the meantime.

The stylus at her throat is what scares me. Utto's holding it so the tip jabs against the thin skin of her larynx. The fucker must have taken it off one of the solicitors.

One of his hands fists in her hair. A low rumbling sound fills my ears. My own growl.

Utto growls back, a deep resonating purr, his chest rising with it.

A take a scant step forward, body tightening in, knees slightly bent as I study Utto's posture, looking for an opening.

Utto's gaze darts nervously around the growing crowd. "Everyone back up. Back up."

I don't move. The crowd around us surges. I don't think anyone even heard him.

Feola's eyes roll back. Finally, she stops fighting for air. Her eyelids drift closed. Her hand falls limp to her side. Her chest ceases its frenzied heaving, but the redness in her cheeks fades, her nostrils flaring slightly as she inhales.

"This is my woman. *My* mate. I'll kill her. I will fucking kill her before I let anyone else have her," Utto bellows.

The stylus stays right there, hovering just over Feola's throat. A nasty choice of weapon. Nothing clean about jamming a pen into someone's neck. I glance around the room. There's a lot of stuff. Digis, papers, and files.

Utto backs up, pulling Feola's limp body with him until he bumps against the dais. The High Adjudicator stares down with curious eyes.

I close in.

"Stay back," Utto shouts. Sweat pours down his forehead. A drop runs down the side of his nose to land in Feola's hair.

In my peripheral vision, Tam and Spiro creep closer.

The Guarda, finally having noticed us, step in, *rezals* aimed right for Utto's head. "Drop the stylus," one of them says.

"Drop the *rezals.*" Utto tightens his grip on the stylus. The fine skin of her neck swells around it. "I'll fucking bleed her dry before I let you have her. Back away." Another millimeter or two, and he'll break the skin.

Her pulse flutters along the vein.

If they took a shot and Utto's arm bucks with the momentum of the blast, it could pierce her throat.

"Don't shoot," I murmur

Utto tosses his head, glaring at Ajax, then the Guarda, then Spiro. "I'm not losing h—"

A dozen things happen at the same time.

One of the Guarda takes a step closer.

Tam appears on top of the dais.

Another Guarda squats low.

Spiro moves in, holding something blunt in his hands.

Tam lifts a finger to his lips.

The Guarda raises his weapon.

"No," I roar, but it is too late.

The *rezal* blast takes off the top of Utto's forehead, spraying Tam with red.

I lunge for Feola, grabbing her around the wrist, hauling her body up against my own, so her neck won't be pierced and her body won't be pulled down as Utto's bulk drops to the floor.

Then she's in my arms, and everything else just fades away. I take her pulse. She's fine. Breathing easy. Warm color. Healthy as ever.

Dimly, I'm aware of someone leading us out of the High Convene and back toward their room.

A knock comes to our chamber door only a few hours after Utto's death. I freeze on the bed, arms around Feola

Tam sticks his head in the opening, his gaze landing on Feola's sleeping form. "Fifty stones of innocence," he whispers. "The Adjudicators didn't waste any time."

"For me? Or Feola?"

Tam grins. "Fifty stones for each of you."

"And?" I hold breath, willing Tam to say Upranimus is done, sentenced to life in Insuractius.

"They're still discussing him."

"Fuck." Until Upranimus is locked away, I'll never be able to relax, never be able to trust that some assassin isn't lurking in the corners.

Feola rolls over on her pillow, a smile on her face that's wider than a mile and brighter than the sun. "This means we're free?"

"Technically. I'll feel better when I know what will happen to Upranimus." An innocent verdict seems unlikely, but the punishment could be as lenient as probation and as harsh as the death penalty.

"So what now?" she asks in that perfect musical voice.

"Triannon. We go home," Tam says unequivocally. "You're coming home, where you'll both be safe. You have one hour before our transport departs." The door snicks softly as Tam leaves us in peace.

Maybe I expected her to be jubilant at the thought of returning home, but her eyes are surprisingly grave.

"Don't you want to go home?"

"Sure, but I'm already home, *Ay-shocks*. Wherever you are is my home."

I shove my nose into her hair, breathe her in. She's my home too. "Won't you be glad to see Triannon?"

Her shoulder lifts. "As long as you're there. Won't you miss Argentus?"

I mimic her gesture. "Wherever you are is my home." I slide my hand under her back, raising her from the bed.

"Where are you taking me?"

"The bathing pool. You stink of Utto. I'm going to fuck you but not while you smell like him."

She wrinkles her nose. "Can you really smell him?"

Utto's sweat dripped all over her hair. She smelled like he rubbed his armpit on her head. "Yes."

The air in the bathing chamber is humid, her hair curling around her face as I set her down.

It only takes a few seconds to slip the straps over her shoulders, and the red dress hits the floor.

Another second after that, and my own clothes are off.

Another second, and we're both in the water.

I spend a long time spreading soap along her skin, sudsing it through her hair. "You won't ever smell like another man again."

Her lips pinch. "And you won't ever smell like another woman."

"God no."

"Never."

"Only me."

"Only you."

CHAPTER FIFTY-TWO

Every single part

FEOLA

Triannon is as warm as I remembered, and just as bold. Every morning, the sky burns violet, the lazy breeze off the vibrant emerald green sea carries the same salty, watery notes as my memory, whispering in the scarlet ferns as they walk together to Ajax's healing bay at the city center.

It's been a full month since we arrived, and still can't quite relax, to accept the safety and comfort of home.

I deserve to be happy. I did nothing wrong. I repeat the words in my head a hundred times a day. But still, every once in a while, I'll turn away from the notes I've been entering in a digi, or the exam room I've been preparing, and a man will be standing just a little too close, just a little too tall, and it feels like a frozen gust of wind rushing straight down my spine.

It doesn't matter that Utto is gone. And Rennie. It doesn't matter that they'll never be able to hurt me again. That instinctive response of fear might be mine for life. I can live with it.

Small price to pay for a lifetime of happiness with Ajax. A lifetime of safety and comfort. Guilt over Torum's friend. Klymeni and he have been found on Vesta—and he's a king of all things, but that's a story for another day.

The senator was found guilty, and sentenced to fifty years of labor on Insuractius Colony. At age sixty-six already, he won't leave the colony with his life. According to all reports, criminals rarely survive more than a decade there, even if they are in their prime.

We're safe. Finally. And Ajax's career survived intact. Spiro may have lost his future-mate, but he's fully recovered, if permanently scarred at the neck with a weakened voice box. He croaks when he speaks.

The Trianni people are learning to trust Ajax with their illnesses, both big and small. And for me, it's a chance to get to know them.

Life is good.

Steps cross the floor behind me, where I am in the bay's supply closet, organizing medicine.

Ajax. I know his smell, the cadence of his steps. And I feel him in my chest, across the Bond. Warm. Excited. Happy.

Planning something.

His hand slides around my waist, to settle on my

lower belly. "Do you trust me?"

"Yes," I whisper, already feeling breathless. His touch, as always, hits me like a jolt of electricity. Dizzying, thrilling, intense. His other hand comes around to cup my breast through the thin fabric of the linen dress I'm wearing.

My nipples harden instantly.

The bay is quiet so late in the day. Abandoned. When he presses his hips against my back, I suck in a fat breath.

"I'll never hurt you," he whispers.

"I know that."

He catches his tongue between his teeth in a grin. "Walk to exam room C, then. I'll be right behind you. I want to watch that sweet ass sway."

When we reach the room, I spin around slowly, conscious of his eyes on my body. My belly flutters at the heat smoldering in those turquoise eyes.

He inclines his head toward the exam table. "Up."

My stomach clenches, but I climb onto the exam table.

He pulls out a pair of examination gloves and snaps them onto his hands. "It's past time I gave you a proper medical examination." The little gleam of humor in his eyes has me laughing.

"Is that so?"

"Yes. It would be remiss if I didn't." He steps up closer. Closer than any healer would ever step to a real patient. "Your nipples are erect."

"They are. And tingly."

"Are you aroused?"

"I'm not sure. Maybe you should check."

"I'll get to that. Raise your skirt, and spread your legs."

Liquid heat pools on my skin, raising goosebumps.

Cheeks flaming, eyes locked on him, slowly, I part my thighs. The fabric of the dress inches higher. Vulnerable, soft skin of my upper thighs comes into view. The hard bulge in his pants leaves no doubt that he can see everything from his angle.

"Disrobe completely."

I pull the dress over my head, my breasts bouncing softly with the motion.

His lips curve in a smile. "Beautiful."

He directs my legs wider. His gloved fingers drifting up, and up, and up. A smooth finger slides inside, where I am, indeed, slippery wet.

He flashes a devil's smile. "This will be a very, very thorough exam. Are you ready?"

I nod, hips lifting against him, wanting more.

"Tell me."

"Yes!" It laughs out of me, happy and bright and for a second, I remember who I was with Ajax before Utto. "Yes, I'm ready."

He slides a second finger inside." "Everything feels normal," he says, in a healer's efficient tones. "Just one more."

A third slick finger presses lower, stroking along my ass, pressing deeper.

I relax against it, pressing in, taking it deeper. The extra layer of fullness has my eyes rolling back and moans tearing from my throat.

Ajax's thumb makes little circles around my clit until my body bucks beneath his heady gaze.

"Mmmm. Everything appears to be in working order. But let's see how you respond to increased stimuli, shall we?"

"Yes, please."

His hands stop moving and slowly withdraw. "As I said. Beautiful. Now get on your knees."

My eyes pop open. "What? No. You can't stop now."

"On your knees." He says it sternly, but the grin on his face is anything but.

"I was close."

"Hands and knees, please."

That voice. I'll do anything when he talks like that, low down and sex gruff.

"Yes, Healer Willo." I offer my coyest smile, thrusting my breasts toward him.

His gaze drops.

"I really think though, healer, that you're wearing too many clothes."

He laughs. "I'll take off the gloves, then."

They snap as he slides them off.

I turn away, rolling over as gracefully as I can manage on an exam table. He pushes my hair over my shoulder, baring me for his gaze.

"Arch your back."

I do.

"Spread your legs wider."

I do, feeling very on display and very vulnerable.

"Lean forward. Put your hands on the table in front of you."

This position puts my hips right in line with his.

He inhales sharply. "Spread your thighs wider."

I shiver but do it, inching my knees apart. A wave of desire courses across our Bond, and I can't stifle the moan that rises in my throat. Instinctively I push my bottom out toward him, presenting to him, the heat of his gaze making me throb.

The sound of a zipper meets my ears.

I glance at him over my shoulder. His face is hard, his gaze hooded as he strokes the up and down the length of his cock.

"You're going to feel some pressure." He steps closer. Only a few breaths separate our bodies. The air between us sizzles, pops and thrums, ripping with the intensity of his voice.

The moment stretches, and nothing happens. I just wait. The anticipation builds and spreads.

"Ajax," I groan. "Ajax, please."

"Shh," he says, sliding a hand down my neck, he lines his cock up against my pussy, and shoves his way inside, hard enough to make me cry out. His balls press against my clit, but he doesn't move again, just grinds in deep, like he's staking a claim.

Motions slow, almost idly, his fingers come up, to

press inward, probing against my ass, pressing in.

I roll my head against the exam table as he sets up a rhythm.

"Reach between your legs and touch your clit."

I do.

"Good girl." He reaches around and palms one of my tits, thrusting in and out, setting up a rhythm that makes the uprights of the exam chair creak and the leather under my hands and knees squeak. It all coils up and both of us grunt out a raw orgasm, as he pumps me full of serum, which triggers a whole new cycle.

But he doesn't stop. He keeps going until I've had another and I'm so weak I can barely move. Serum slides down my thighs, when he pulls out. Still hard. Nowhere close to being done. How many times can an Argenti come? I have no clue. Many.

"And the last part of the exam?" He scoops up serum with his free hand, and uses it to coat a second finger, sliding it into my ass.

I've grown to love the pressure of his fingers there.

"Are you ready?"

"Yeah." I can do this.

"Good." The healer persona is gone. All that's left now is Ajax the man, hard and hot. My man. "I'm going to fuck your ass now," he whispers, fingers deep inside. "You're ready. You can take me." His voice drifts over the sensitive skin of my back. "I won't hurt you."

"I know." My hands tighten into fists.

He pulled his fingers out, and his weight shifts behind me. The head of his cock presses against my entrance, pushes, slippery with serum. Wincing, I push back and he slides inside, not deep, just an inch or two.

"You're so tight." He hisses. "So tight it almost hurts."

He slides in deeper, inch by inch, pausing and rocking with every forward motion. I've never felt so full in my life, and he just keeps on pushing deeper. Whispering words of praise, kissing my neck, stroking my clit, until it's my hips rocking, moving back and forth.

"That's it. Oh, fuck. That's it. Keep on taking me deeper." His voice and his hands set me on fire. I can't stop it. It's like some strange force of nature, or force of instinct. I need to take him in as far as he could go. There's pain, a little, but right there, lurking just behind it, is something richer, something darker.

I grit my teeth, sobbing out, taking more, until his balls slap against my dripping pussy.

He trails kisses down my neck, stroking my breasts, whispering and murmuring until my body quits fighting the intrusion and the muscles quit cramping.

The sensation shifts. The discomfort of the fullness changes, and in its place is a sense of being deeply possessed, completely treasured, protected and safe.

"You ready?"

"Gods, yes. Fuck me, Ajax."

He draws his cock out and thrusts it home. My eyes roll back, fingers clenching against the intensity of it, but there is no resisting it, no fighting it. I can only hold on tight as the most intense orgasm of my life fights its way out of me, right out of the depths of my soul, unnaturally hard, unnaturally fast.

"Shh. Holy shit, Feola. Slow down. Fuck, I don't want to hurt you." He holds my hips still, pulling out in a long, slow movement, and thrusting forward.

"You won't hurt me. Just fuck me."

He curses darkly. But his hips move faster, thrusting hard. Finally, this is what I want. This is what I need. He thrusts in such long, hard strokes that my breasts rock back and forth, and his balls slap against my skin, my groans become incoherent uncivilized grunts.

I curse and sweat against the onslaught until finally, it all condenses into a single fireball of intense pleasure that explodes outwards. The already almost painfully tight muscles of my ass clench around the impossibly thick length of his cock. The orgasm pushes pleasure against pain in a confusing, debilitating tide that blinds me in its sheer intensity. I've never felt anything this intense since our Bonding.

He holds onto me with a hard hand on my hips, as he thrusts deeper.

I drop forward on the exam table but he holds my hips still for his use as his thrusts go erratic. His cock swells deep inside me and the first searing-hot blasts of his serum flood my insides.

It's too much. The serum on top of all of it. There. My fingers and toes curl, all my muscles shuddering. Hips moving wildly against his. He drops down to take his wait on his hands around me, the hard lines of his chest resting against my back, his lips and teeth find my shoulder, and he bites. Hard. As he shoves in so far I scream, his thrusts growing frantic as more serum tears out of him, filling my ass with blinding wet heat.

It's like being exorcised, or tortured, or exalted all at the same time. Maybe. Tortured with pleasure. He finds one of my breasts, strumming my nipple, soothing my back from the dark depths of the last orgasm.

It's only when it's over that I realize I got ahold of his forearm somehow during my contortions and sank my teeth into it. A pair of half-moons flanks the red mark I sucked to the surface.

"You marked me," he whispers, stroking a finger over my shoulder. "I marked you, too."

He starts to withdraw, and I grumble out a complaint, not ready for him to leave yet, not when I've only just gotten used to his presence there.

He settles in, twisting us so I'm on my side, and his hips press tightly against mine, his cock still lodged deep in my ass. "I thought I died for a minute. And I didn't even mind."

"I won't let you die."

I smile, eyes shut, warm and replete.

"Did that hurt?"

"No. Well, maybe a little, but in a good way." I

yawn. "Ajax?"

He hums sleepily.

"Swear we will never break the Bond. Not for anything."

"Never."

I wrap my hand around his. This is how Bonds are supposed to be. Warm. Safe. Trusting.

And unbroken.

Thank you for reading!

Turn the page for a glimpse of Tor and Klymeni's unforgettable (and super steamy!) love story, The Taming.

"I hate you," I groan, unable to stop my body from bowing against him, my bottom from thrusting out.

He grinds his hips, and the long, hard girth of him presses against me, so hot that I can't help but imagine it doing just what nature designed it to do.

I've spent far too much time imagining it. I want it, though I'd never say it. I want him inside me.

"You don't," he whispers in my ear.

We have this argument hourly, it seems. He insists I want him. My body agrees.

His lips drift down my jaw. "You want me, Klym, just as badly as I want you." He turns me onto my back, looming over me to trail his tongue down my sternum, over my breasts, his hair tickling over my skin.

"I know exactly what I feel for you, and it isn't want. It's ahhhh——"

When he closes his mouth over the rise of my breast, dimples flickering in his cheeks, I sigh.

"——loathing." It comes out long and throaty, lacking all conviction, but it's something. "And... and..."

He chuckles.

"Revulsion," I whisper.

His finger slides inside me, where I'm wet from earlier, and another drifts lower. My ass. A place I'd have sworn last week I'd go to my death bed never letting anything inside. I'd have been lying.

"Weird response to revulsion."

CHAPTER ONE

Escape, of course

KLYM

I poke my head around the corner of the galley to peer down the main passageway of the spaceship. There's not much to see. Steel surfaces, dark grated floors, and the pilots' seats on the bridge.

And, of course, the man to whom my father sold me. Like one might sell a pig or a fruit or a shoe.

Spiro—the back of his golden head shines under the lights as he stares rigidly through the viewscreen into space.

The prisoner, Torum, is isolated in the rear, where they've kept him for days, ever since we left his ship on a dusty planet. He's shackled in the darkness on a cot outside the engine room.

If I have any hope of escaping my unwanted Bonding with Spiro, it lies with Torum.

Sneakiness and stealth don't come naturally to me. Well, strictly speaking, that's not entirely true. Walking quietly comes just fine—I am a trained *lady,* after all, and quiet is similar to sneaky. It's the intent that's different.

Sneakiness is not a personal skill of mine. I was educated to converse with dignitaries, take holo-photos, organize parties and always, *always,* be polite—all of which is perfectly useless now.

But people can change when they must.

And I *must.*

So I tiptoe, and my feet make scarcely a sound as I slip down the passageway.

Another glance over my shoulder confirms Spiro hasn't moved. I hold the little paring knife I pilfered from the galley concealed in the folds of my dress. Spiro's brother and his mated woman disappeared into their cabin long ago. This is the perfect time. They'll be lost in a mating haze.

My skirts whisper over the metal floor as I round the wall, passing beyond Spiro's line of sight.

He won't come looking for me. He's learned to avoid me. The only thing I ever say to him is: *I will not Bond with you. I belong to another man. Please take me to him.*

I say it on repeat until I annoy even myself.

He steadfastly refuses to see that I will never accept him.

If he'd only see reason and return me to my real fiancé, my home, the life I was promised, I wouldn't be forced to take this drastic step. But he won't, so we've been frozen in silent stalemate. So much silence.

Really, it's his fault for being unreasonable. I have no choice.

And while Spiro doesn't speak, Torum certainly does.

Every time I pass, he speaks. Whispers of promise. Murmurs of hope. Taunts of freedom. All of it in that dark, accented voice, like grit and gravel and sharpening steel.

I shiver, as I always do, at the very idea of him. A bounty hunter. A *Vestige* bounty hunter. An alien from the most hated, feared, reviled enemy my people had ever known, the ones who sent the plague that killed off nearly the entire female population, plunging our race into near-extinction. I've heard Spiro and his brother discussing him—violent, unpredictable.

He looks it—and then some.

Wild. Untamed. Feral.

Everything I ever imagined of the Vestige.

I step into the darkened passageway, and there he is, as still and unyielding as if he were carved of marble like the statues of the ancients in the museums back home, a relic from a time when men were harder and life more brutal, when their bodies were honed by battle and savagery.

I bite my lower lip, hesitating. It's not *do or die*—it's *do or languish*.

Inky-black hair cascades to his shoulders, and an impressive set of shoulders they are. Twice as wide as my own, and thickly bound with hard, bulging muscles that rise and fall in a thin white shirt.

A black tribal tattoo snakes up his neck.

His head is tilted down. Asleep? *Do the Vestige even sleep?*

There are so many rumors back home that I don't know what to believe. Rumors of dark deeds, inhuman deeds, evil deeds. Still … it's a risk I have to take.

What does one say to a prisoner? I consider clearing my throat to get his attention—

"Come closer." His voice, low and raspy, strips the decision away from me. More of a rumble, really, that vibrates and tickles all the fine hairs on my body, like a feather stroked up my spine.

My fingers come up to touch my pearls as I strain to catch his words. His eyes are still closed. They haven't opened. "How did you know I was here?" I whisper. "I was quiet."

"I can smell you."

My shoulders stiffen. "You can*not*."

"Can too."

"I have impeccable hygiene. I do *not* smell." I never smell.

"Do too." Finally, that face angles up, sharp jaw, hard cheekbones, slanting black brows, and a leer. His eyes open, black and unfathomable. "You smell like fruit." A little scowl forms between his eyes.

"Oh." Well, that's kind. I smile. "Thank you."

"And pussy."

I nearly gasp—but I catch myself just in time. I shouldn't know that word. It's from one of the dirty stories a friend once snuck into the Institute. I hide my surpise with a pat of my hair in the coiled bun at the nape of my neck and push my chin out.

Clearly, he is nothing like my sweet Agammo. Even Spiro is too gallant to use such a word, at least not in my presence. "I'll assume that means something polite and complimentary."

Those dark eyes burn like a physical caress. "It wasn't polite. But complimentary? Absolutely."

I try not to wrinkle my nose.

His teeth flash in the dark. "You know what it means."

I toss my head. "Can I trust you?"

"No."

The thing is, a liar would have said yes. "Why not?"

"Your father is the War Chief of all Argentus." His eyes rover over my body as thought he can see beneath my clothes.

"But I'm not the War Chief, and I don't even like my father."

He moves his enormous boots, shifting his shoulders. "Tell me, what happens if a Vestige and Argenti mate?"

It's an old joke. And not a very funny one. The Argenti ... well, when we mate, our women lose their minds and souls in an orgy of sex that leaves them tied forever to the man. I find that no laughing matter—especially when the man in question is one she may not have chosen—like Spiro. As for the Vestigi—supposedly, their women possess similar capabilities as Argenti men, only in reverse. I don't know what their men can do. "I didn't come here to be crass."

His laugh ripples across the airwaves. "Why did you come, then?"

I hold up the knife, and it's my turn to smile. "For escape, of course."

His lips curve wider, and white teeth flash in a predatory grin. "Now I'm listening, *amiera.*"

CHAPTER TWO

Honor's for fools and losers

KLYM

I listen carefully to his murmured commands and tuck the knife into his boot.

A few hours later, Spiro removes Torum's shackles with a dour frown and escorts him to the bathing chamber at gunpoint. He lets him eat and drink. Again, with a rezal trained clearly on his chest.

As Torum finishes his dinner, I tuck the sum total of my possessions into the pockets of my dress. My travel documents and my treasured holo-cam, which holds every last holo-vid and memory I have of my mother. I pat her pearls around my neck, ensuring they're safe, and tell Spiro I'll tidy up after the meal, and in so doing, move just a shade closer to the prisoner than necessary. Precisely as he told me to.

Spiro looks surprised and strangely pleased at my offer to assist or make words other than my annoying repetitive mantra. He probably I'm softening to him, poor man.

For a split second, my body blocks his view.

It happens so fast my teeth clash together, and my vision swims. Torum yanks me against the big, rock-solid mass of his chest, close enough for me to smell the woody, spicy smell of his body. His hand fists in my hair, and Spiro stands no chance. He's far too noble.

"I'll kill her," Torum purrs, and I genuinely believe him.

My visible terror is one hundred percent genuine.

Rough fingers slip along my neck, pressing over a vein until my vision darkens and my knees buckle. "Don't fuck with me, *migané*."

Pure dread slicks up my spine at the hateful growl.

Spiro's boots creak.

The knife—*the one I gave Torum*—hisses as it flies through the air to lodge firmly in Spiro's throat. I barely even feel his's body move.

Spiro drops to his knees.

So much blood.

Moments later, I'm staring down at my shaking hands as the escape pod pushes off from the main body of Spiro's ship, one tiny little vessel wading through the infinite colorless void.

As the thrusters activate, my bones rattle, and my teeth clatter.

What did I just do? What was I thinking?

I wasn't thinking about anything at all, except escaping and finding my way back to Agammo.

I've never, not once in my entire, dignified boring life, done anything cruel. Until now.

The blood.

Blood was everywhere, spreading beneath his prone body. My mouth twists, but I can't get it out of my head. Spiro clutched his hands to his bleeding neck, sputtering. And the look he gave me as he dropped to his knees. A whole lifetime had burned in the true-blue depths of his eyes. Surprise. Accusation. Confusion. Disappointment. Concern. *For me.*

Even as he bled out, he was worried about me. Spiro, whatever else lies between us, is a good and decent man of my planet. And I just left him bleeding and took off with a wild unknown. A question mark of an alien, capable of anything.

I didn't throw the knife that landed in his neck. But I may as well have.

I close my eyes, squeezing my hands into fists, forcing my face to relax from its grotesque mask. I'll never get that look on his out of my head.

Spiro will be okay. He has to be okay. I didn't want him to get hurt. It was an accident. Surely that matters on the scale, doesn't it? I didn't *mean* to cause any harm.

I just wanted to get away. That's all. Get away, back to Agammo, the man *I chose,* so we can start a family, and I won't have to be alone anymore. But the blood. So much blood. His brother is a healer—he'll be fine. I hope to all the gods, he'll be fine.

"Quit sniffling. It's annoying." The deep, gravelly voice of the man who *did* throw the knife interrupts my thoughts.

I open my eyes but refuse to look at him, focusing instead through the escape pod's porthole at nothing but emptiness punctuated by stars too distant to offer comfort. It doesn't help to be reminded that the universe is enormous. And I'm small, so very small. And home and Agammo and all our dreams are very, very far away.

"I am not sniffling," I snap. Or am I? Maybe. I wipe at my cheeks. They're wet.

"Good. Don't." Torum leans back from the console, looking smug.

I breathe through pinched nostrils. "You needn't be *rude.*"

The dark pools of his eyes glint evilly, and his unfashionably long black hair gleams under the multi-colored lights on the console, the harsh planes of his face almost glowing, and he laughs.

"You didn't need to *hurt* him, either," I say, trying to tamp down the burst of panic at being lost in space with this rude monster.

"Wrong, *amiera.* I *did* have to hurt him." He props a black-booted foot on his knee. His head nearly brushes the top of the pod. His elbow bumps against the bulkhead. He takes up far too much room, and seems to only want to spread out more. "If I didn't hurt him, he'd have killed me."

"You could at least have the dignity to look upset."

He snorts. "Why would I be upset? I'm happy. Jubilant. He and his brother had my hands cuffed behind my back for days. You have any clue what that feels like?" He rolls his shoulders. "I'm fucking free."

"He didn't deserve to be hurt like that."

"It wasn't personal. It was him or me. Two people. Different goals. Nothing but knives. If I hadn't hurt him that bad, they'd be coming after us right now. That knife in his throat will keep them busy long enough for us to get away." His brows quirk. "What did you think would happen when you turned on him?"

"I didn't *turn* on him. I just wanted to get *away* from him."

"Then you ought to be celebrating. Congratulations. You're away from him. We're on our way to my ship back on that planet you all left it on. And then I'm done with you."

I shake my head at his flagrant lack of morals. He's barbaric.

Then his words sink in. *Done with you.*

"You mean done with me *after* you take me home."

"You can go wherever you want. But I'm not taking you anywhere."

Panic sets my heart pounding as I imagine myself floating alone through space. "You promised," I breathe.

"I promised to take you away from that ship. Not to take you to Argentus. You know what they'd do with me if they caught me? I'm not getting tortured for *you*."

He says *you* as if I am so vile as to be beneath contempt.

A sob of panic rises in my throat, and I swallow it, tracing my fingers over the pearls. "You'd still be there with your hands tied behind your back if it weren't for me."

He turns away, the sinuous shapes of the tattoo twisting on his neck moving as he shifts in the seat, elbowing it irritably.

"Have you no concept of honor on Vesta, then?"

"Honor's for fools and losers. I'm neither."

I straighten my shoulders and try to match his insouciant tone. "What *do* you intend to do with me?"

His amusement fades. A muscle ticks in his hard, unshaven jaw.

I press my advantage. "You can't just leave me on a deserted planet and forget about me."

He fiddles with the gauges on the console, mouth hard. "I could."

I stiffen. "You *wouldn't.*"

A lazy grin flashes across his face.

"I would have no way to get home. Even you couldn't be so cruel."

His dour glare implies that perhaps, in fact, he really could be just that cruel. His biceps flex and ripple through his thin shirt as he runs his massive hands through his hair. "*Inns yiurian a ghiann.*"

The part of his words I catch cut like a knife. *You'd deserve it and worse.* My Vestigi was more than adequate for school, but the last word is not one with which I am familiar. The tone, however, leaves no doubt it is a curse.

"The enemy tongue," I say, "was part of my comprehensive education. Curse words, however, were omitted. My tutors failed to predict that I would come across a man of your *vast* vocabulary."

He laughs, dimples dancing on his face, and unleashes another violent stream of Vestigi.

I pluck at the folds of my dress because it's that or cry. "Do try to use words someone who wasn't raised in a gutter might understand."

Another stream of amused unintelligible Vestigi.

It doesn't matter.

He can curse all he wants.

He can hate me as much as he likes, as long as he doesn't abandon me. I need him only until I can get in contact with Agammo. Then sweet, gentle Agammo will come for me. We will Bond as we've always intended. And all of this will be nothing more than ugliness left in the past. Forgotten. We'll be free together, and we'll build a family.

"Please, if you'll just help me get somewhere safe and help me contact home—I'm sure my fiancé would see you well rewarded."

"Your fiancé is bleeding out as we speak," he growls.

Deep breaths. "Spiro will be fine." *He has to be.* "His brother is a good healer. I meant my real fiancé. Agammo."

"How many fiancés do you have?" He scrapes a hand along the hard edges of his bristly jaw.

I stiffen.

"Never mind. I don't care. Just keep your mouth shut."

Preparing to keep my voice calm so even a brute can understand, I inhale sharply. "I'm sure there's some neutral place where you c—"

He doesn't even look at me, but his jaw ticks again. "What part of 'mouth shut' confused you? If I have to be stuck with you until I can figure out how to get rid of you, at least I don't have to listen to your traitorous tongue."

I shrink away from the vehemence behind his words and straighten my dress so the ivory lace falls evenly to the floor, over my crossed ankles.

I pat my hair to check that the coiled bun wasn't destroyed during our escape. All the instructors at the

Institute said my hair was one of my best features. Turquoise, thick and sleek.

There's no call for bad manners. *Fight rudeness with smiles*, that's what the Merentide Ladies' Institute of the Galactic Future taught. Leaning forward in my seat, I wave a hand through the air to capture his attention.

He frowns, eyes wary.

I incline my head. Manners are a form of armor. I gather them closely. If I can't speak, it doesn't mean I can't communicate. I point to my tightly shut mouth.

Clearly, compromise is the only way to handle this heathen.

His frown deepening, he studies me from the top of my head to the bottom of my toes.

I turn away and dissolve into silence, just as he demanded and do what I always do when I'm upset— pull out the holo-cam my father gave me for my last birthday. I pass the time filming an impressive view of a foggy, glittering pink cloud of an elliptical galaxy winking on the right side of the porthole. It helps, focusing on the familiar feel of the hand-sized holo-cam, seeing the images take form, pushing aside the guilt and the fear, and instead imagining the documentary of my travel I might make when all of this is over.

It's my only available escape, so I cling to it.

Miraculously, aside from a few dubious glares, he doesn't object.

I'm as good as my word, or rather, my *not*-word. I don't open my mouth once. At least not to do anything other than eat my rations. Not for the two days we sit side by side in the cramped bridge of the tiny escape vessel, as he grunts and curses and growls like an angry beast about what he calls *the shitty seat*. Not when I discover there is no water for washing, only a sanitizing spray for our hands. Not even when I am forced to use the tiny closet of a toilet chamber well within his earshot.

And certainly not during the two nights we sleep side by side in the seats of the tiny pod.

I certainly don't speak as the escape pod thunders into the atmosphere of the pale planet where we left his ship, flames blasting on the outside of the hull, the silvery surface roaring up to meet us, and the interior growing so hot I start to fear we'll be cooked alive, and only my fingers clutched around my holo-cam, filming it all, keeps me from screaming. Nor when the landing parachute engages, and our violent descent lurches to an even more violent stop, though I am more terrified than I've ever been in my entire life.

We hit the surface with a loud, metallic bang that rattles my brain, and then it's over. We've landed in a dust cloud beside his hulking matte-black spaceship on the silver and purple planet of Araa-Ara.

I follow him off the escape pod, holding the holo-cam steady in front of me, clambering through the tiny porthole hatch, and trail him across the hot, dusty stretch of terra.

His eyes narrow on the holo-cam, as they do every time he sees it, but he doesn't comment, merely gestures me gruffly ahead of him inside his ship, where it is blessedly cool.

I hesitate, unsure of what to do.

He stalks down the passageway and disappears behind a metal door.

When I hear a loud splash, I back away. Is that his bathing chamber? Is he naked in there? Heat rises up my cheeks. Agammo wouldn't like this at all. Not one bit. In all the years he came to the Institute to visit me, we've only been alone together a handful of times. And he's always been staunchly proper.

And now here I am. All alone. With a big, mean alien who is anything but proper.

I gather my lacy skirts in my hands and walk to the main hatch of the ship at the exit to wait outside until he finishes.

And then, pray to all the gods he'll let me take a bath too. I've never been so filthy in my life.

The air outside is fiery hot, and the sun, only three-quarters of the way through its arc, hovers, blinding and merciless overhead.

I walk around the edge of the ship to stand in the shade. Dusty soil rises around my legs in great powdery gusts.

The clime in my city, Merentide on Argentus, is far more civilized. Cool and breezy, at least in the spring and autumn months, when a cool breeze blows off the Meren Gray River. Even in summer, it never approaches this heat.

I tug at the bodice of my dress. A bead of sweat runs down my neck. My clothes will be ruined at this rate. Not to mention the smell if I keep sweating in the silk lace and skipping baths.

Glancing back at the ship, I undo the tiny row of pearl buttons down the bodice and tug off my overdress, with its high neck, long bell-shaped sleeves, and lacy designs, over my head, leaving me in only a loose chemise.

On impulse, I ruck up the chemise, and untie the tight laces of my corset, don't even give myself time to think before I tug it off. Thick red welts run along the skin over my ribs. I loathe stays.

I hurry to re-button the bodice over my chemise, which is little more than an ankle length, sleeveless shift, that leaves my entire neck and upper chest bare, as well as my arms, not to mention the tops of my breasts, but it's the only bra I have. I don't dare leave it off.

On Argentus, this would be scandalous, but Torum despises me. He won't even look at me twice.

A stray draft cools the sweat on my skin. Heavenly. I can move. And breathe. Feeling guilty all over again, I roll the long white stockings down my thighs and leave them around my ankles like socks.

Another breeze blows and sends air up between my thighs, cooling sweaty skin. Decadent.

I trace the toe of one of my slippers through the soil. A little cloud puffs up around it, but small blue flowers peak out, tossing petals to swirl through the air.

I smile despite myself and gather a few of the tiny blossoms. Smaller than my pinkie nail. When I pull a long tendril of a vine, another cluster of flowers comes too. I wish I could send some to Spiro. He must be in recovery by now—he *must*.

There's only the subtlest of scents when I lift them to my nose, but the soft blooms calm me for the first time in days. Surely Spiro is fine. I gather handfuls of the spreading vines in a bouquet of pale white leaves and bold blue blossoms that trail from my hands like water.

In the distance, lavender trees glimmer against the horizon, and beyond them, a darker, violet hill rises with a sparkling waterfall and a white building complete with shining blue domes. A fairyland. A foreign fairyland light-years from home.

I raise the holo-cam to capture it, already picturing how I can splice together the peaceful footage with the violent landing. Maybe in a decade, back on Argentus, safe with Agammo, we'll watch these vids and laugh and wonder at the beauty of places so far from home.

If Torum weren't such a beast, this would be the adventure of my lifetime. I'd be like the heroines in the books I read, free to wander on a foreign planet, explore the ruins, roam at will, unsupervised. I've never been anywhere outside the home in which I was born, and the Institute.

Until now.

"Where the hell are you?" A bellow from the mouth of the ship diverts my attention. "Klymeni!"

Torum charges around the entrance, black hair, long and wet around his neck, wearing a pair of black trousers—and nothing else.

His bare chest gleams in the harsh sunlight. Sleek muscles ripple as he storms around the corner, gripping a sword with one hand and a gun with the other. And that tattoo covers not just his neck. It snakes down the entire right side of his chest, along his upper arm, and even part of his rippling abdomen, disappearing into the waist of his trousers. I've never seen a tattoo before in my life, but now I've seen many.

And scars. The man has so many scars. Small ones and large ones. One trails down his right pectoral, and another bisects one of his abdominal muscles.

He stops dead when he sees me, his gaze dropping to the top of my bodice. My skin heats at the look in his eyes.

"What the he—Are you picking *flowers*?"

I open my mouth, on the edge of explaining, and remember that I've been commanded not to speak.

Angling my chin at him, I gesture toward the vista before us, at the hills in the distance.

His brows draw together.

I smile sweetly and gather my clothing and flowers. Holding his gaze, I walk toward the ship's entrance. Hauteur might be a silly defense, but it's all I have.

Besides, I want a bath of my own. And he's in my way.

"Where do you think you're going now?"

My smile never flickers. Not even when I get close enough to smell his woody, soapy, post-bath scent. He's so tall I have to tilt my head back to keep my eyes on his. I lift a cool brow.

And walk right past him, through the hissing hatch door, down the passageway with its icy blast of cool air, and slide the door of the bathing chamber shut behind me.

Only there do I rest my back against the wall. Torum is unlike any man I've ever come across. Unlike the elderly instructors at the Institute, he isn't kind, patient, and gentle. Unlike Agammo and Spiro, he isn't courteous, gentlemanly and predictable. No, Torum is something else entirely—but at least for now, I need him.

He's my only hope in the universe of getting home.Keep reading here:

Join Immy's VIP READER'S ROOM for information about sexy new releases, behind the scenes insider-access, giveaways and more.

www.ImogenKeeper.com

https://www.goodreads.com/author/show/15601917.Imogen_Keeper
https://www.bookbub.com/authors/imogen-keeper
https://www.facebook.com/ImogenKeeper
https://www.instagram.com/imogenkeeperauthor/
https://twitter.com/Imogen_Keeper